KNIFE EDGE

Also by Shaun Hutson

Assassin
Breeding Ground
Captives
Deadhead
Death Day
Erebus
Heathen
Lucy's Child
Nemesis
Relics
Renegades
Shadows
Slugs
Spawn
Stolen Angels
Victims
White Ghost

KNIFE EDGE

SHAUN HUTSON

LONDON NEW YORK SYDNEY TORONTO

This edition published 1997
by BCA
by arrangement with Little, Brown and Company

CN 5099

Typeset in Palatino by M Rules
Printed and bound in Great Britain by
Clays Ltd, St Ives plc.

This book is dedicated, with the utmost respect, to the memory of Sam Peckinpah.

It isn't Durango, it's London, but I hope you would have approved. Wherever you're watching from . . .

'The IRA have decided that as of midnight, 31 August, there will be a complete cessation of military operations. All our units have been instructed accordingly.'

IRA statement, 11 a.m. August 31, 1994

'Man still has one belief. One decree that stands alone. The laying down of arms, is like cancer to their bones . . .'

– Megadeth

Acknowledgements

These might seem a bit short and sweet compared to usual but those who've helped either before, after or during the writing of this novel, you know who you are. Those of you who've forgotten who you are . . . you're listed below:

Extra special thanks to my manager Gary Farrow. A man who can always turn the screw a few more notches than anyone else I know. Cheers, mate.

Many thanks to my publishers for their continued support. Especially to Barbara Boote and to my own 'Wild Bunch', my sales team. Look upon them, other publishers, and weep.

Special thanks to Cathy Cremer, Jo Bolsom and Wendy at Sony, and Dee, Zena, Karen Crane and Sarah Cousar (thanks *and* congratulations). Sanctuary Music, Iron Maiden and my most valued friend, Wally Grove (wherever he may be at the moment). Thanks also to Duncan Stripp, Martin Phillips, Jez, Terri, Rachel and Rebecca.

Thanks to Jack Taylor, Tom Sharp, Amin Saleh and Lewis Bloch. Not forgetting Damian and Christina Pulle.

Many thanks to Broomhills Shooting Club, especially Martin Slack, Mark and Maurice. Although 'thanks' might not be the word I'm looking for in Maurice's case . . .

Special thanks to Hailey Owen, a 'muse of fire' in her own right. To Deena and to everyone at Amex Platinum

Services for organising us so brilliantly. Many thanks to Factotum too.

Indirect thanks to Metallica, Queensryche, Clannad, Enya, L7 and Megadeth. Not forgetting Martin Scorsese. As if I could.

Thanks also to the Rihga Royal Hotel in New York and Margaret in Lindy's in Times Square.

Many thanks to Liverpool Football Club. To Sheila, Jenny and Joan in the Bob Paisley Lounge. Also many thanks to Steve 'red mist' Lucas, Paul 'Kevin Kuley' Garner and my co-driver and assistant maniac, Aaron Reynolds.

Thanks seems too inadequate a word to use when it regards my mum and dad but it'll have to do for now.

Extra special thanks to my wife Belinda for, well, just about everything really. And to my precious, beautiful daughter, whose smile in the mornings sometimes makes it just that little bit harder to kill and maim (figuratively speaking of course . . .)

The last thank you is always for you, my readers. As ever, for those who've been there from the beginning and those just joining the fight, welcome.

Let's go.

Shaun Hutson

KNIFE EDGE

7.03 a.m.

It was like being struck in the face by a handful of razor blades.

Sean Doyle stood motionless beside the dark blue Datsun for a moment, eyes narrowed against the biting wind. He zipped up his leather jacket, the wind whipping his shoulder-length brown hair around his face.

He brushed it away and glanced up at the sky.

Fuck. Not even light yet.

Great swollen banks of grey cloud were scudding across the blackened heavens, propelled by the powerful gusts of wind.

Doyle felt a spot of rain against his cheek and brushed it away. He wondered how long it would be until the threatened downpour arrived.

Reaching into his pocket he pulled out a packet of cigarettes and jammed one between his lips.

The raging wind made it almost impossible to light the Marlboro, the flame of the lighter sputtering even when Doyle cupped a hand around it. He sucked hard when the cigarette ignited, the tip glowing.

Doyle spat out a small piece of tobacco and drew deeply on the Marlboro, allowing the smoke to fill his lungs.

Christ, it was cold.

He leaned on the roof of the Datsun and glanced around.

The houses in London Road were unremarkable and

1

relatively uniform in appearance. A number had been converted into flats, as had many like them in this area of Brent.

From where he stood, Doyle could see the twin towers of Wembley Stadium less than a mile away, barely visible in the early morning gloom.

Half a mile behind him lay Wembley Central station. He could hear the intermittent rumble of trains passing through, the sound carried on the icy wind.

Early morning commuters travelling to work.

Some of the occupants of these dwellings in London Road would be joining that mass exodus to the centre of the capital soon. Some already had passed him, glancing around curiously at the cars parked in the road.

Some glanced across it.

Doyle continued to draw on his cigarette, his dark grey eyes scanning the street, the houses.

So quiet.

So ordinary.

Lights were on in some windows as the neighbourhood readied itself for the daily routine. A routine that remained the same for the duration of these people's working lives.

Get up, go to work, come home, go to bed.

There was a reassuring, if soul-crushing, regularity to the whole thing; a little bit of security in the midst of the insanity that was day-to-day living.

Doyle hated routine. Always had. He hated the regimentation work brought with it, the discipline that was constantly expected. The realisation that he was merely a cog in a different type of wheel did little to lighten his mood.

He watched a young woman scurrying down the road

towards a bus stop, waiting patiently with her coat pulled tightly around her.

A car passed by, the driver yawning, rubbing his eyes with one hand.

He cast Doyle a cursory glance, wondering perhaps who this long-haired, leather-jacketed individual was.

For his own part, Doyle watched as the car disappeared around a corner, brake lights flaring briefly in the gloom.

He took one last drag on his cigarette then dropped it, grinding it out beneath the sole of his boot.

Behind him another train rumbled past. It moved slowly, seeming to reflect the lethargy of its passengers, as if their indifference was somehow seeping into its metal innards.

Doyle felt more rain against his cheek and brushed it away, his fingers tracing the long scar that ran from the corner of his left eye down to the point of his jaw.

There were many more scars not immediately visible.

Both physical and emotional.

Pain.

The one constant in his life. The one ever reliable, ever present fucking companion.

So much pain.

Doyle glanced at his watch and clambered back inside the Datsun.

As he did, the Beretta 92F burst-fire automatic in a holster beneath his left arm bumped against his side.

Conciliation

Dromoland Castle, County Clare,
The Republic of Ireland:

They were the last three in the dining room.

The waiter watched as the trio of men, all immaculately dressed, ages ranging from thirty to forty, sat around a table close to the window of the oak-panelled room.

The curtains were open, offering a view of the man-made lake and part of the golf course beyond.

The sun was setting, reflecting on the still surface of the water like fire on glass.

In these winter months the darkness came early but the death of daylight was no less spectacular.

Apart from the three men there had been only two other tables to serve that evening. The hotel was quiet. The tourists wouldn't begin to descend for another month or two. For now the natural serenity of the ancient building was intensified by the lack of guests frequenting its magnificently appointed corridors and halls. All too soon the swarms of Americans would arrive, all of whom were convinced they had Irish ancestors in this or some part of the country.

The waiter smiled to himself as he tidied one of the other recently vacated tables.

A couple in their late twenties had sat there and the waiter had been particularly struck by how good looking the young woman was. He'd cast an envious eye in the direction of her companion as they'd left the dining room.

Now he glanced across to the three men and noticed that they had finished their desserts. He wandered over to collect the plates.

'Did you enjoy your meals, gentlemen?' he asked.

'Superb,' said Patrick Macarthy, wiping some crumbs from his beard.

His companions echoed his sentiments.

'Could you bring us three brandies, please?' Macarthy asked as the waiter gathered the plates.

'What's this, Patrick?' Liam Black said, smiling. 'A celebration?'

Macarthy sat back in his seat, glancing up as the waiter propped the last of the plates on his arm and retreated from view.

'I think we've every cause for celebration,' he said, clasping his fingers together before him on the table. 'We've won. This peace is on our terms and I'm glad it's over.'

Macarthy had been a member of Sinn Fein for the last eight years and, prior to that, he'd spent six years in Long Kesh for possession of firearms. Now, just three days away from his fortieth birthday, he still had the lean and hungry look of a fighting man which not even the flecks of grey in his beard could diminish.

His companions were younger, both members of the coiste seasta, a standing committee which ratified major Sinn Fein decisions.

Liam Black was a tall, powerfully built man with thick brown hair.

Eamonn Brady was thinner. Pale and narrow-featured with sad eyes.

'Are you sure it is over?' Brady asked, pulling agitatedly at the corner of his napkin. 'If the Prods have anything to do with it . . .' He let the sentence trail off.

'It's just a matter of time now,' Macarthy told the younger

man. *'Tying up loose ends. We'll see a united Ireland before the beginning of the next century.'*

The waiter returned with the brandies and set down the crystal balloons before disappearing once again.

Black warmed the liquor in the glass, cupping one large hand around the base.

'That was all I ever wanted for my kids,' Macarthy continued. *'That was what I fought for when I was a soldier, what I campaigned for when I got out of the Maze.'* He took a sip of his brandy, brushing his lips with his thumb and forefinger as he replaced the glass.

'How are the kids?' Brady asked.

'They're grand,' Macarthy said, wistfully. *'My daughter started school three weeks ago and my son's just been picked to play for his school's hurling team.'*

'He must get his athletic prowess from his mother then,' Black chuckled.

'You cheeky bugger,' said Macarthy, patting his stomach. *'Look at that, still flat as a washboard. Pure muscle.'*

'Pure bullshit,' Brady retorted.

Macarthy raised his glass and sipped once more at the brandy.

The blast was deafening.

A thundercrack which seemed to reverberate not just around the dining room but also over the lake, echoing away like rolling thunder.

The window behind Macarthy shattered, the first bullet striking him in the back of the head, at the base of the skull.

It exploded from his mouth, blasting two teeth free, smashing the brandy glass.

A thick gout of blood spouted from the wound, tiny pieces of pulverised bone spinning through the air like bloodied confetti.

The impact drove him forward, slamming his shattered face

into the table which immediately upended, sending more glasses flying into the air.

Three more shots followed in rapid succession.

One caught Black in the chest, staving in his sternum before exploding from his back just below his shoulder blade. He remained motionless for what seemed like an eternity then dropped to his knees, hands clapped to his chest as if trying to hold in the blood.

Brady threw himself down as two more bullets sent glass flying into the dining room. He looked across at Black who was on his knees, head bowed as if in prayer, blood pouring down his chest and stomach.

Macarthy lay face down a foot or so from him, eyes open.

Brady felt his stomach somersault as he looked at the back of his companion's head.

Where the bullet had entered there was something thick, swollen and pinkish-white bulging from the hole.

He realised it was brain.

Brady vomited.

Outside, the thunderous echo of the firing died away on the cold air.

The sound of an engine drifted across the lake as a car sped away into the enveloping gloom.

7.10 a.m.

The noise from the Datsun's heater was irritating him.

It needed fixing.

The constant rattling pissed him off.

The weather pissed him off.

Being stuck in the car at this time in the morning pissed him off.

There wasn't much that *didn't* piss him off if he was honest.

Sean Doyle leaned forward and pushed a cassette into the car stereo, twisting the volume knob. Music filled the car, loud and threatening.

'Almost called it today . . .'

Doyle slid down in his seat, one foot propped against the dashboard. He flicked some mud from the side of one cowboy boot trying to remember how long ago it had been since he'd cleaned the boots.

'Turned my face to the void, along with the suffering . . .'

The trail of people passing by on either side of the road, heading for work, or wherever, was still little more than a trickle. It wouldn't become a stream for another hour or so. Some looked in at him, others seemed more intent on trying to walk down London Road while glancing back over their shoulders in the direction of number ten.

From where he sat, Doyle had a clear view of the house.

'And the question, why am I? . . .'

It was a simple red-brick dwelling with a white porch and white-framed windows. There were no lights on inside. The sodium glare of street lights reflected in the glass like a candle flame in blind eyes.

Doyle flipped open the glove compartment, pulled out a packet of hard-boiled sweets and popped one into his mouth.

There were more cassettes in there, tape cases, a crushed box which had once held a McDonald's fruit pie, a few balled-up pieces of paper with scribbles on them.

And a box of 9mm shells.

Just the usual shit.

'So many times I've tried and failed, to gather my courage, reach again for that nail . . .'

Doyle reached for the box of ammo and slid it open. He reached into his inside pocket and pulled out a spare magazine for the Beretta. Slowly, he began to feed shells into it.

'Life's been like dragging feet through sand, and never finding a Promised Land . . .'

Each of the bullets was hollow-tipped.

Doyle also wore a holster around his left ankle, hidden by his jeans and boot. In it nestled a .45 PD Star. The pistol was less than four inches long but Doyle had its six-shot magazine loaded with hollow tips too.

It would take the back of a man's head off from twenty yards.

He knew it would because he'd seen it do just such a job.

How many times?

A dozen? Two dozen?

He'd lost count.

Who fucking cared?

Doyle certainly didn't and if *he* didn't, it was for sure no other bastard was going to.

He had no idea how many men he'd killed over the years. With guns, with knives. With his bare hands. He knew some of their names, others were just faces.

He'd been close enough to some of them to smell them, to look in their eyes. To see that combination of fear and pain.

Pain.

The constant companion.

Death was part of his job.

As a member of the Counter Terrorist Unit, Doyle had seen it in more guises than he cared to remember for more years than he could be bothered to recall.

How long?

Five years? Ten?

A hundred?

He smiled to himself.

For every death he'd dispensed, he'd seen one. A colleague, innocent men and women, sometimes children.

And *her*.

The only one he'd ever really cared for.

Georgie.

He pushed the last shell into the magazine and dropped it into his pocket.

Fuck it.

He closed his eyes momentarily and she was there.

She was always there, especially in quiet moments. He hated the nights more than ever now. Thoughts of her came to him in the lonely stillness and even though he fought to keep those thoughts at bay they battered against his consciousness.

She'd been dead more than eight years now.

Hadn't she?

You should know. You held her that night, you looked into her eyes. You felt her blood on your hands. You smelled her.

'Fuck it,' Doyle hissed under his breath and reached for another cassette, jamming it into the stereo, turning the sound even louder.

'I hope the end is less painful than my life . . .'

Doyle saw movement in his rear-view mirror and turned in his seat.

The paper boy was about twelve, maybe younger. A tall lanky lad who was standing looking towards number ten London Road.

He could see figures moving about on the path in front of the house.

Uniformed figures.

Doyle swung himself out of the car and the boy looked at him with an expression coloured by fear.

Doyle ran a hand through his long hair, sweeping it back from his forehead. The cold wind sent it lashing back around his face.

'You got any spare papers in there?' he asked, nodding towards the boy's bag.

The paper boy looked at him blankly.

'I want a paper,' Doyle told him.

I need something to pass the fucking time.

The boy shook his head.

'Do you deliver to number ten?'

The boy nodded.

Doyle held out a hand. 'I'll have theirs. They won't be needing it today.'

The paper boy hesitated a moment then reached into his bag and handed the *Mirror* to the counter terrorist who took it and slid back behind the wheel.

He turned to the sports pages and began reading.

The paper boy stood motionless for a moment longer then tapped on Doyle's window. 'What's going on?'

'Nothing for *you* to worry about,' Doyle said. 'You'd better deliver the rest of those papers.'

'Are you sure number ten don't want theirs?' the boy persisted.

'Trust me,' Doyle said, watching as the boy nodded and rode off.

The counter terrorist glanced first at his watch then at number ten London Road.

The house was still in darkness.

Doyle sighed irritably.

How much longer?

Mediation

Broadcasting House, Belfast:

As the lift descended, William Hatcher looked across at the young woman standing opposite him.

She was in her early twenties he guessed, perhaps younger.

The same age as his own eldest daughter, he mused.

The young woman had a clipboard clasped firmly to her chest and, as the lift descended slowly, she never took her gaze from the line of numbers above the door, each one lighting in turn as the lift fell from floor to floor on its even journey.

Hatcher coughed, cupping one hand over his mouth.

The young woman still didn't look at him.

'Thank you for coming in,' she said finally, still staring fixedly at the row of numbers. 'I know you must be busy at the moment.'

'You could say that,' Hatcher said, a small smile on his lips.

'Have you done many interviews before?'

He raised his eyebrows.

He'd been a Unionist MP for the past six years, he'd done his share.

'Did I sound like a novice?' he chuckled.

The woman's cheeks coloured but still she didn't even glance his way.

'No, I meant, well, you know . . . with the peace settlement coming off and that. . .' She was struggling for the words but Hatcher intervened to help as she stumbled.

12

'I've done two already today,' he informed her. 'I've another four to go.'

'All in Belfast?'

He shook his head, realising then that she wouldn't notice the gesture as she was still gazing at the numbers above the lift door.

'All over,' he told her.

The lift finally bumped to a halt at the ground floor and only then did the young woman look at him, glancing at him sheepishly and smiling. She ushered him from the lift and together they walked along a short corridor towards reception.

'How long have you been doing this job?' he asked her.

'This is my third day,' she told him. 'I just take guests in and out, get tea and coffee for people, that kind of thing. Nothing important.'

'What's your name?'

'Michelle.' Her cheeks coloured once more.

'Well, Michelle, I'm sure you'll do a fine job,' Hatcher told her, handing her his clip-on Visitor Pass as he reached reception.

Two uniformed security men were standing on either side of the exit, both of whom nodded affably in Hatcher's direction as he passed.

'Mr Hatcher,' said Michelle quietly, lowering her voice almost conspiratorially. 'Can I ask you something?'

For the first time she looked directly into his eyes and he noticed how clear and blue her eyes were.

Hatcher was a tall man and she was forced to look up at him.

He nodded, waiting for the question.

'Is there really going to be peace?'

Hatcher hesitated a second, transfixed by those blue orbs which had been so hesitant to focus on him earlier but which now seemed to burn right through him.

'Yes,' he said finally, hoping that he'd injected the right amount of sincerity into his voice.

13

She smiled.

'Thank you for coming in,' she said in a practised tone before she turned away and walked back towards the lift.

Hatcher nodded towards his driver who was already on his feet and heading for the exit doors which he pushed open for the MP.

The two men stepped out onto the pavement.

'How long before the next interview, Frank?'

The driver looked at his watch. 'An hour and a half,' he said, as he opened the back door of the Mercedes for Hatcher to slip inside.

'Stop off somewhere on the way,' the MP told him. 'We'll get a sandwich and a drink, shall we?'

The driver smiled, closed the door and hurried around to the other side, pausing a moment as a van passed by close to the Mercedes.

Hatcher reached into his inside pocket and glanced at his itinerary for the day, squinting at the small print, muttering to himself as he had to retrieve his glasses from the glove compartment.

Forty-six years old, eyesight going. What was next? The hair?

He smiled and flipped open the compartment.

It was then that the car exploded.

The blast was massive, violent enough to lift the Mercedes fully ten feet into the air, the rear of the vehicle flipping over slightly.

The driver was blasted off his feet by the detonation, hurled into the street by the concussion blast.

The Mercedes disappeared for a second, transformed into a blinding ball of yellow and white flame, pieces of the chassis hurtling in all directions before the remains of the vehicle thudded back to the ground, one wheel spinning off.

Cars screeched to a halt in the street, and one of the security guards from the BBC building ran to the door shielding his face from the flames, which were dancing madly around the obliterated remnants of the car.

He saw something glinting near his feet, something hurled fully twenty feet by the ferocity of the explosion.

It took him a second to realise that it was a wrist watch.

A moment longer to grasp the fact that it was still wrapped around what was left of William Hatcher's left arm.

7.26 a.m.

Doyle knew he may as well be dead.

Perhaps if he'd had the guts he'd pull one of the pistols he wore, stick the fucking barrel in his mouth and finish it here and now.

End of story.

He flicked through the paper again.

He'd read the print off the fucking thing once. He could remember every headline, every pointless story. It was the usual bullshit. Politics. Gossip. Exclusives.

The country was recovering from the recession.

Bollocks.

Some tart from a TV soap was marrying a talentless one-hit wonder who'd just had a number one record.

Bollocks.

A celebrity was confessing how drink and drugs had almost wrecked his career but now he was cleaning up his life.

Bollocks.

Doyle tossed the paper to one side.

It was all shit.

15

Life was shit.

There had been a story in there about the peace in Ireland, mention of a United Ireland. An end to the troubles.

Doyle took a drag on his cigarette.

After all these years it was actually over.

Wasn't it?

So where does that leave you?

Doyle had even heard rumours that the Counter Terrorist Unit was to be disbanded. It was superfluous to requirements now. Its members were to be pensioned off. Discarded.

He sighed.

What the fuck was he going to do?

It was all he knew. All he'd known for so many years. Where did he go from here? What did life have to offer him now that the fighting was finished?

It was something he'd considered briefly and, each time, the realisation had troubled him.

He was finished without it and that only angered him more.

Retire at thirty-seven. Sit on your arse and count your scars. Sit in your flat and go slowly insane until the day came when the only course of action was to suck on the barrel of a .44.

Over the last twenty years he'd faced death so often, risked his life more than any man should have to, but the prospect of that final ending had never frightened him. For the last eight years, since Georgie had gone, it had seemed preferable to the emptiness, the loneliness.

Doyle had never been afraid of dying but the thought of being discarded, of having outlived his usefulness, was almost unbearable.

There was something inside him, a cancerous rage which gnawed at him and found appeasement in the violence of his work. With that work gone he could see little future. Could see no way of fighting off that anger which both fuelled him and fed off him.

Better off dead than discarded.

He stubbed out the cigarette in the ashtray then pulled it free and emptied the contents out of the side window, all over the road.

His back ached.

It felt as if he'd been sitting in the car for hours and, again, he checked his watch, as if by constantly gazing at the Sekonda he would accelerate time itself.

There were still no lights on in number ten London Road.

The only movement was *outside*.

The sky was still dark, still mottled with bloated rain clouds.

Every now and then droplets would hit the windscreen and Doyle watched them trickle down the glass.

He lit up another cigarette then leaned forward and turned up the volume of the car stereo.

'. . . *all of the people who won't be missed, you've made my shitlist* . . .'

A car drove past but Doyle hardly heard the engine above the thundering stereo.

There were fewer vehicles heading down the street now and he wondered if the road had finally been closed at either end but decided that wasn't the right tactic.

Things had to look relatively normal outside to anyone peering into the street.

A white van approaching from behind him, moving slowly. Doyle watched it in his rear-view mirror, counted two people in the front. A man was driving, a woman seated next to him was pointing.

The counter terrorist squinted in the gloom and noticed that she was gesturing in the direction of number ten.

He took a long drag on his cigarette, holding the smoke in his lungs.

'. . . *all the ones who put me out . . .*'

The van had stopped about twenty yards behind where Doyle was parked.

'. . . *all the ones who fill my head with doubt . . .*'

He saw the driver clamber out, wander around to the rear of the van where a second man climbed free into the street. The woman was walking ahead of them, glancing back and forth as if searching for something.

Doyle shook his head and swung himself out of the car.

He wondered what had taken them so long.

Unification

Portadown, Northern Ireland:

Major John Wetherby dropped the files on to the top of the desk, the thump reverberating around the room.

Wetherby was a tall, powerfully built man with pale, pinched features, his hair greying slightly at the temples. He stood with his back to the other two men in the room, both of whom looked first at the officer then at the files.

The younger of them, Captain Edward Wilton, reached for the top file.

'Read it,' said Wetherby without turning round, and Wilton hesitated for a moment, as if fearing his superior possessed eyes in the back of his head, before he realised the Major must have seen his reflection in the glass of the window. 'Read them all,' Wetherby continued, his tone subdued.

Wilton began flicking through the file.

His colleague merely sat, hands clasped on the top of the table, gazing at his superior's back.

Captain James Armstrong didn't need to read these files. He knew what they contained. What those contents meant and how important they were.

'How many is it now?' Armstrong asked.

'Including Hatcher and the two Sinn Fein men, eleven,' Wetherby informed him, turning back to face his colleagues. 'And Christ knows how many more to come if something isn't done soon.' The Major exhaled wearily. 'Just when it seems

there's finally going to be peace, just when it looks as if we're finally going to be able to get out of this bloody place, this happens.' He jabbed a finger towards the files.

'Are we sure who's behind it?' Wilton asked.

'I wish there was some room for doubt but I'm afraid there isn't,' the Major told him.

'We're just lucky the media hasn't got hold of it,' Armstrong offered.

'As far as the media is concerned, it's a leftover from the conflict,' Wetherby said.

'Two dead Sinn Fein men, both shot,' Wilton began, as if he was reading some kind of bizarre shopping list. 'An Ulster Unionist MP blown to pieces by a car bomb, five known IRA prisoners released from Long Kesh all shot, and three UVF men assassinated, one stabbed, one blown up and the other one shot. No common MO?'

Wetherby shook his head.

'It's only going to be a matter of time before each side starts blaming the other,' Wetherby added. This bloody peace is fragile enough as it is; there are those on both sides who don't need much more pushing to start hostilities again.'

'It looks as if someone already started them,' Wilton said, closing the file.

Wetherby sat down, fingertips pressed together.

'These killings will go on unless we do something to stop them,' the Major said. 'As head of Military Intelligence here I feel we must act before it's too late. Before anyone else on either side is killed and, more importantly, before this peace settlement is jeopardised any further.'

'What options do we have?' Wilton asked.

'As far as I see it we don't have a choice,' Wetherby replied. 'There is only one course of action open to us.'

The other two men sat motionless, gazing at their superior.

'In three days' time seven more IRA men are due to be released,' Wetherby continued. 'It's my guess they'll be the next target. They're to be transported from Long Kesh to the border by minibus, escorted obviously. It's a tempting target.'

'Just like the other five were,' murmured Armstrong.

Wetherby nodded slowly. 'I don't see what else we can do,' he said wearily.

'You said there was only one course of action open to us?' Wilton echoed, vaguely.

'These killings must stop before the media make any connections. They'll have a field day with this and, if it gets out, God help us all,' the Major said, crossing to his desk. 'There is no choice.' He flicked a switch on the console. 'Cranley, send in Sean Doyle.'

7.41 a.m.

Doyle saw the woman looking at him as she and her two companions approached.

Come on, you fucking vultures.

The first man, short, stocky and wearing a waxed jacket, was carrying a small case with him. The other man, bespectacled and crew-cut, was holding the camera.

As the woman drew nearer, Doyle could see she was already wearing a radio mike, the power pack tucked into the pocket of her jeans. She had a thick scarf wrapped around her neck as added protection against the chill wind. Doyle watched as her long dark hair flowed behind her, stirred by the wind.

The cameraman raised the machine and it was then that Doyle stepped forward.

'Will you turn that off, please?' he said as politely as he could.

'Who are you?' the woman asked, gazing at him intently.

The camera moved round to focus on him.

'Turn it off,' Doyle repeated, raising one hand.

The man with the spectacles complied.

'My name's Patricia Courtney,' the woman told him. 'We're with an outside broadcast unit from Thames Television and . . .'

Doyle nodded, ran appraising eyes over her.

About five four, auburn haired. Pretty.

'Are you involved in this?' she asked him, nodding towards number ten.

'You *could* say that. How the hell did *you* find out about it?' the counter terrorist enquired.

'We have our sources,' she smiled.

It was a warm smile.

Doyle didn't return the gesture.

'You can't film here.'

'Who says we can't?' the cameraman demanded.

'I just fucking told you, didn't I?' Doyle hissed.

'You still haven't told us who you are,' Patricia insisted.

'I'm the bloke who's stopping you filming.'

'Can you show us some ID?' she persisted. 'You could be anyone.'

Doyle slid the Beretta from its holster and aimed it at the reporter, who gasped and took a couple of steps back.

'That's my fucking ID,' Doyle rasped. 'Now piss off.'

'I want to speak to someone in charge of this operation, I have a right—' Patricia began.

Doyle cut her short. 'You've got no rights here, now fuck off before I get mad.'

'I could have you reported,' she said challengingly.

'Try it.'

'Look, mate, we don't want any trouble, we're just trying to do our jobs,' said the man in the wax jacket, trying to inject a note of calm into the proceedings.

'Then do them somewhere else. And I'm not your fucking mate.'

'Just one quick shot of the house, that's all we want,' Patricia said, her eyes flicking nervously towards the automatic.

'Forget it,' Doyle instructed, holstering the pistol.

'Are you in charge here?' the cameraman said. 'Because if you're not, then I want to speak to your superiors, I—'

Doyle grabbed the man with one hand, gripping his jacket, pulling him close. Their foreheads were almost touching.

'Have you ever tried to eat one of these fucking cameras?' he asked, his eyes narrowed.

The cameraman tried to pull away but Doyle kept a firm grip on him.

'If you don't get out of here,' he continued, 'I'm going to stick this camera so far down your throat you'll be able to photograph your fucking breakfast. Got it?'

He pushed the man away, watching as he sprawled against one of the other parked cars.

'You're a real hard nut, aren't you?' wax jacket said, helping up his colleague.

'Do *you* want some too?' Doyle snarled, glaring at him. The man didn't answer.

'We're just trying to do our jobs,' the reporter told him.

'You've told me that once. Just piss off. Go and make something up, that's what you bastards usually do, isn't it, if you can't get the story you want? Go on. Crawl back

23

under your stone.' Doyle stood staring at the woman for interminable seconds.

'You haven't heard the last of this,' the cameraman said defiantly, making sure he was several steps away from the counter terrorist.

'I'm shitting myself,' Doyle said sardonically. He dug in his pocket for the Marlboros and stuck one between his lips.

'We won't be the only ones, you know,' Patricia told him. 'This place will be swarming with media inside an hour. You won't be able to keep all of them away.'

'In an hour it won't matter,' Doyle said cryptically.

'This is a big story,' she told him. 'You can't hide it. The *public* have a right to know what's going on here.'

'If you've finished your speeches why don't you get back in your van and fuck off,' said Doyle, tugging open the door of his car. 'And I'll tell you something else, if you come back here, you'd better hope *I* don't see you.'

They turned and headed back towards the van, the reporter shooting him one last venomous glance.

'Nice talking to you,' Doyle said smiling. Then, under his breath, 'Bastards.'

He slid behind the wheel of the Datsun once more.

Waiting.

Intervention

Portadown, Northern Ireland:

As Doyle entered the office he was aware of three pairs of eyes upon him. He even saw a look approaching bewilderment on the face of Wilton, who then glanced across at Wetherby.

The Major nodded a greeting to Doyle, no less taken aback by the counter terrorist's appearance but having had the benefit of knowing what to expect.

They'd met before.

It had been in a Mayfair office that time, at the main Head-Quarters of the CTU, he guessed three or four years ago. The officer was surprised at how little Doyle had changed. He still wore a leather jacket, jeans and cowboy boots, his hair was a little longer if anything and there were the odd flecks of grey in his stubble. Otherwise, no change.

The scars were still there.

Not that Wetherby had expected them to have magically vanished during the intervening years, he just didn't remember quite how savage one or two of them were. At least those that he could see.

'Gentlemen, this is Sean Doyle, a member of the Counter Terrorist Unit,' the Major said and indicated a chair nearby, where Doyle sat down. The officer then introduced his two colleagues.

Doyle looked impassively at Wilton and Armstrong then reached inside his jacket for his cigarettes.

'It's still Major Wetherby then, I see,' said Doyle, lighting his cigarette. 'No promotion yet? Perhaps you're not brown-nosing enough.' He smiled.

'Still as insolent as ever, Doyle,' Wetherby said flatly. 'Some things never change.'

'All right, let's cut the bullshit, what do you want?' Doyle demanded. 'You didn't get me in here to talk about old times, did you?'

'These killings,' Wetherby said. 'The Sinn Fein men, the UVF and IRA members, you're aware of them?'

'I'd have to be pretty fucking stupid not to be.'

'Who do you think's behind them?' Wetherby asked.

Doyle looked directly at the officer.

'You're Army Intelligence, aren't you? I thought you were going to tell me.'

Wetherby didn't rise to the bait. 'I'm asking for your opinion.'

Doyle shrugged. 'Extremists on both sides,' he said, finally. 'Not everyone wanted peace out here.'

'Do you think the fighting's still going on then?' Armstrong wanted to know.

'Not like it was, of course not,' Doyle said dismissively. 'But that's not to say a few of the boyos don't still fancy a bit of a ruck between themselves. Some of the Unionists think this peace deal sold them down the river.'

'What do you think?' Wetherby insisted.

'About the peace settlement? I couldn't give a fuck one way or the other. Do you know what it's done for me? Put me out of a fucking job.' He smiled thinly and took a puff on his cigarette.

'You don't suspect the IRA or the UVF?' Wetherby enquired.

'I said extremists,' Doyle told him. 'It was never just those two, there were more splinter groups on both sides than you

could count. Who knows, it could be some nutters on either side.'

Wetherby looked across at his colleagues.

'Look, what the fuck is this all about?' Doyle demanded. 'I want to know what it's got to do with me.'

'You worked for Army Intelligence before,' Wetherby said. 'You were very successful.'

'Don't tell me,' said Doyle laconically. 'You're going to give me a medal.'

Wetherby glared at him then continued. 'We need your help again, Doyle.'

'Why me?'

'As I said, you were successful before, you know your way around the whole country, not just this province.'

'Your parents were Irish, weren't they?' Wilton said.

'Yeah. So what?' Doyle rounded on him.

'You understand the mentality of these people, the ordinary people and the terrorists,' Wetherby continued.

'Get to the point for fuck's sake,' Doyle snapped. 'You want me to find out who's behind these killings, right?'

'Not who's behind them, we already know that,' the Major told him and, for once, noticed a flicker of surprise on the counter terrorist's face. 'Just find them and find them fast. If news of this gets out, this whole country will go up in smoke, maybe not just this country but the rest of Britain too.'

'You know who's been hitting these fuckers?' Doyle said incredulously. 'Then why don't you do something about it? Why not send in some fucking SAS to sort it out.'

'It's not as simple as that,' Wetherby told him. 'Speed is of the essence but so is secrecy. That's why I chose you for this job.'

'The SAS boys aren't exactly likely to let it slip down the pub, you know, Wetherby,' Doyle told him.

'*You wanted some work, Doyle, I'm offering you some,*' the Major said irritably. '*You were right, this peace has put you out of a job. With the fighting gone, you're nothing. You need this as much as we need you.*'

The counter terrorist held the officer's gaze for long seconds.

'*Go on,*' he said quietly.

'*You've got two days to complete the job.*'

'*You're fucking joking,*' Doyle snorted. '*It could take more than two days to search Belfast, let alone the whole country, these bastards could be anywhere in Ireland, North or South. They could be Protestant or Catholic, IRA or UVF, and you expect me to find them in two days?*' He got to his feet. '*Forget it, Wetherby.*'

'*Two days is plenty of time,*' the Major told him. '*We'll tell you where to go, where to pick up the trail, we've got files and as much information as you need.*'

'*What the fuck is this?*' Doyle said quietly, eyes narrowed.

'*We know who's behind these killings, I've already told you that. What you have to do is make sure that no one else finds out. It isn't the IRA or the UVF who are responsible for these murders.*'

'*Then who is?*'

'*It's a British soldier.*'

7.58 a.m.

The daylight was grey, like dirty sheets. Still full of lowering clouds, the sky was a clear warning of things to come.

Doyle watched the rain hitting the windscreen of the Datsun, the rivulets coursing down the glass.

He'd switched off the cassette for the time being and was listening to the news on Radio 5. The draw for the next round of the Coca-Cola Cup was coming up after it and the counter terrorist seemed more concerned with *that* than what was happening in the world around him.

It was the usual shit.

Just like the papers.

Same shit, different day.

Politics.

Showbiz.

Bullshit.

He looked across at the windows of number ten London Road.

The windows of one of the rooms upstairs were open. Every other set was firmly closed. In the darkness the windows had been uncovered, exposed to the gloom, Now that light was grudgingly filling the sky, it was being shut out. At least from that particular house.

There was a brief mention of number ten London Road on the news.

Doyle looked disdainfully at the radio as if hoping his mood would be transmitted to the newsreader.

It was a short piece.

They didn't have enough information as yet. There would be more bulletins as the day went on.

I bet there will.

With the coming of daylight he could see the entire road.

Both ends had been sealed off now, uniformed police moving around without any pretence of furtiveness. Doyle counted at least twelve men in clear view and he knew there must be more he hadn't yet seen.

Also parked further up the road were two ambulances,

a couple of police cars and a large white Transit van with police markings.

Doyle puffed on his cigarette and turned up the volume on the radio as the news came to an end.

The weather forecast was for more rain.

Doyle shuffled uncomfortably in his seat and sat forward slightly as the announcer proclaimed that the draw for the next round was about to take place.

Doyle glanced out of the window and saw men moving about, taking up positions.

He was surprised at how silently it all took place. It was as if the car was hermetically sealed. No sound from outside could penetrate.

He pulled distractedly at the top of one boot as the draw began.

Arsenal would play Spurs.

Doyle continued to watch the policemen, some of them glancing towards the curtained windows of number ten as they moved, swiftly, nervously.

Newcastle would play West Ham.

Still Doyle had seen no movement at any of the windows. He wondered how well the rear of the house was covered. The back garden led down to train tracks; it would be difficult escaping that way.

Watford would play Liverpool.

'Come on, you reds,' he whispered under his breath.

And Manchester United . . .

Doyle switched off the radio.

Who gave a fuck about that shit?

He shoved a cassette back into the machine and turned up the volume further.

The tap on his side window startled him and he turned to see a uniformed policeman standing there.

The counter terrorist wound down his window.

'Mr Doyle,' said the policeman. 'Will you come with me, please?'

Doyle looked at his watch then at the constable.

'About fucking time,' he snapped and hauled himself out of the car.

Was the waiting over at last?

Eradication

Portadown, Northern Ireland:

'Bullshit.'

Doyle looked directly at Wetherby as he spoke the word.

'His name is Robert Neville,' the Intelligence officer said, pushing a file towards the counter terrorist. 'Corporal Robert Neville, a para. Age thirty-eight, married with a daughter. Enlisted March fourteenth 1977. Joined the Paratroop Regiment and came through the training with the highest marks of anyone in the same batch of new recruits. He subsequently specialised in explosives.'

Doyle had begun to read the file, scanning the pieces of paper there.

'Wounded four times,' Wetherby continued. 'Recommended for promotion to Sergeant in January 1993.'

There was a photo of Neville amongst the reports.

Doyle studied it.

Neville had a square face, his jaw flat, his ears tight to his head. His hair was short as Doyle would have expected. Dark and lustrous. A faint smile was distinguishable on the paratrooper's lips. A small scar ran from the corner of his mouth to his chin.

'There's a psych report in there too,' Wetherby told Doyle. 'But as far as anyone can tell, he's no crazier than anyone else in the army.'

'How can you be so sure he's responsible for these killings?'

Doyle asked, his tone subdued. 'How do you know it isn't some extremist faction on either side?'

'The bullets they dug out of the men that were shot had Neville's fingerprints on them,' Wetherby explained. 'Some cartridge cases were found by the Gardai at the scene of a shooting in the Republic. They had his prints on too.'

'And the bombings? How can you be sure he was responsible for those? He's not the only geezer out there who knows how to use Semtex.'

'Forensic reports by the RUC and Army Intelligence found evidence that Neville—'

'What kind of evidence?'

'You sound as if you're trying to defend him,' Wetherby said.

'You could be wrong,' Doyle snapped.

'We're not,' Wetherby assured him.

Doyle tossed the file back in the officer's direction.

'So what the fuck do you want me to do?'

'Find Neville, before the IRA, the UVF, the media or all three find out the truth.'

'And if I do find him?'

'Kill him.'

Doyle regarded the officer coldly. 'Just like that?' he said softly.

'You've done it before, Doyle. Don't tell me you're going soft,' Wetherby chided. 'How many men have you killed? Twenty? Thirty?'

'This is different.'

'Why?'

'The others weren't British soldiers,' Doyle snarled.

'What difference does *that* make?' Wetherby snorted. 'It's one man's life. We're talking about a country here, Doyle. Over three thousand people have died since 1969. Half of the people *involved don't even know why. Now, after all those deaths, there's peace. That peace can't be destroyed. Not at any cost. Neville is threatening that peace. He has to be removed. If not, all the deaths, all the sacrifices, the talking, it'll have been for nothing. We can't let one man jeopardise that.'*

'Save the fucking sermons, Wetherby,' Doyle rasped.

'You've suffered enough yourself,' the officer continued. 'Don't you want it finished?'

Doyle didn't answer.

He reached for a cigarette and lit it.

'You said there was nothing left for you, Doyle,' the Major reminded him. 'Look on this job as a swansong. A last shot. You're right. There is nothing left.'

'And what if I refuse?'

'You won't,' said Wetherby, smugly. 'Two days, Doyle.'

Doyle snatched up the file on Neville and headed for the door.

'You're right, Wetherby,' he said, pausing as he turned the handle. 'I'm nothing without the fighting, maybe that's how Neville feels too; perhaps that's why I don't want to kill him, because I understand how he feels. The difference between you and me is that I might be nothing when all this is over but you, you'll be a nothing for the rest of your fucking life. You've always been nothing and that's the way it'll stay.'

And he was gone, the door slamming behind him.

8.04 a.m.

'Who's in there with him?'

Doyle took a drag on his cigarette, his eyes fixed on number ten London Road.

From the single window of the Portacabin it was clearly visible, as were the dozens of uniformed policemen who had taken up position around it, some as close as the pavement. They were using parked cars as cover.

The Portacabin was about twelve feet long, half that in width and, despite the fact that it contained just three men other than Doyle, it seemed crowded inside. Somehow a small table had been brought in and upon that a map of the area and several files had been laid out.

A uniformed man stood at the door, removing his cap to run a hand across his bald head. Doyle wasn't sure of his rank but guessed he must be fairly high up in the pecking order.

The other two occupants of the Portacabin were plain-clothes. Both of them, the counter terrorist guessed, three or four years older than himself. The first of them was an overweight, dark-haired man who looked as if he hadn't shaved for a week. His companion, DI Vic Calloway, was taller, thick-necked and sporting a nose which looked as if it had been flattened with a frying pan.

Calloway's more portly assistant, who was sipping tea from a Styrofoam cup, seemed more interested in Doyle than in number ten London Road. Detective Sergeant Colin Mason wondered who the hell this long-haired newcomer was and, more to the point, what business he had here. Mason stuck the tip of his tongue into the cavity which had formed in one of his back teeth and wondered how much longer he could avoid a trip to the dentist. The fucking thing was starting to ache.

The uniformed man seemed to tire of standing at the door and wandered out into the road, closing the door behind him.

'I said, who's in there with him?' Doyle repeated, looking at Calloway.

'Just his wife and kid as far as we know,' the DI said, reaching for his own tea, sipping it, wincing when he found it was cold.

'Julie and Lisa Neville,' Doyle murmured.

Calloway nodded.

'Has he made any contact with you?' Doyle enquired. 'Any demands?'

'Not yet,' Mason replied. 'What makes you think he will?'

'He's taken his wife and kid hostage, I think it's safe to assume he wants something,' Doyle said sardonically.

'Like what?' Calloway snapped. 'You're the expert, aren't you? You're supposed to know all about him.'

'How come the Counter Terrorist Unit is involved anyway?' Mason echoed. 'What makes Robert Neville so interesting to your lot?'

'I've followed him halfway across fucking Ireland during the last thirty-six hours,' Doyle snapped. '*I* was the one who tracked him here.'

'Then why didn't you call *us*?' Calloway said angrily.

'Because Neville's *my* business.'

'Not now he's not,' the DI insisted.

'Why were you chasing him anyway?' Mason wanted to know.

'That's classified,' Doyle said dismissively.

'Fuck off, Doyle,' Mason snorted. 'Who do you think you are, James Bond?'

'I *know* who *I* am,' Doyle rasped. 'And I've got a pretty good idea what *you* are too, you fat cunt.'

'I don't have to take that shit off him,' Mason shouted at his superior. 'Long-haired, scruffy fucker.'

Doyle smiled, watching as Mason's face turned a deep shade of crimson.

'Both of you, just knock it on the head, will you?' Calloway snapped.

'Tell fucking Pavarotti to calm down then,' Doyle said, still smiling.

He and Mason locked stares.

Calloway looked at each of them in turn.

'Finished, children?' he said irritably.

The other two remained silent.

'Right, now let's get down to work, shall we?' the DI continued. 'How much do you know about Neville, Doyle?'

'What do you want to know?'

'Why you were chasing him would be a help.'

'I told you, that's classified information,' Doyle insisted. 'Let's just say I need to talk to him about something important.'

Like the future of Ireland?

'Can you give us *any* details about him?' Calloway persisted.

'Tell me what you know, I'll fill in the holes if I can.'

'That's nice of you,' Mason chided.

Calloway shot him an angry stare then picked up one of the files from the small table.

He began reading.

Details about Robert Neville, background, upbringing, training.

It was the usual shit.

Doyle listened, his attention still fixed on the house.

Calloway dropped the file back on to the table when he'd finished.

'Well?' he said.

Doyle shrugged.

'Anything to add? Any *holes* to fill in?'

Doyle wasn't slow to catch the note of scorn in the policeman's tone. He smiled.

'He's armed,' Doyle said.

'How do you know?' Calloway asked.

'I know *him*.'

'How well do you know him, Doyle, how do we know *you're* not involved with this somehow?' Mason said. 'I mean, you knew he was here, you knew he was armed and yet you still didn't contact us. Why?'

'You know, you're a rare kind of man, Mason,' Doyle said. 'You actually *are* as fucking stupid as you look, aren't you? Jesus Christ, the last fucking thing I wanted was coppers swarming all over the place. I didn't want Neville panicked, I didn't want him to know anybody had found him. The last thing I wanted was for him to look out of his window and see uniforms. Who called you lot in anyway?'

'A neighbour reported seeing someone trying to break into the house,' Calloway said. 'A patrol car investigated. When they tried to get inside they were shot at. They called for back-up.' The DI shrugged. 'It just escalated from there.'

'If Neville shot at them he obviously wasn't trying to hit them,' Doyle said quietly. 'Because if he had been, you'd be scraping their brains off the road now.'

'We surrounded the house, closed off the road at both ends,' said Calloway, then his tone changed. 'Anyway, if you were sitting out here all the time, you must have seen what was going on, you must have heard the shots.'

Doyle didn't answer.

'What would you have done on your own, Doyle?' Mason said challengingly. 'Stormed the place?'

The counter terrorist reached for his cigarettes and lit one, blowing smoke in Mason's direction.

'So, what do we do now?' Calloway said.

Doyle perched on one corner of the table, eyes still locked on number ten London Road.

'We wait,' he murmured.

8.31 a.m.

'They're going to kill you, Bob.'

Robert Neville turned from the window and looked at his wife.

Julie Neville brushed some strands of blonde hair from her face and shifted uncomfortably on the sofa, her eyes never leaving her husband.

He pulled the .459 Smith and Wesson automatic from his belt and worked the slide, chambering a round.

Julie swallowed hard as she saw him advancing towards her and, for fleeting seconds, she thought he might strike her.

Neville leaned close, his face only inches from hers.

'*They're* going to kill me, are they?' he said quietly and, as he spoke, she could smell the whisky on his breath.

She lowered her gaze slightly.

Neville reached out with his free hand and gently stroked her cheek with his finger.

God, how smooth her skin felt. Like a marble statue.

'Do you *want* them to kill me?' he whispered.

She shook her head almost imperceptibly.

'Do you?' he said, more insistently.

'No,' she snapped, glaring at him. Her expression gradually softened. 'I just want you to let us go,' she finally breathed. 'If not me, then at least let Lisa go, she didn't ask to be a part of all this.'

'She's happy enough, I haven't harmed her, I'd never harm her,' Neville said. 'I'd rather die first. You and Lisa are all I've got.'

'Then why are you holding us prisoner here?' Julie asked, attempting to mask the anger in her voice. But it was anger tinged with anxiety.

And fear?

'You were the one who wanted to leave,' Neville reminded her. 'You were the one who was going to take Lisa away from me.'

'It was for her own good, Bob.'

'Bollocks. I'm her father.'

'Then why do you hurt her?'

Neville gripped Julie's jaw in one firm hand, his forehead pressed almost against hers.

'You tell me when I've ever hurt her,' he rasped. 'I've never laid a fucking finger on her.'

Julie tried to pull free of his grip, away from the smell of whisky.

'What about your drinking?' she snapped. 'Or are you too pissed now to remember it?'

He stepped back.

'Every time you were home on leave you spent all day and night drunk,' Julie continued. 'Since you left the army it's all you've done. How many bottles a day is it now, Bob?'

'What the fuck do you expect?'

She regarded him warily.

'You talk as if I'm the only one,' he said angrily.

'You're the only one I'm married to. I don't care how other soldiers cope with it. I don't care how many of them get pissed, fuck other women, get into fights. I only care about you.'

'Is that why you were going to leave me?' he said softly.

40

'Leave me and take Lisa with you. Don't tell me you care about me, Julie. Not when you were going to take away the only thing in this miserable, useless fucking life that I ever cared about, that I ever loved.'

He held her in that unrelenting gaze.

'Do you still love me?'

She swallowed hard. 'Yes.'

'Liar,' Neville rasped, the knot of muscles at the side of his jaw pulsing angrily.

'You've changed,' she told him. 'You're not—'

'Not the man you married?' he hissed. 'Are you surprised I'm different? After what I've seen, is it any wonder? I've risked my fucking life for this country, for the army, for people who'd spit in my fucking face one day and laugh with me the next. And I was supposed to take it. And I did, because that was what I was ordered to do. That's what we were *all* ordered to do. We were in Northern Ireland to keep the peace. Jesus, that's a fucking laugh. What a great job we did. How many thousands have been killed out there since 1969? And what about here? How many have died in car bombs or pub bombings? How many men, women and children?'

He sat on the sofa beside her. 'Do you know how many friends I lost out there? How many other men who were just doing their jobs? Ten, fifteen? I can't even fucking remember myself. Not *all* of them. But some things you never forget. Like holding a bloke's hand while you're waiting for him to die, waiting for the fucking medics to come and try and put his head back together because some fucking sniper's bullet has blown most of it apart.'

Julie could see tears in his eyes.

'There was one lad,' he continued, his voice low. 'He was about twenty-two, Tony Lane. That's one name I *can* remember. Our unit was called to some ruck that was going on near the Divis flats. It was his first tour, he was nervous. We pulled in four guys we'd been told were PIRA. We searched them. Tony found a box of matches on one and he opened it to see if there was any ammunition inside. They'd do that, hide a couple of rounds in there. The matchbox had a charge inside it. No bigger than my thumbnail. But there were sewing needles in there too. When it went off, Tony caught most of them in his face. The needles went through both his eyes. He survived. The doctors said he was lucky.' Neville snorted. 'Blind, but lucky. I held his head in my lap while we waited for help and all the time he was crying. Trying to cry with needles stuck in his fucking eyes and there was so much blood you couldn't see the tears. He just kept saying that he didn't want to die and he kept calling for his mum. That's the curious thing, you know, when guys get shot, when they're dying, they don't call out for their wives or their girlfriends; they call for their mums. And do you know, while I knelt there talking to him, staring at him, the only thing I could think of? Thank Christ it was *him* and not me.'

Neville got to his feet and began pacing the room, slowly.

'He got a commendation, I think they gave him some kind of medal. I bet that really made up for losing his sight. A medal and some poxy fucking pension if he was lucky. And all the politicians crowed about how brave we all were and the army told us what a good job we were doing, but now it's all over no fucker wants to know. They don't want to know about us now. We did our job and that job's over. Now we should all get on with our lives. As simple as that. They don't realise we've *got* no lives any more. I hated being in Northern Ireland but at least I was doing what I'd been trained for. They train you, shape you, indoctrinate you and then, when it's over, they expect you to switch off. Like some kind of fucking machine.'

He crossed to the window and peered out, noticing the policemen moving around outside.

'Well, not this time,' Neville hissed. 'This is one machine they're *not* going to switch off.'

8.58 a.m.

'Is he insane?'

Sean Doyle looked up and saw that the question was directed towards him.

'Neville?' he mused, then shook his head.

'How can you be sure?' Calloway asked. 'If he's crazy, he's unpredictable, there's no telling what he might do next.'

'He's not crazy,' Doyle said, a note of assurance in his voice. He was sitting on the floor of the Portacabin, back propped against one wall, legs stretched out in front of him. On the floor next to him was a half-empty cup of tea and a sausage sandwich. The meagre provisions had been brought by a uniformed man five minutes earlier.

Calloway was seated on the only chair in the Portacabin.

DS Mason was perched somewhat awkwardly on the corner of the desk.

'If Neville's crazy, then so is every other guy in the Parachute Regiment,' the counter terrorist said, taking a bite of his sandwich.

'How many others have held their wife and kid at gun-

43

point lately?' Mason sneered.

'You don't know how his mind works,' Doyle said.

'And *you* do?'

'I've seen what he's seen, been through what he's been through.'

'You sound as if you feel sorry for him,' Calloway said.

'I *understand* him, there's a difference. That doesn't mean I agree with him,' Doyle murmured.

'I reckon he's a fucking nutter,' Mason interjected.

'You read his files,' Doyle said, munching on the sandwich. 'There was nothing in there to suggest he was unstable, was there?'

'I'm sure Fred West was a good laugh after a couple of pints,' the DI said, derisively. 'All I know, Doyle, is that we've got an armed man in that house over there, holding his wife and daughter hostage.'

'Our job is to get them out safely,' Mason added.

'The wife and kid are *your* concern. I'm only interested in Neville,' Doyle said, swallowing some tea.

'You still haven't told us exactly what that interest is,' Calloway reminded him.

'If I were you, Calloway, I'd be more concerned about the woman and child.'

'So, what ideas have you got? How do we get them out without getting them both killed?' the DI wanted to know.

Doyle shrugged.

'Come on, hotshot, you're supposed to be the expert,' Mason chided.

'Look, porky,' Doyle sneered, seeing the colour spreading through the DS's cheeks. 'This is a fucking siege, in case you hadn't noticed. There's a pissed-off para shut up in his house with two hostages, surrounded by plods and, as far as we know, armed to the fucking teeth. You make the wrong move and you're going to have a bloodbath on your hands. He'll kill the woman and kid first, then he'll either top himself or he'll start on you boys. My guess is he'll start putting it about if you try to storm the place, so I hope you've got a good supply of body bags. Neville's not playing fucking games and, until we find out exactly what he wants, there isn't a thing any of us can do but wait.'

'For how long?' Mason snapped. 'He could be holed up in there for days.'

'Give it another couple of hours then shut off all electricity and gas. We might as well make it as uncomfortable for him as possible,' Doyle offered.

'And the wife and kid?' Calloway said. 'It'll be uncomfortable for them too.'

'They're being held prisoner by a geezer with one or more guns, can life get *that* much worse?' Doyle mused. 'If someone had a gun to *your* head would you really notice if the fucking heating was on or off?'

'What else?' Mason asked.

'You need to know *where* they are inside the house,' Doyle said, getting to his feet. 'You've got plans, haven't you?'

The DI nodded and indicated the plans on the table.

Doyle glanced at them.

Three rooms downstairs. A sitting room to the front. A dining room and a kitchen. The front door opened into a reasonably large hall. The stairs were directly ahead. Beneath them was what appeared to be a toilet.

The upper level consisted of three bedrooms, two facing the front, and a bathroom.

'If you rush the place he's got two very good vantage

points to pick you off from,' Doyle said pointing at the front bedrooms.

'The houses on either side have been evacuated,' Calloway interjected. 'The others five up and down on either side of number ten are empty, the occupants have already left for work. The place is isolated.'

'Is the rear covered?' Doyle asked.

'We've got men in both of the gardens on either side,' said the DI. 'Neville couldn't get out that way even if he wanted to.'

Doyle didn't answer. 'What's that?' he asked, tapping the plan.

The two policemen peered intently at the sketched area.

'It's an attic,' Calloway said. 'So what?'

'Somewhere else to hide,' Doyle said.

'So, what do we do?' the DI asked.

Doyle looked at number ten London Road, gazing at the curtained windows.

'Try and get some men closer,' he said quietly.

'But you said he might open fire on them if they rushed it,' Mason reminded the counter terrorist.

Doyle smiled thinly.

'I'm not talking about going in the front door,' he said. 'There's another way.'

9.06 a.m.

Robert Neville raised the automatic as he saw the policeman moving slowly towards the house.

Squinting, Neville steadied himself, lining up the sights until the pistol was aimed at the uniformed man.

His finger tightened a fraction on the trigger.

It would be so easy.

One shot, maybe two.

Start it off now.

They *must* have armed men out there, Neville mused. They must know *he* was armed. What they didn't know was that, in addition to the .459, he also had a .357 Sterling revolver and a Steyr MPi 69 sub-machine gun.

They were in for one hell of a fucking surprise when things finally kicked off.

The MPi could fire over 550 rounds of 9mm ammunition a minute.

Come in, boys. Join the fucking party.

The policeman he'd drawn a bead on was standing beside a car talking to a colleague.

Neville reckoned he could take them both out with ease.

Just a little more pressure on the trigger . . .

'Why don't you just kill us and get it over with, Bob,' said Julie, sitting watching him.

'I don't want to kill you, I never have,' Neville said, softly, the pistol still trained on the policeman.

'Why did you come back?'

He finally turned away from the window and faced her.

'It would have been easier for you if I'd just disappeared, wouldn't it? Better still if I'd been killed out there.'

'I never wanted that. I never wanted you dead, I just wanted you to realise that it was over between us. I tried, Bob. I tried harder than a lot of wives would have. I stuck by you when you left the army.'

'Out of duty?' he chided.

'I didn't enjoy watching you drink yourself into a stupor every day,' she told him. 'I should have left when you disappeared. Why did you go back to Ireland? You'd been out of the army for six months but you went back. Why?'

'There were some things I had to do,' he told her.

'Did you miss it that much, Bob?'

He rounded on her angrily.

'Yes,' he snarled, taking a step towards her. 'Everything I *was*, I left behind when the troubles ended. That's why I went back. There was nothing for me here, there still isn't.'

'What about me and Lisa?'

'You were going to leave me,' he roared, his face contorted, eyes bulging.

For the first time that morning, Julie felt genuine fear.

She could feel the colour draining from her face.

'I'm not going to give in,' he rasped. 'It's all I knew, all I wanted. It's what I was trained for. I can't spend the rest of my life like this. I'm too young to die but I'm frightened of living. I don't know how to live without it, without the fighting. I could carry on from day to day, wait for cancer or a stroke or some other fucking thing, but I won't. All I want is to die like a man.'

'Why do you have to die at all?'

'Because there's nothing else for me and, when I go, I'm taking as many with me as I can.' He sat down wearily on the end of the sofa.

'Including me and Lisa?' Julie asked quietly.

He didn't answer, merely sat there staring at the floor, the .459 still gripped in one fist.

'Life's overrated,' he said, smiling bitterly. 'But people take it for granted. They take men like me for granted. The public is as bad as the media and the politicians. When there's a war on everybody wants to slap you on the back, buy you fucking drinks, tell you how brave you are, and do you know why? Because the cunts are pleased it's not them. And then, when everything's over, they don't want to know you. You're not front-page news any more, you're no good to politicians because they can't use you to vote-catch. And you're no good to the public because they find new heroes. And they expect you to go away quietly and not bother them again because once all the fighting's over, they don't want to be reminded of it. There were fucking victory parades after the Falklands, after the Gulf. How many fucking victory parades have there been for the soldiers who were in Ulster? Who gives a fuck? Who's *ever* given a fuck?'

His voice was rising steadily in volume. 'I'll make them care. I'll *make* them remember,' he shouted.

'Dad.'

He turned as he heard the word, pushing the .459 into his belt.

Lisa Neville was standing in the living-room doorway.

She looked at her father, then across to the sofa where her mother sat.

There was bewilderment in her eyes.

'I heard shouting,' she said quietly.

'It's all right, sweetheart,' said Neville. 'You go back upstairs to your room.'

'Mum, can I have an apple?' Lisa said, twisting some strands of hair around her finger.

Julie nodded, tried to smile.

'You get it, darling.'

Lisa scooped a Golden Delicious from the bowl on the coffee table and scurried back upstairs. They both heard her footfalls then the banging of her bedroom door.

Neville looked at Julie but neither spoke.

He wandered back to the front window and looked out once more.

It wouldn't be long now, he thought.

He glanced up towards the ceiling and smiled.

9.24 a.m.

Doyle didn't know the names of the two men with him.

He didn't care.

They were both uniformed and in their late twenties. One fresh-faced and slightly built, the other broader across the shoulders. The bulletproof waistcoats which they both wore added to the bulk.

Doyle had seen both of the policemen inspecting him as Calloway had briefed them and then he'd heard names mentioned.

Scott and Wilde? Something like that.

Who cared?

They both carried Sterling 81 rifles.

Doyle held a two-way radio in his hand, the volume turned down as low as possible.

The three men were less than fifty yards from number ten London Road, ducked low as they sprinted towards number six, passing other policemen, some of whom were crouched down behind the many parked cars which clogged the street.

Doyle saw more guns.

The counter terrorist slowed his pace when he reached the short path leading towards the front door of number six. There was a high fence to one side of the house which would shield their approach. It also hid the garden from view should anyone be looking from a rear window of number ten.

Doyle knew that Neville would have ensured he could see in all directions. He would have picked his vantage points carefully.

That's what Doyle himself would have done.

He smiled to himself.

The gate which led to the rear of number six was open and Doyle eased up the latch and beckoned the two policemen to follow him.

The garden was a mess. The lawn was overgrown, the flowerbeds infested with weeds. A child's swing was at the bottom of the garden, the seat swaying gently back and forth in the wind, the rusty chains creaking noisily.

The fence which separated this garden from that of the next house was six feet tall, weather-beaten, rotten in places.

Doyle gripped the top and hauled himself up, glancing swiftly over into the garden of number eight.

Beyond it there was a low privet hedge.

'Fuck it,' hissed Doyle, dropping back down.

'What's wrong?' asked Scott, the larger of the two armed policemen.

'Don't fuck about when you get over this fence,' Doyle said sharply. 'There isn't much cover. Just head straight for the back door and keep your heads down, otherwise you're likely to get them blown off.

Doyle pulled the Beretta from its holster and worked the slide, chambering a round before slipping it back beneath his left arm.

Wilde looked at his companion then at Doyle.

'What if Neville opens fire?' he asked nervously.

'You're wearing body armour, aren't you?' Doyle said. 'Just hope he doesn't aim for your head.'

'Do we return fire?' Scott wanted to know.

Doyle shook his head.

'Then what's the point in us having these?' Wilde blurted, holding up the rifle.

'Just do what you're told,' Doyle snapped, turning towards the fence once again.

He gripped the top, dragged himself up and over it, landing lightly on the other side. As soon as he hit the ground he ducked down and scuttled towards the rear of the house, casting a swift cautionary glance towards one of the back windows of number ten.

No signs of movement.

Had Neville seen them approaching?

Cat and fucking mouse.

Doyle saw Scott heaving himself over the fence, the rifle slung around him.

He jumped down, landed heavily and overbalanced, sprawling on the grass.

'Get up, you prat,' Doyle hissed under his breath as the policeman hurried across to join him.

Wilde followed a moment later, banging the fence hard with one foot as he swung himself over.

Doyle looked up towards the back of number ten.

Are you waiting for us, Neville?

Doyle half expected to hear a shot ring out, to see Wilde fall.

Instead the policeman sprinted over to join the other two men. He was breathing hard and Doyle suspected that it wasn't the exertions which were causing it.

The younger man's face was pale.

'Now what?' said Scott.

'We get inside,' Doyle told him.

'But Neville's in number ten,' Wilde protested.

'Do you want to go and ring his fucking doorbell then?' Doyle snapped.

The younger man lowered his gaze, contenting himself with staring around the garden instead.

There was still washing on the line. Just a solitary blouse and, for some reason, a single white sock.

A plastic tricycle lay overturned on the well-manicured lawn. Close to it a black and white football.

Children's possessions, thought Wilde.

He could feel his heart pounding hard against his ribs and he gripped the rifle tightly.

Doyle was staring at the back door, which was wooden with glass panels in the top half.

Using one elbow he broke the panel above the lock and snaked his hand through, turning the key.

He pushed open the door, took one last look up at the rear of number ten, then ushered the two armed policemen inside ahead of him.

If Neville had seen them arrive he was keeping quiet about it, thought Doyle.

What little surprises have you got in store, you fucker?

Doyle stepped inside number eight and flicked on the two-way.

'Calloway, it's Doyle, come in, over.'

The radio hissed and crackled and Doyle fiddled with the buttons on it.

He heard the DI's voice.

'Doyle, this is Calloway. Over.'

The counter terrorist held the two-way close to his mouth.

'We're inside number eight,' he said.

9.29 a.m.

Robert Neville sat on one end of the sofa and poured himself another glass of Scotch.

'Join me?' he said, smiling crookedly at his wife.

Julie shook her head and looked away from him, shifting position. She could feel the first twinges of cramp in her left calf and began to massage the affected area slowly.

Neville suddenly got to his feet and crossed to her, gripping her chin in his hand, forcing her head around so that she was compelled to look into his face. Into his eyes.

They locked stares, then he released his grip and walked towards the window, whisky glass in one hand.

'Bob, just promise me one thing.'

Neville turned to look at her.

'Promise me you won't hurt Lisa. I don't care what you do to me but—'

'Don't you?' he said sharply. 'You really don't care. What's the matter? Do you put that little value on your own life? I thought it was just me you didn't give a shit about.'

She sighed resignedly. 'I know you'll kill me if you want to, I'm just asking you not to hurt Lisa. She is your daughter, in case you'd forgotten.'

'So, *you* want *me* to promise?' he said cryptically.

She watched as he downed what was left in the glass then crossed to the wooden sideboard and refilled the tumbler.

There was a photo perched on top of the mahogany cabinet.

A wedding photo.

Neville picked it up and studied the figures in it.

Himself and Julie. So long ago. How long? He could barely remember.

Neville in his uniform. Julie resplendent in a knee-length blue dress.

Nine, ten years ago.

Jesus, where had the time gone?

The photo had been taken outside Camden Register Office. There'd been fewer than a dozen people there. Family, what little they had. Friends, those who'd bothered to turn up.

Neville replaced the photo.

'It hasn't *all* been bad, has it?' he asked softly, eyes still fixed on the picture.

'What?'

'Our life together.'

'No. We've got Lisa.'

'We just never had each other, did we?' he said, his tone hardening rapidly.

'You were never here, Bob.'

'I was doing a job, for Christ's sake. You knew what I did when you met me. You knew I was in the army.' He turned to face her.

'You were different then,' she told him.

'Bullshit.'

'We were *both* different people, Bob.' She opened her mouth to speak again but he held up a hand to silence her, his ears attuned to the slightest noise.

He moved across the room, towards the living-room wall, then he cupped a hand to it and listened.

Movement on the other side.

He leaned closer, trying to distinguish the sounds.

Then, silence.

He wondered if the noise had come from the front of

the house, but something told him his initial instinct had been correct.

Sounds of movement from the house next door?

Neville retreated from the living room for a moment.

When he returned he was carrying the MPi 69, his face set in a stern expression.

Julie looked at the automatic weapon and shuddered involuntarily.

Neville slipped off the safety catch.

It seemed the waiting was over.

9.41 a.m.

Doyle noticed that there were still cups and plates on the kitchen table of number eight. Even a bottle of milk was propped in the centre of the table, bowls of half-eaten cornflakes close by.

The resident must have been evacuated during breakfast.

On one of the plates a fried egg had congealed along with several rashers of bacon and a couple of sausages.

The counter terrorist picked up one of the sausages and pushed it into his mouth, chewing hungrily.

He looked around the room. Crayon drawings were stuck to the cupboard doors with Blu-Tack. Fridge magnets in the shape of letters had been placed randomly on the white metal of the cold unit.

Wilde noticed some small metal cars on the floor beneath the table, discarded by their owner during the flight from the house.

The room smelled of cooking.

He and Scott followed Doyle through into the living room, which looked slightly less chaotic.

The television was still on, the sound turned down.

Beneath it the digits of the video, he noticed, were set at the wrong date and time.

There were photos on the wall showing the family who had fled.

Mother, father and two children.

The parents were in their late twenties, he guessed, the kids about eight or nine. A boy and a girl.

Doyle glanced around the room, also taking in the details, then he crossed to the front window and peered out.

The view he had was roughly the same as that of Neville in the building next door. Uniformed policemen, a number of cars. Even the Portacabin which he'd left not so long ago was just visible from here.

The counter terrorist saw a door behind him and assumed it led to the hallway.

He pushed open the door and found that his assumption was right.

As Scott and Wilde watched, he closed the door again then flicked on the two-way.

'Calloway, it's Doyle, come in.'

There was a sharp hiss of static then he heard the policeman's voice.

'What have you got, Doyle?'

'Any sign of movement from Neville?'

'Not yet.'

'If there is, you let me know straight away, got it?'

Doyle flicked off the two-way then pushed open the hall door once more, edging towards the stairs, climbing them cautiously, cursing under his breath when the first one creaked alarmingly.

The two policemen followed him, also treading carefully.

As they reached the landing, Doyle looked up and saw a trapdoor leading to the attic.

The four doors which faced the three men were all closed. He nodded towards Wilde, then the closest door.

Scott searched the other two rooms.

'Nothing,' Scott whispered, joining Doyle who was still gazing up at the trapdoor.

Wilde rejoined them a moment later and merely shook his head.

'Give me a leg up,' Doyle said quietly and Scott clasped his hands together, stirrup-like, allowing the counter terrorist to put one booted foot there, then he lifted.

Doyle pushed the opening of the trapdoor with one hand, using the other to grip the side of the attic entrance, then he swung himself up into the gloom of the loft.

The darkness up there was impenetrable, the dust thick.

It clogged in his nostrils but he put a hand over his mouth to stop himself coughing.

Doyle reached into his jacket pocket and pulled out his lighter, striking it, holding it high above his head.

The sickly yellow light it gave off was barely sufficient to cut through the inky blackness and it only gave him a puddle of brightness about a foot in diameter in which to move.

He picked his way slowly across the attic floor, the lighter growing hot in his hand.

There were boxes everywhere, piled high, some overflowing. He saw magazines, tools, clothes and even old blankets stuffed into them. Some of the boxes were ripped, their contents having spilled out on to the dusty floor of the attic.

A pile of old copies of *Men Only* stood close by and Doyle glanced down approvingly at the face of the young woman who adorned the cover, her features covered by a film of dust.

There was a loud squeak from beneath his foot and he froze.

Shit.

The sound seemed to be dulled by the dust in the air but, to Doyle, the noise sounded deafening.

He looked down to see that he'd trodden on a plastic rabbit. Another child's toy. As he removed his foot it squeaked again, almost protestingly.

Fucking thing.

The wall which separated the attic of number eight from the attic of number ten was about six feet away now.

Doyle could see that the bricks there were still bare, untouched by paint, encrusted only with dust and grime.

He stood close to the wall and pressed the flat of one hand to the cold bricks.

These houses were more than eighty years old. The walls must be at least a foot thick, he mused, tapping a brick with the knuckle of his finger.

If they were going to get into the house next door through here they'd need to blast the fucking thing.

So much for plan A, Doyle mused, turning and heading back towards the hatch.

It was then that the two-way crackled into life.

He snatched it from his pocket, turning the volume down as low as it would go.

'Doyle, this is Calloway, come in.'

The counter terrorist took two swift steps towards the hatch.

'Doyle.'

'Shut it for fuck's sake, I can hear you,' Doyle rasped. 'I'm in the attic of number eight, Neville will hear you *too* if you don't keep it down.' He crouched on the edge of the hatch, the two policemen looking up at him. 'What the hell's going on?'

'Something's happening,' Calloway told him. 'The door to number ten is open. Someone's coming out.'

9.47 a.m.

Julie Neville stood motionless in the doorway of number ten London Road, her coat pulled around her shoulders, her gaze flicking back and forth.

She could see a number of uniformed men ahead of her.

She wondered how many were carrying guns.

How many of those guns were trained on *her*.

She stood motionless, silhouetted in the doorway.

Waiting.

'Walk to the front gate,' Neville said, ducked inside the house, the Steyr aimed at her.

She did as she was told, slowly, falteringly. Her heart was hammering so hard against her ribs she feared it would burst.

'What the fuck is he playing at?' DI Calloway murmured under his breath as he stepped from the Portacabin.

DS Mason practically had to run to keep up with him as the taller man took long strides which ate up the ground.

'Perhaps he's going to set demands,' Mason said breathlessly.

'Or he's giving himself up,' Calloway said humourlessly.

They were less than thirty yards from the front of number ten now. Both men could see Julie Neville standing about six feet from the front door, the wind whipping her long blonde hair around her face.

Calloway reached for the two-way and flicked it on.

'Doyle, he's sent out the woman.'

No answer.

'Doyle. Doyle, can you hear me?'

Still nothing.

From his vantage point in the front bedroom of number eight, Doyle could see Julie Neville standing on the path. Every now and then she would take a step forwards, getting closer to the gate.

Was Neville setting them up?

Doyle saw Calloway and Mason drawing nearer.

What the fuck was Neville doing?

Doyle heard the two-way hiss, heard Calloway talking to him.

He finally reached for the radio and flicked it on.

'Watch yourself, Calloway,' he said quietly. 'Neville could be pulling you in.'

'What do you mean?'

'You get close enough, he'll open fire. Watch it.'

'Can you see him from where you are?' Calloway asked.

'No. Only the woman.'

Julie had reached the gate by now. She gripped it as if to steady herself then glanced back over her shoulder towards the house.

Doyle frowned as he saw her beginning to unbutton her coat.

Calloway and Mason were mere yards away from her now.

Julie turned and looked behind her, then pulled her coat free.

Doyle could see a small black oblong between her shoulder blades, held in place by what looked like masking tape. The object was roughly the same size as a TV remote.

There was a tiny red light blinking on it.

'Oh Jesus,' he murmured, snatching up the two-way.

You fucking sly bastard, Neville.

'Calloway, stay away from her,' Doyle said urgently. 'She's wired.'

'What are you talking about?' the DI demanded.

'She's got a fucking bomb strapped to her back,' Doyle rasped.

9.52 a.m.

DI Calloway held the two-way close to his ear, his gaze fixed on Julie Neville.

She was only three feet from the policeman now and he could see how pale her features were, her eyes red-rimmed and slightly sunken. She was holding the gate as if for support, fearing that if she loosed her grip she would fall. He could see her trembling and he realised it was not because of the chill wind.

'Are you sure?' Calloway said into the two-way.

'Sure about what?' Mason wanted to know.

The DS could hear only his superior's side of the conversation; Doyle's hissed words were little more than a static blur.

'Are you all right, Mrs Neville?' Calloway asked, the two-way still pressed against his ear.

Now *he* was reluctant to move, as if any sudden action might cause not only the death of this woman but also of himself and Mason.

'Just stay where you are.'

The shout came from inside number ten.

From Neville.

Calloway looked towards the house, trying to catch a glimpse of the man who had just bellowed out the order but he could see nothing.

'Show them, Julie,' Neville called.

Julie turned slowly until her back was to the watching policemen.

They both saw the small black object taped to her back, the red light winking menacingly on it.

'It's a bomb,' Neville called.

'I know what it is,' Calloway called back.

'He's bluffing,' Mason hissed under his breath.

'He's *not* bluffing, you stupid cunt.'

Mason turned to his left and saw Doyle standing there, his gaze also fixed on the hapless woman before him.

'How do you know it's a bomb?' snarled Mason.

'Trust me,' Doyle murmured.

I've seen enough of the fucking things up close.

Including the one that nearly killed me.

'Neville's not playing games,' Doyle said.

For long seconds the three men stood motionless, all staring at Julie.

'Go on then, Neville,' shouted Doyle. 'Press the fucking button. Blow her up.'

'What the hell are you doing?' Mason said angrily, grabbing at Doyle's jacket. 'He'll kill her.'

'Get your fucking hands off me,' Doyle growled, pushing the DS away. He glared at him, those dark grey eyes

63

boring into the smaller man like lasers. 'He's not going to kill her. Not yet.'

'Why not?' Mason demanded.

'Because *she's* his ticket out of here, nobhead,' Doyle hissed.

'What do you want?' Calloway called.

'How good's your memory?' Neville shouted back. 'I've got a list.'

'Go on,' Calloway said, his gaze still fixed on Julie, who was trembling before them.

'I want a car, safe passage out of here and no tails,' Neville said. 'If I see so much as a copper on a fucking pushbike I'll kill them both.'

'Is the kid wired too?' Doyle shouted.

'What difference does it make?' Neville replied.

'How do we know you won't detonate the bomb anyway?' Mason chipped in.

'You don't,' Neville told him.

Doyle took a step to his right, trying to see inside the house, to see where Neville was standing.

One clear shot was all he needed.

And if you miss?

Julie had pulled her coat back on by this time, in a vain attempt to keep out some of the chill. She was quivering madly, her face the colour of rancid butter.

'A car, safe passage out of here and no tails,' Neville repeated.

'We heard you,' Calloway called back. Then, to Doyle: 'We could put some kind of tracking device in the car.'

'He'd be expecting that,' Doyle replied. 'Just give him what he wants.'

'As easy as that?' Calloway protested.

'If you don't, you're going to be sweeping her up with

64

a fucking dustpan and brush,' Doyle said, nodding towards Julie.

She looked helplessly at the three men.

'Even if he kills *her*, he's still got the kid in there with him,' Doyle reminded them. 'Do you want *that* on your conscience, Calloway?'

'Do *you*?' the DI countered.

'All I want is Neville,' Doyle told him. 'Now give him a fucking car. Let's get this shit over with.'

'You've got ten minutes to make up your minds, then I blow her to pieces,' Neville shouted.

'You haven't got the balls,' Doyle shouted back.

Julie looked frantically at the counter terrorist.

'Go on, Neville, spread her all over the street,' Doyle persisted. 'And then what? Kill your kid? If you do, you've got nothing to bargain with. And, as soon as they're gone, I'm coming in after *you*.'

'Who the fuck are you anyway?' Neville shouted angrily.

'Doyle. Counter Terrorist Unit. I know you, Neville. I know how your mind works. *I've* been where *you've* been, for what it's worth.'

'You don't know anything about me, Doyle,' Neville roared back.

'I know more than your wife. I even know how many times you shake your dick when you've had a piss.'

'You're full of shit. Now get me that fucking car or I'll kill her,' Neville bellowed. 'You've got nine minutes now.'

'Even if you get away from here, I'll still find you,' Doyle assured him.

'Try it.'

'I'll guarantee it.'

'Eight minutes,' Neville called.

Doyle walked away from the gate and looked at Calloway.

'Give him the car,' he said flatly.

10.01 a.m.

Doyle leaned against the door of the Portacabin and sucked hard on his cigarette, watching as Calloway finished his phone conversation.

'Sorted?' Doyle asked disinterestedly.

'The Commissioner isn't too happy about this,' Calloway told him. 'Letting Neville go.'

'You're not letting him go, you're agreeing to his demands in order to protect the lives of hostages, aren't you?'

'If he gets away . . .'

'He *won't* get away,' Doyle asserted.

'I wish I was as sure as you,' Calloway answered.

'He won't get away because hotshot here is going to get him, aren't you?' Mason chided. 'Captain fucking Marvel is going to track him down, isn't that right, Doyle?'

The counter terrorist looked at the DS contemptuously.

'*You're* going to track him down, *you're* going to hunt him,' Mason continued. 'What do you think this is, a fucking Western?'

'If it was, you'd be the fat, bungling sheriff, wouldn't you, porky?' Doyle quipped.

'All right, girls, knock it off,' Calloway said irritably. 'Let's just get on with it. The car's here.'

'Let me take it to Neville,' Doyle offered.

'You'll try and kill him as soon as you get near him,' Calloway snapped. 'One of the uniformed boys can do it.'

'Calloway,' Doyle said, taking a step towards the DI. 'Let me do it.'

The two men's eyes locked.

'You'll try to kill him,' the policeman said quietly.

Doyle shook his head. 'Not until the hostages are safe. You've got my word on that.'

Still Calloway hesitated. 'Earlier on, when we were outside the house,' the DI said, 'you told Neville you'd *been* where *he'd* been. What did you mean?'

Doyle shrugged. 'He was in Ireland, I was in Ireland,' he explained. 'He'd been wounded there. So was I.'

'Badly?'

Doyle smiled.

If you could see the fucking scars . . .

There was a knock on the Portacabin door and a uniformed constable stood there, a set of car keys in his hand.

Mason took them from him and handed them to Calloway.

'Let me take the car to him,' Doyle persisted.

Calloway waited a second, then tossed the keys to the counter terrorist who nodded and stepped outside.

The policemen followed, watching as Doyle slid behind the wheel of a dark blue Montego.

'No fucking heroics,' said Calloway. 'Our concern is the hostages.'

Doyle nodded. 'He'll ditch it as soon as he can, you know.'

'I know that,' Calloway told him.

Doyle started the engine and revved it, exhaust fumes filling the cold air.

'You tell those fucking snipers to keep their fingers off the triggers,' Doyle said. 'If one of them gets jumpy

I don't want him shooting me by mistake.'

'Yeah, that'd be a tragedy, wouldn't it?' Mason chided.

Doyle eyed him coldly. 'You know what, fatso?' he said. 'When I finish with Neville, I might just come back for *you*.'

He stuck the car in gear and pulled away.

'Doyle,' Calloway shouted after him. 'Just take it easy. Remember the hostages.'

Doyle slid a hand inside his jacket and touched the butt of the Beretta.

Fuck the hostages.

He drove the Montego up onto the pavement, bringing it close to the front gate of number ten.

He left the engine running, eyes fixed on the front door. Waiting.

'Come on, Neville,' he said under his breath. 'I've got something for you.'

The front door remained closed.

10.06 a.m.

Doyle was leaning against the bonnet of the Montego when he saw the front door open.

He had both hands dug deep into the pockets of his leather jacket but, as the door opened a little wider, he slid one hand inside the garment, almost unconsciously touching the butt of the automatic.

'I hope they've been given their instructions,' Neville called from inside. 'No shooting or I press this fucking detonator.'

'You're safe,' said Doyle.

Come out, you fucker.

'Step away from the car,' Neville ordered, finally

68

stepping into view.

Doyle saw him for the first time.

Perhaps if he pulled the Beretta now. He could get off a couple of shots before . . .

Before Neville pressed the detonator?

Before he opened up with the Steyr?

'Where are the hostages?' Doyle demanded, watching as Neville edged cautiously from the front door, a hold-all gripped in his free hand.

'They're safe. Inside,' Neville said, motioning with his head. 'Unless someone gets trigger-happy.' He held up the detonator control.

Smaller than the palm of his hand. A tiny black box with a winking red light on it and a red button. Neville's thumb was poised over that button.

Neville was walking slowly up the path now, his gaze never leaving Doyle.

'Why did you do it, Neville?' Doyle asked. 'Why did you kill the IRA men, the Sinn Fein guys, the UVF blokes? Why?'

'Is that why they sent *you*?

'They want you kept quiet,' Doyle told him.

Neville chuckled. 'They're scared of me, aren't they? Terrified I'll fuck up their little peace plan.'

Doyle nodded.

'How long were *you* in Ireland?' Neville asked.

'Five years, six, seven. Who cares?'

'Undercover?'

Doyle nodded again.

Neville opened the passenger-side door of the Montego and tossed the hold-all on to the seat, never allowing the barrel of the Steyr to leave Doyle.

'You saw what went on out there,' Neville continued.

'Don't you understand why I killed them? Why I don't want peace? I was shot at, screamed at, spat at and fuck knows what else while I was there but as soon as their little peace treaty is signed, they expect us all to forget about it. Bollocks to that.'

'I understand what you're talking about,' Doyle said quietly.

'Maybe you do but *they* don't,' Neville told him, sweeping one arm towards the watching horde of policemen.

Doyle could see the detonator in his hand.

'And the fucking army don't understand either, that's why they sent you to kill me, isn't it?' Neville hissed.

'Yes,' Doyle answered bluntly.

'What are you carrying?' Neville asked, nodding towards Doyle's jacket. 'Show me.'

Doyle eased open the jacket and pulled it to one side, allowing Neville a sight of the Beretta.

'Pull it,' Neville said, smiling.

'So you can cut me in half with that, fuck you,' Doyle said, nodding towards the sub-gun.

'I'm giving you a chance,' Neville told him. 'Come on, you want to kill me. Try it.'

'Don't tempt me.'

'You know you can't. If you shoot me I'll still press this detonator.'

'Press it. I couldn't give a fuck if you blow up your wife, your kid and the whole fucking street,' Doyle rasped. 'I came for *you*.'

'Then take your chance while you've got it.'

'There'll be another time.'

Neville regarded him coldly. 'Why are you doing this?' he said finally. 'Why do you want to kill me? We're on the same side. We always were. We still are. What are they going to do with *you* now all this shit in Ireland is over? How long before someone comes to kill *you*?'

'They wanted peace and they've got it, Neville. You jeopardised that peace. That's why I'm here.'

'I thought you understood me.'

'I do but I've got a job to do and I'm going to do it.'

Neville slid behind the wheel of the car, the detonator still in one hand.

He's put the sub-gun down. Shoot him now.

'How long before they want you dead too, Doyle,' Neville said. 'You're as useless now as *I* am. Whatever we *were* was back in Ireland, in the fighting.'

Doyle gritted his teeth, the knot of muscles at the side of his jaw pulsing.

What's wrong? The truth hurt?

'*I'm* the only thing left for you, Doyle,' Neville said, a slight smile on his face. 'If you kill me what else is there for *you*?'

'Fuck you, Neville,' Doyle snarled.

'Too late. The politicians already did that.'

The car pulled away, moving slowly down the road, past dozens of watching policemen.

'Shit,' Doyle murmured under his breath.

Policemen were hurrying towards the house now.

The counter terrorist himself turned and walked up the short path towards the front door, pushing it, surprised when it swung open.

He stepped into the hall.

There was a faint, sickly sweet odour in the air which was familiar to him.

Something . . .

He pushed the living-room door open.

Again that sickly sweet smell.

Julie and Lisa Neville were sitting on the sofa, wrists and ankles tied, both of them gagged with pieces of cloth.

The first of the policemen entered the house close behind Doyle.

The counter terrorist was already untying Julie's hands.

She ripped the gag free. 'Get us out of here,' she wailed, her eyes bulging.

'It's all right,' Doyle said, frowning as he finally recognised the cloying smell.

The marzipan odour.

'He's rigged the house,' Julie shouted, snatching up her daughter and bolting for the front door.

'Jesus Christ,' hissed Doyle.

The odour was plastic explosive.

The building must be packed with it.

'Get out!' Doyle bellowed.

Robert Neville looked at his watch.

He'd driven about two miles.

No sign of anyone following.

The police would be inside the house by now.

He pressed the detonator button.

10.16 a.m.

The explosion was deafening.

The entire upper floor of number ten London Road seemed to rise into the air, propelled by a blast of such thunderous proportions it sounded as if the sky itself had been split apart.

Roofing tiles, pieces of guttering, lumps of wood and

stone all erupted upwards in a shrieking funnel of fire, the concussion blast rolling across the street, knocking those nearby off their feet, deafening them.

Doyle lay face down, arms covering his head as he waited for the debris to begin raining down.

What had gone up, after all, had to come down and, seconds after the massive detonation, pieces of brick, wood and all manner of materials began raining down from the heavens.

A screaming plume of flame shot twenty feet skyward, mushrooming outwards into a thick cloud of black and reddened smoke, the pall spreading rapidly across the heavens like ink across blotting paper. A noxious man-made cloud from which the debris seemed to be pouring.

Doyle glanced up and saw bricks landing on parked cars.

A length of timber fully six feet from tip to tip crashed through the windscreen of a police car, the men nearby ducking even lower, one of them falling heavily as a lump of tiling struck his shoulder.

Glass from the upper storey of the house also sprayed outwards and Doyle hissed in pain as a sliver laid open the back of his right hand. He kept the bleeding appendage clapped to his head until the last of the smoking debris had come to earth, though.

Slowly, he picked himself up and turned to look at the house.

Close by, Julie Neville was clutching her daughter to her, her eyes also fixed on what remained of the house.

Three policemen were gathered around her, one of them holding a blanket which he was attempting to wrap around her shoulders.

Calloway and Mason moved cautiously across towards

Doyle, who was standing in the street slowly bandaging his hand with a handkerchief.

Sirens were wailing in the distance.

Lisa Neville was crying.

Doyle looked across at the child impassively as she and her mother were helped away.

'Are you OK?' asked Calloway, nodding towards Doyle's injured hand. Blood was soaking through the material.

The counter terrorist nodded slowly, his eyes still riveted on the destruction the bomb had wrought.

'Neville's fucking crazy,' Mason rasped. 'Christ knows how many people he could have killed with that bloody bomb . . .'

'I don't think he wanted to kill anyone,' Doyle said quietly.

'Are you stupid?' the DS shouted. 'Look at that fucking house.'

Doyle grabbed the smaller man by the lapels and dragged him close, pressing his forehead against the policeman's nose.

'Yeah, look at it, fuckhead,' he rasped. 'Look at the way it's blown.' He pushed the DS away.

'What the hell are you talking about?' Calloway asked.

'The blast went upwards,' said Doyle, making an expansive gesture with his hands. 'Up and out. The houses on either side are barely damaged.'

'I don't get it,' Calloway said, gazing at the wreckage.

'The bottom floor is still intact. My guess is he only wired the attic, maybe only the roof,' Doyle said. 'That's a neat piece of work. Clever.'

'I'm glad you approve,' Calloway said irritably, walking towards the house.

He stepped over burning timber as he approached the front door.

Beneath his feet, broken glass crunched loudly. It was like walking on a crystal carpet.

The stench of burning was heavy in the air and millions of tiny cinders were spinning around like filthy snow.

Calloway coughed as he inhaled the acrid smoke.

Doyle moved inside the house, into the sitting room.

'Watch it, Doyle,' Calloway said. 'The fucking ceiling might give way.' He glanced up nervously but the counter terrorist seemed unconcerned.

There were several deep cracks in the plaster, a diaphanous white dust drifting down from these rents.

Doyle moved back out of the sitting room and headed for the stairs, taking them carefully, feeling them give, hearing them groan protestingly beneath his weight.

Halfway up he stopped, but from this vantage point he could see what was left of the upper storey, the light pouring in through the gaping hole made by the explosion.

The walls were blackened and there were dozens of tiny fires on the landing carpet, even on the walls. Pictures which had hung there lay smashed on the floor, and there was more glass scattered around.

And everywhere, the acrid stench of smoke clogged in Doyle's nostrils.

'What did he use?' Calloway asked.

'Semtex, I could smell it when I came in. He'd have needed three or four pounds to do this kind of damage.'

'It looks like somebody fired a fucking cannon through the roof,' Mason interjected.

'This was a controlled explosion,' Doyle said almost admiringly. 'Neville would have known exactly what damage he was going to do, what angle the blast would take. Like I said, this is a clever bit of work. When they said he was an explosives expert they weren't taking the piss.'

'Where the hell would he have got Semtex?' Mason asked.

'The same place he got those guns,' Doyle said indifferently. 'And my guess is he's got more of it somewhere.'

Doyle turned and headed back out of the house.

'How can you be so sure?' Calloway prompted.

'I know Neville.'

As he headed up the path he noticed that there was a small teddy bear lying amidst the debris.

It was blackened on one side but Doyle stooped and picked it up, rubbing as much of the soot away as he could.

He dropped it into his jacket pocket and headed towards his car.

'Doyle,' Calloway shouted after him. 'Where are you going?'

'There's somebody I need to talk to.'

'What about Neville?' the DI continued.

'He can't have gone far.'

Doyle slid behind the wheel of his car and started the engine.

Calloway watched as the Datsun pulled away.

10.29 a.m.

The cat had obviously been dead for a number of weeks.

The stench it gave off was almost palpable.

Neville wondered how it had managed to get inside the lock-up in the first place. The building had always been secure.

It had needed to be.

The two large wooden doors at the front of the building had been held firmly shut by a series of locks and a rusting chain he'd used to manacle the handles. There was a window in each door, but the glass was so caked in dirt it was practically opaque.

Inside, the walls were bare brick, dark with mildew in several places which looked like mouldering cankers on the stonework.

Neville was certain he hadn't been followed.

Positive he hadn't been seen abandoning the car, or entering the lock-up.

He'd heard the explosion when he'd detonated the bomb.

Hard to miss it, he mused.

They'd come looking for him now and that was what he wanted.

The police would come.

Doyle would come.

I'll bury the fucking lot of you.

In one corner of the lock-up, boxes were stacked high. He'd put them there himself the last time he'd been here about a month earlier.

No one had seen him come or go then and if they had, there would have been nothing unusual to alert them.

Neville crossed to the boxes and began pulling them away, dismantling the makeshift rampart with gleeful speed.

As each discarded box hit the floor it sent up fresh clouds of dust, motes twisting lazily in the rancid air.

The object hidden behind the boxes was covered by a tarpaulin.

Taking hold of one corner, Neville tugged hard on the canvas.

More dust billowed upwards but Neville merely smiled.

The Harley Davidson's sleek bodywork gleamed, even inside the dismal confines of the lock-up.

Neville placed one hand reverentially on the petrol tank, feeling the cold metal against his palm.

The FLTC Tour Glide was dark blue, the chrome exhaust pipes even more striking against the bodywork. The entire machine, capable of over a hundred miles an hour and weighing just under a ton, seemed to give off an aura of power and Neville looked at it admiringly for a second longer before flipping open the top box.

From inside he pulled out a pair of thick leather trousers, which he hastily slid over his jeans before fastening himself into the matching jacket.

The folds of the jacket easily hid the .459 automatic which he wore beneath one arm and the .357 revolver strapped to his right side in another shoulder holster.

The Steyr he slid into the top box.

The leather creaked loudly inside the stillness of the deserted building as Neville moved about, finally lifting the black helmet into view.

It glistened like a black skull.

With it wedged firmly on to his head, only his eyes were visible through the visor.

Neville swung his leg over the Harley, settled himself on to the seat and flicked the ignition switch.

The four-stroke V-twin 1,340cc engine roared into life, the sound reverberating inside the lock-up.

He twisted the throttle, exhaust fumes spewing from the tail pipes, the roar building steadily.

Five thousand rpm.

Like a fucking dream.

Beneath the helmet, Neville was laughing.

10.47 a.m.

Doyle thought about knocking but finally he just eased the handle down and peered around the door.

At first Julie Neville didn't see him and Doyle stood looking at her while she sat by the small bed pushed up against one wall.

She was gently stroking her daughter's forehead, gazing at her as she slept.

The room was tiny. Apart from the bed, it contained only a small wooden cabinet, a couple of plastic chairs and a small table. A cold cup of tea was perched on the table top.

Doyle glanced around the room, taking in the posters warning of meningitis, AIDS and smoking.

Leamington Park Hospital. Even in this side room he could smell that all too familiar antiseptic smell he associated so strongly with these places of healing.

He hated that smell.

Christ alone knew it was familiar enough.

Doyle had seen the inside of enough hospitals in his time.

A couple of them he'd thought he'd never leave.

He looked at Julie again.

She ran a hand through her long blonde hair and turned slightly, as if suddenly aware of his presence.

She nodded towards her sleeping daughter and pressed a finger to her lips, indicating that Doyle should remain silent.

'We need to talk,' he said softly, motioning towards the corridor beyond.

Julie got to her feet, took one more look at Lisa, then followed him out.

'Is she OK?' the counter terrorist asked as Julie closed the door behind her.

'They gave her something to help her sleep.'

'And what about you? How do *you* feel?'

She smiled thinly. 'Well, considering my husband tried to blow me up, demolished my house with explosives and nearly killed half a dozen coppers too, I'm fine.'

Doyle fixed her in his gaze.

She was pretty.

Like Georgie?

He offered her a cigarette.

'You're not supposed to smoke in here,' she told him, glancing around as if afraid someone would see them.

Doyle held the packet of Marlboros steady and she finally took one.

He jammed one between his lips then lit both with his lighter.

Julie took a long drag. 'I needed that,' she said, smiling.

It was her turn to run appraising eyes over *him*. The cowboy boots, the worn leather jacket. The long hair.

He needed a shave, she mused.

'I've already spoken to the police,' she said finally. 'They questioned me in the ambulance on the way here.'

'I'm not the police. I'm with the Counter Terrorist Unit.'

'What's that got to do with me?'

'Fuck all. But it's got a lot to do with your old man.' He raised his eyebrows. 'Want a coffee? There's a machine round the corner.'

'I shouldn't leave Lisa.'

'She'll be OK,' he reassured her. 'We can come straight back.'

Julie hesitated a moment longer then nodded.

They began walking.

10.51 a.m.

'Where did they find it?' asked DI Calloway, barely looking up from his cup of tea.

DS Colin Mason replaced the phone and exhaled deeply.

'About three miles from here,' he said. 'Dark blue Montego. It was definitely the car.'

'You didn't expect him to stay in it, did you?' Calloway sipped at his tea. 'What the fuck is his game?' the DI mused. 'If Doyle's right about that explosion—'

'*If* he is,' Mason snapped.

'He seems to know what he's talking about.'

'Cocky bastard.'

Calloway leaned back in his seat and glanced at his companion. 'It's a pretty safe bet Neville's not on foot now.'

'Do you reckon he had another car hidden somewhere nearby?'

'Well, he wouldn't be walking the streets with the gear he's carrying, would he?'

'His missus wasn't much help,' Mason said dismissively.

'We'll go back and talk to her again. I want to know what else Doyle thinks about this shit. Maybe he's got some idea what Neville's next move will be.'

'I don't trust him.'

'Why not? He's on *our* side, you know.'

'I'm beginning to wonder,' Mason grunted. 'Where the fuck did he get to anyway? I reckon he knows more than he's telling.'

Calloway sipped at his tea. 'Maybe we ought to do some checking up on Doyle too,' he murmured.

Mason smiled crookedly. 'If he *is* involved with Neville then *I* want the bastard myself.'

Calloway raised his eyebrows. 'Good luck,' he muttered, reaching for the phone.

Julie Neville watched as Doyle fed coins into the vending machine, waiting as a plastic cup dropped into view and watery brown fluid dribbled in. According to the selection he'd pressed, it was meant to be coffee.

She took the cup from him and sipped at it, wincing as it burned her lips.

Doyle got his own drink and motioned towards the plastic seats close to the machine.

From the window at the end of the corridor, Julie could see out over the hospital car park. An ambulance was pulling in to Casualty, blue lights spinning furiously. She turned away as she saw the uniformed attendants lifting a stretcher from the rear of the emergency vehicle.

'I don't know what you want to hear,' she said to Doyle who was lighting up another cigarette.

'The truth would help,' Doyle told her.

'About Bob? I'm not even sure I know that myself. Why are *you* so interested in him?'

Doyle ignored the question, sipping his coffee instead.

'Did he contact you very often when he was away? Letters, phone calls, that kind of thing?'

82

'In the beginning,' she said, smiling wanly. 'He used to write two or three times a week. But it's always like that at the beginning, isn't it?'

Doyle kept his gaze on her.

'When he came home on leave he used to bring me flowers,' Julie mused. 'Every time he'd bring something. Flowers, chocolates or earrings. I must have more earrings than any other woman in London. And they were always the same design. Silver hoops. Bob never did have much imagination.' Her tone had darkened slightly.

'What about recently?'

'About two years ago the letters started to dry up. He'd write once every couple of months, ring if I was lucky. He even stopped coming home on leave.'

'Do you know where he went?'

'He could have had another woman for all *I* knew.'

'Do you think he did?'

She regarded him warily. 'Does it matter?' she snapped.

'As a matter of fact it does.'

'What's he done? I mean, I know about this morning, but there's something else, isn't there?'

'Do you think he had another woman?' Doyle persisted.

'He found it hard enough to make friends, let alone relationships.'

'He made one with you.'

'If you want to call it that.'

'You were married, you've got a child. You must have loved him.'

'Once.' She took a swig of her coffee.

'January twenty-seventh, ten years ago,' Doyle said.

'How do *you* know?'

'You'd be surprised what I know. It goes with the job.'

'Well, if you know so much, why the questions?'

'There are still some gaps. You might be able to help me fill them.'

'You know so much about me. I don't know anything about you.'

'There's no need for you to,' he said, a thin smile touching his lips.

'I'm nosy,' Julie retorted, running her hand through her hair.

Christ, she reminded him of Georgie when she did that.

'I know your name and I know you want to find my husband, that's it.'

'That's all you *need* to know.'

She reached out and looked at his left hand, lifting it slightly. 'No wedding ring.'

Doyle pulled his hand away gently. 'No wife.'

'Girlfriend?'

He shook his head.

'There must be someone, Doyle.'

'There've been a few. I don't keep a bloody score-card.'

'Anyone special?'

'There *was*. She died.'

'I'm sorry. When?'

'Seven, eight years ago now.'

Nine. Ten. A fucking eternity.

'How did it happen?' Julie's voice was soft.

'She was shot,' he said flatly.

Shot to fucking pieces.

'We were working together at the time,' he continued. 'There isn't a day goes by that I don't think about her.' He turned his gaze on Julie and she found herself looking deeply into his grey eyes.

'What was her name?'

84

'Georgie. Georgina.' A faint smile played across his lips then vanished hurriedly.

What the fuck are you doing?

Doyle drained the contents of his cup and tossed it into the waste bin.

What are you going to do? Tell her your fucking life story? Get a grip.

'You said your husband didn't have many friends,' Doyle began, angry with himself.

Don't let the mask slip.

'The ones he *did* have, did you know them? Meet them?'

Julie hesitated a moment. 'Most of them were in the paras with him, I only met a couple.'

'Names?'

'It was a while ago.'

'Try to think, it might be important.'

'He was really close to a guy called Baxter. Ken Baxter.'

'Any details about him you can remember?'

'They were in the paras together. I met him a few times when he came home with Bob. They were in the same company.'

'Baxter,' Doyle muttered. 'That'll do for a start.' He got to his feet. 'I'll walk back round with you.' He nodded towards the other end of the corridor.

Julie got to her feet and they set off for the room where Lisa still slept.

'What'll happen to him if he's caught?'

'*When* he's caught,' Doyle corrected her. 'It depends who gets to him first. The police or me.'

11.06 a.m.

Neville slowed down as he approached the red light.

Inside the helmet his own breathing sounded laboured and he flipped up the visor, allowing some exhaust-choked air inside.

He could feel the reassuring bulge of his weapons against each side, hidden beneath his jacket.

As he drew up at the lights at the junction of Kilburn High Road and Belsize Road, Neville glanced at the vehicles aligned on either side of him.

A pale blue Volvo driven by a woman who was constantly turning around to bellow at two kids in the back seat.

Behind her a red Astra driven by a man with a haggard expression who was speaking animatedly into a mobile phone, alternately glancing at his watch and the lights which seemed to be stuck on red.

A white Transit van was on the other side of him, loud music blasting from inside.

The driver, a Jamaican wearing a baseball cap with the letter X emblazoned on it, regarded him balefully.

Neville met his gaze.

The Jamaican jerked his head up and down as if offended by the motorcyclist's gaze.

'What you lookin' at, man?' he said sharply.

Neville didn't answer. He continued to stare.

Nigger bastard.

The light had changed to red and amber, engines revved.

Neville kept his eye on the driver.

Neville gunned the throttle and sped off, swerving in front of the van, causing the driver to brake hard.

In his wing mirror he caught sight of the Jamaican gesturing angrily after him.

Neville smiled to himself, guiding the bike effortlessly through the traffic, moving along Belsize Road at a steady speed.

He didn't want to attract attention to himself.

Not yet.

There was a police car ahead of him.

So fucking what?

They had no idea who he was, who this leather-clad rider was.

More traffic lights ahead.

The police car was slowing down.

They *couldn't* know who he was.

Could they?

Neville wondered for fleeting seconds if he should speed around the police car, shoot across the lights. He thought better of it.

Another red light was coming up.

The police car had stopped too.

Neville pulled up alongside it and glanced quickly in at the driver.

Young, fresh-faced.

The driver glanced at him and at the bike then he nudged his companion, pointing to the Harley.

Neville swallowed hard.

They knew.

They fucking knew.

The light was still on red.

The driver was winding down the window now, his companion leaning across also.

Neville kept his gaze straight ahead, one hand fumbling gently with the zip of his jacket. He only had to ease the .459 free. Three or four shots into the car would do it. He was less than two feet from them.

Any minute now.

The driver had wound down the window fully by now.

Neville eased the zip further down.

'Excuse me,' the driver said.

Neville ignored him, his hand closing over the butt of the automatic.

'I say, excuse me,' the policeman persisted.

Neville turned to look into his eyes.

You're dead, he mused.

The driver held his gaze. 'It's a nice bike. Harley, isn't it?'

Neville looked puzzled momentarily.

'Harley Davidson,' the driver continued. 'It's not an Electra Glide, is it?'

Neville shook his head.

'Tour Glide,' he answered.

'Told you,' said the driver, turning to his companion.

Neville kept his hand around the butt of the .459.

'Cheers,' the driver said and wound the window back up.

The lights turned green, the police car moved off.

Behind him, Neville heard a loud blast on a hooter and he too pulled away, drawing alongside the police car again then swinging right into Chalk Farm Road.

The police car moved off in the opposite direction.

Get a grip.

They couldn't know. Not yet.

Neville was angry with himself for his own nervousness.

Just calm down.

You've got a good headstart on them. They don't even know what they're looking for.

He smiled.

And by the time they do, it'll be too late.

He glanced at his watch.

It should take him another fifteen minutes to reach Euston.

11.12 a.m.

Doyle recognised the voice immediately and a slight smile flickered on his lips as he leaned against the plastic shell of the phone cubicle.

A nurse glanced fleetingly at him as she passed by and Doyle wrinkled his nose as he caught a scent of the contents of the bedpan she was carrying.

'Are you OK, Doyle?' asked Major John Wetherby, his voice sounding metallic at the other end of the phone.

'You heard what happened?'

'It was difficult to miss it. Why didn't you kill Neville when you had the chance?'

'There *was* no fucking chance, Wetherby, that's why the cunt's still breathing. Now listen to me, I need your help.'

'How inconvenient for you,' Wetherby sniggered.

'Cut the bullshit, will you, just listen. I spoke to Neville's wife and—'

'She doesn't know who you are, does she?' Wetherby interrupted.

'She knows I'm with the Counter Terrorist Unit, what the fuck was I supposed to tell her? That her husband had won nutter of the year award and I was presenting it on behalf of the army?'

'Does she know why you want Neville?'

'No.'

'And the police?'

'Neither do they. Now will you shut the fuck up and listen to me.'

'This mustn't get out, Doyle. If—'

'I *know* that,' the counter terrorist snarled. 'Don't worry, your little secret is safe with me, Wetherby. Now listen to me. Neville's missus reckons he was a bit of a loner but there was one guy he *was* friendly with. A para by the name of Kenneth Baxter. I need to know as much about Baxter as you can tell me. If he's still serving. If he is then where? If he isn't then I need to know where I can find him. All the usual shit.'

'Why the interest in Baxter?'

'If he's a friend of Neville's it's not out of the question Neville might try and find him.'

'Why?'

'For fuck's sake, Wetherby, do I have to spell it out?' Doyle spat out exasperatedly. 'For support, for somewhere to hide out, to have a cuppa and a piece of fucking cake with. What the hell do you think? Neville might be trying to figure out his next move, it'd help him if he had some friendly faces around him, wouldn't it?'

'I should think Neville knows *exactly* what he's going to do next,' Wetherby said smugly.

'Just find Baxter for me, will you? I'll call back in thirty minutes.'

'Doyle, have you any idea where Neville is now?'

'If I had, would I be standing here talking to you?'

Doyle hung up.

11.22 a.m.

As Doyle approached the door he slowed his pace, listening for any sound from inside the room.

There was none.

He eased the handle down gently and stepped in.

Julie Neville was sitting close to the bed where her daughter slept.

To Doyle it looked as if both of them were in the same position as when he'd first entered the room. As if his conversation with Julie had never happened. As if a moment of time had been acted out and simply discarded.

This time when she turned towards him, she smiled.

A wide, bright smile.

Welcoming.

The counter terrorist said nothing, crossed to the bed and looked down at the sleeping form of Lisa Neville.

The long honey-blonde hair, one small hand gripping an edge of the sheet which was pulled up to her neck.

Doyle reached out and touched that small hand.

Julie watched him, a mixture of bewilderment and surprise on her face.

She studied the scars on his face. Deep scars.

She wondered how he'd got them.

There was even one on the hand which had reached out to touch her daughter.

'She looks like you,' Doyle said quietly, his eyes never leaving the child.

'You never had kids then?' Julie asked.

Doyle smiled. 'No need,' he said. 'No need, no time, no inclination.'

One more person to worry about. One more to lose.

'What about your girlfriend? The one that was killed, didn't she . . .'

'I never found out if she had much of a maternal streak,' he said bitterly.

'You said you worked together, was she in the same line of work? Counter terrorist?'

He nodded. 'She was the best I ever worked with,' he said softly.

Right. That's enough of the bullshit.

He ran a hand through his long hair as if the gesture was designed to wrench him from this mood.

Get a fucking grip.

'Neville loved her, didn't he?' Doyle said nodding towards Lisa who stirred slightly in her sleep.

'More than anything.'

'More than *you*?'

She looked shocked.

'After all, *you* were the one he strapped the bomb to, not her,' Doyle said.

'He would have done anything for Lisa.'

Doyle reached for his cigarettes, lit one, then offered the packet to Julie.

She declined.

'What did he say to you when he was holding you hostage? What did he talk about?'

'He was angry.'

'I figured that out myself.'

'Angry with the army,' Julie snapped. 'With the Government, with the public. With everyone. He thought he'd got a raw deal from the army. He kept on about having been trained to kill but then being discarded. He was mad because no one wanted him any more.'

'Including you?'

'It had been over between us for a couple of years. I put up with it as long as I could, for Lisa's sake. I suppose it was the last straw for him, me telling him I was going to leave him and take Lisa with me.'

'Did you think he was crazy?'

'I didn't know what to think. His moods changed like the bloody weather.'

'He never hit you or Lisa?'

'He wouldn't do that. It wasn't his *style*.' She smiled humourlessly. 'He'd never have slapped me.'

'Just wired you up with explosive. *I'd* rather have been slapped.'

'What do you want to hear, Doyle? That he was a maniac, that I was terrified of him? That I hated him?'

'Did you?'

'I felt sorry for him.'

'That's worse.'

'Fuck you,' she hissed.

They locked stares, then Doyle glanced at his watch.

'I've got to make a phone call,' he said, moving towards the door.

Julie watched him go.

'You're a bastard, Doyle,' she said as he opened the door.

'Who's arguing?' he shrugged.

It was as he stepped out into the corridor that he saw DI Calloway heading towards him.

11.37 a.m.

'What the hell are *you* doing here?'

Doyle eyed the DI disinterestedly and reached for his cigarettes.

'I asked you what you were doing here, Doyle,' Calloway repeated.

'Interviewing the witness.'

'That's police business, it's nothing to do with you.'

'You're right, it is police business but she's Neville's wife and he *is* my business.'

Doyle noticed that the DI was alone. 'Where's the other half of the partnership?' he asked, taking a long draw on his cigarette.

'Mason's gone back to New Scotland Yard for now. He's got a few things to sort out there.'

The two men eyed one another warily for a moment longer, then Calloway's expression softened slightly.

'Is she saying much?' he enquired, nodding towards the door.

'Not much that's any help.'

'No idea where Neville might be?'

Doyle shook his head. He thought about mentioning Kenneth Baxter then decided against it.

Let the fuckers find out themselves.

'I've got a phone call to make,' Doyle said, walking past Calloway.

'What *is* the big secret about Neville?' the DI wanted to know. 'Why are you after him?'

Doyle smiled. 'Let *me* worry about that,' he said quietly.

'I could do you for obstruction,' Calloway said menacingly.

'You couldn't do me for gobbing on the fucking pavement,' Doyle said dismissively, brushing past the DI.

'We're supposed to be on the same side,' the policeman called after him.

Doyle ignored him and kept walking.

As he turned the corner of the corridor he saw that the public phone was in use.

'Shit,' he muttered under his breath, sidling close to the user, a man in his mid-fifties who kept peering anxiously in Doyle's direction.

Come on, get a fucking move on.

Doyle drew on his cigarette and leaned against the wall, gazing at the man who was glancing all around him, anything to avoid making eye contact.

When he finally finished he gave Doyle an apologetic smile as he stepped away from the phone.

The younger man picked up the receiver and began feeding coins into the machine, aware that the other man was staring at him.

Only when Doyle turned and glared back at him did the man hasten his retreat along the corridor and out of sight.

Doyle jabbed the digits and waited.

An officious-sounding voice greeted him at the other end.

'I want to speak to Major John Wetherby,' Doyle said. 'Tell him it's Sean Doyle.'

The other voice said that Wetherby was busy.

'Then interrupt him. This is urgent.'

The officious voice insisted Doyle should hold.

'I'm using a public phone, you prick, now get Wetherby and stop fucking about. This is very urgent.'

There was a moment or two of silence on the other end, then Doyle heard a more familiar voice.

'Doyle, I—'

He didn't let the Intelligence officer finish. 'What have you got on Kenneth Baxter?'

'Well, he wasn't hard to trace. It makes for interesting reading, Doyle.'

'Cut the small talk. Where is he?'

'He's in London. He's lived there for the past twelve months. Kenneth Edward Baxter, age thirty-eight. Born May—'

'I don't need his fucking life history,' Doyle snapped.

'It's relevant,' Wetherby replied angrily.

'Is he still serving?'

'That's the interesting bit. Kenneth Baxter was court-martialled eighteen months ago, while he was a serving paratrooper. He was found guilty and sentenced to six months in a military prison in Aldershot. After his release he was dishonourably discharged from the army.'

'Jesus Christ, what did he do?'

'Well, like our friend Neville, Baxter was an explosives expert too. The only problem was, he was selling explosives, army explosives, to the IRA *and* the UVF.'

'For fuck's sake.'

'There was some talk of him selling weapons too but that charge was never proved.'

'So where is he now?'

'Like I said, he's living in London. He works for a private security firm called Nemesis.'

'They obviously didn't ask for references.'

'He's been there for about eight months.'

'Addresses?' Doyle fumbled in his pocket for a piece of paper. He found an old betting slip in one back pocket of his jeans and pulled a Bic from his jacket, scribbling away as Wetherby relayed the information. 'Anything else I should know?' he said finally, shoving the worn pink slip back into his pocket.

'Just find Neville,' Wetherby said.

'Doyle!'

The counter terrorist turned as he heard his name being called.

He looked around to see Calloway hurrying up the corridor towards him.

'Got to go,' Doyle said into the phone and hung up.

Calloway looked flushed around the cheeks.

'What's going on?' Doyle asked.

'I just spoke to Mason at New Scotland Yard,' the DI told him. 'He called me on my mobile. Neville rang there five minutes ago. He says he's ringing back in a couple of minutes. He wants to talk, but he'll only talk to *you*.'

'What the fuck does he want to talk to me for?'

'He said something about a bomb.'

11.41 a.m.

Doyle stood beside the black Granada, gently rocking from one foot to the other.

'This is bollocks,' he muttered, glancing around the hospital car park.

A red Metro had just pulled up close by and he watched as two elderly women clambered out, one of them carrying a Cellophane-wrapped bunch of flowers.

'He's not going to call back,' Doyle insisted, watching as the women linked arms and headed off towards the hospital's main entrance.

Calloway was seated behind the steering wheel, his eyes fixed on the mobile phone which lay on the parcel shelf, as if by mere power of thought he could make it ring.

'Come on, come on,' Doyle muttered.

The phone rang.

Calloway snatched it up.

'It's him,' DS Mason said on the other end of the line. 'He wants to speak to Doyle.'

'Patch this through the radio too,' Calloway instructed. 'And get a fucking trace going on the call.'

'He won't be on long enough for that,' Doyle said.

'He will if you keep him talking,' Calloway snapped, handing the mobile to the counter terrorist.

The DI himself grabbed the radio and pressed 'Receive'.

Doyle looked at the phone for fleeting seconds then pressed it to his ear.

'Neville,' he said.

'Is that you, Doyle?' the voice at the other end said.

'You asked for me, didn't you? Why bother *me* with your bullshit?'

'Because I know *you'll* listen.'

'What makes you think that? What if I switched you off right now, shithead?'

Calloway waved his hand frenziedly, fearing that Doyle would carry out his threat, but the counter terrorist held the phone firmly to his ear.

'Why did you try to kill your wife and kid, Neville?' Doyle enquired.

'I didn't, you ought to know that.'

'Yeah, I know that. What do you want, a fucking medal for your handiwork? So, you can blow the roof off a house without damaging anything nearby. What do you do for an encore?'

'You'll see,' Neville said softly. 'I used ten pounds of Semtex to lift that roof, I've got plenty more.'

'How *much* more?'

'Enough to put a fucking crater where the centre of London used to be.'

'How much?' Doyle persisted.

'A hundred and fifty pounds of it.'

Doyle and Calloway looked at each other but if Doyle was surprised it didn't register in his expression.

'Jesus fucking Christ,' whispered the policeman, swallowing hard.

'So, what are you going to do with this explosive then, Neville?'

'I know you're tracing this call.'

'Good for you. Then you'll know that I'm going to find you.'

'You're not going to find me. Not you or any of the fucking coppers listening to this conversation.'

'Look, just tell me what the fuck you want, will you? You're starting to bore me,' Doyle said.

'I want my daughter back.'

'No chance,' Doyle said flatly.

'In fifty minutes a bomb will explode somewhere in the centre of London,' Neville informed him. 'If you don't give me my daughter back then another one will explode every hour after that. Different locations. Different lives, Doyle. You know what it's like. You've seen what bombs can do. A lot of people are going to die if I don't get my daughter back.'

'Fuck you, Neville.'

'One bomb every hour,' Neville continued. 'You'll never know where. And if you haven't seen sense by eight o'clock tonight, if I haven't got my daughter by then, if you're not sick of filling fucking body bags, then that's when the big one goes up. Eight tonight, Doyle. One hundred pounds of C4. Now get my daughter.'

The radio crackled.

'We've got the trace,' DS Mason said triumphantly.

'Where's he calling from?' Calloway asked anxiously.

'Euston station,' Mason almost shouted. 'The bastard's on Euston station.'

Doyle looked at the humming mobile phone. 'He hung up.'

Calloway glanced at his watch. 'We've got fifty minutes to find that bomb,' he said frantically. 'What the fuck do we do?'

'My guess is it's near him,' Doyle said. 'I reckon the bomb's at Euston.'

11.43 a.m.

Doyle tossed the mobile towards Calloway then turned and sprinted towards his own car.

'Listen,' said Calloway into the radio. 'I want every available mobile unit in the vicinity to close in on Euston station. Also, contact BR, tell them what's going on. Get that fucking place evacuated. If the bomb goes off there . . .' He allowed the sentence to trail off.

The DI watched as Doyle leaped behind the wheel of the Datsun, revving the engine, reversing wildly.

He sped off, almost colliding with an ambulance.

'I want the emergency services on alert too,' Calloway continued. 'And the bomb squad. And *you* get to Euston as fast as you can, I'll meet you there. Doyle's already on his way.'

The DI twisted the key in the ignition and the Granada's engine roared into life.

As he guided the vehicle out of the car park he glanced at his watch. Could Neville be bluffing about the bomb?

He hoped so but he doubted it.

'Shit,' he hissed.

There wouldn't be enough time.

The bomb *must* be close to Neville, Doyle thought as he drove.

Chances are it was to be detonated by remote control and most electronically triggered devices only had a range of about a hundred yards. Two hundred absolute tops.

It was on that bloody station somewhere.

Doyle looked at his watch.

Forty-eight minutes.

He banged his horn, trying to force the van ahead of him to pull over.

The traffic was heavy.

Too fucking heavy.

Even if he reached Euston quickly the chances of finding Neville there were slim, the chances of finding the bomb in time even slimmer. There were a hundred different places he could have planted it.

The lights ahead of Doyle were on amber, the rest of the traffic was slowing down.

Fuck it.

He pressed his foot down hard on the accelerator and the Datsun shot through on red.

The counter terrorist heard horns behind and to one side of him sounding like some organised chorus of dissent.

Forty-five minutes before detonation.

The first of many.

Neville had said one every hour until eight o'clock.

Doyle did some quick arithmetic in his head as he screamed past a cyclist.

One every hour.

Seven bombs and then the big one.

'That's a lot of lives, Doyle.'

Neville's words came floating back to him.

'You know what it's like.'

The counter terrorist's grip on the wheel tightened.

'You've seen what bombs can do.'

Seen, smelled, felt.

He had the scars to prove what it was like to be on the receiving end.

If he didn't find Neville quickly, there were going to be many people with more than scars to show.

11.51 a.m.

Neville saw the policeman as he reached the bottom of the steps.

The motorcycle officer was about the same height as Neville, his white helmet gleaming beneath the fluorescents in the underground car park.

Neville slowed his pace, watching as the policeman walked slowly around the Harley Davidson, his own bike parked close by.

The air reeked of diesel fumes and oil. Black cabs were dropping off passengers then heading down the ramp to collect more in this underground area of Euston.

Neville had left the bike there, not expecting any trouble, not expecting anyone to find it until he was ready to leave.

He took another step towards the Harley, watching as the cycle cop continued walking around, inspecting.

When he turned to face Neville, the ex-para could see

that the uniformed man was in his early twenties.

He flipped up his visor as Neville approached.

'Is this your bike, sir?' the policeman asked, running appraising eyes over the leather-clad newcomer. 'You realise it's parked illegally?'

Did he know? Was this a ruse?

'Have you any identification on you?' the uniformed man wanted to know.

Neville reached for the zip of his jacket, aware of the bulky weight of the .459 and the .357 beneath each arm.

He was looking fixedly at the young policeman.

Two businessmen who had just alighted from one of the taxis passed by, glancing disinterestedly at the tableau.

'Why did you park here?' the officer continued.

Neville eased the jacket open slightly.

The policeman's radio crackled and he pulled it from his belt, flicked it to 'Receive'.

Neville stood gazing at him.

The policeman nodded as he heard what was being said to him by the voice at the other end.

Nodded.

Neville kept his gaze fixed on the uniformed man.

He knows.

The policeman looked straight at him.

For interminable seconds it was as if both men had frozen.

He fucking knows.

A woman struggled from a cab, the driver helping her with her massive suitcase. Both glanced at the motor-cyclists nearby.

From above, Neville heard some words being called urgently over the station Tannoy but his eyes were still riveted on the policeman.

'Your ID, sir,' the policeman said, the radio still pressed to his ear.

Neville slid his right hand inside his jacket and pulled the automatic free.

He saw the look of surprise on the young policeman's face as the pistol was hefted before him, the barrel yawning wide.

Neville fired.

The sound was amplified by the enclosed concrete space and the gunshots exploded like a sonic blast, deafening everyone in the confined area.

The woman with the suitcase screamed, her cries drowned out by the blasts.

The first bullet hit the policeman in the left shoulder, tore through and erupted from his back, cracking a portion of his scapula, taking gobbets of flesh, bone and material with it.

It was quickly followed by a second, which thudded into his stomach, doubling him over, fingers clutching at the wound, one slipping inside the hole as blood poured freely down his body.

He dropped to his knees, his visor falling forward and Neville could see the uniformed man staring at him almost in bewilderment through the Perspex.

He fired one shot through it.

The clear material shattered, the bullet powering into the policeman's cheek, punching his lower jaw, blasting several teeth free.

Blood seemed to fill the helmet and he fell on to what was left of his face.

The woman was still screaming.

The taxi driver had run back and leaped behind the wheel.

Other cabs in the drop-off area were accelerating towards the ramp, anxious to escape, one even tried reversing up it.

Neville swung his leg over the Harley's seat, started the engine and twisted the throttle.

The bike screamed on to the road, skidding slightly, back wheel spinning.

The woman had stopped screaming now, and was standing motionless, gazing down at the body of the policeman, her eyes bulging wide in their sockets as his spreading blood reached her shoes.

A taxi driver jumped from his cab and ran up the ramp into the street, the breath rasping in his lungs, eyes searching the clogged traffic.

He was the first to spot the approaching police car.

By now others had heard the sirens.

11.54 a.m.

The speeding police car mounted the pavement to avoid the traffic in Hampstead Road, the driver twisting the wheel, guiding the vehicle down the sharp incline towards Euston's underground car park.

The sound of screeching tyres joined the strident scream of the sirens as the Astra sped down the ramp.

PC Stephen Garside glanced to his left as they swept through the subterranean area.

He saw the prone figure of the motorbike cop lying in a pool of blood.

'Shit,' he grunted and reached for the radio.

The car roared down another ramp, the vehicle skidding slightly on some spilled oil at the bottom.

'There's an officer down,' said Garside, gripping the door as the car turned the corner, throwing him sideways. 'Underground car park at Euston, it looks bad. Over.'

'Puma three, message received. Where are you now? Over,' the voice at the other end said.

'In pursuit of a motorbike. We have reason to believe the rider is responsible for the injuries to the officer. We're heading out of the underground car park at Euston and—'

He grunted as the car cannoned off a wall before spinning back on to the road.

'Fuck's sake, Phil,' Garside grunted, glaring at the driver.

'Do you want to drive?' PC Phillip Brenner said, eyes fixed on the speeding bike ahead of him.

'Heading up into Hampstead Road again,' said Garside into the radio. 'Request assistance. Over.'

The Astra reached the top of the ramp and sped between two cars, clipping the front of a Nissan, shattering one headlamp.

Neville looked over his shoulder and saw the pursuing police car, its lights spinning wildly on its roof, the siren wailing.

The ex-para gunned the throttle and took the bike into a tight left turn into Euston Road.

The Harley narrowly avoided a Rover heading in the opposite direction, the tip of one handlebar scraping the paintwork of the vehicle and almost causing Neville to overbalance but he kept control of the bike and roared on.

The police car followed.

More traffic lights ahead.

The lights were flickering from amber to red.

Neville shot through, the needle on the speedo nudging sixty.

The Astra followed.

Another police car turned out of Eversholt Road, its sirens also blaring and, for fleeting seconds, Neville could see the nervous faces of the two men inside.

The ex-para smiled inside his helmet and sent the bike roaring almost diagonally across the road.

It struck the kerb, skidded, then the wheels gripped and he was riding hell for leather along the pavement, pedestrians scattering before him, some shouting, some screaming, some gesturing angrily.

He turned the bike back on to the road and swept past St Pancras.

The two police cars followed, the first of them closing the distance between car and bike. Neville saw this in his wing mirror and slid one hand inside his jacket, pulling the .459 free.

He looked quickly behind him then fired off four rounds, the pistol bucking uncontrollably in his hand.

Two shots ricocheted off the road, the third took off the police car's left wing mirror and the fourth struck the radiator grille.

Neville continued to pump the trigger.

His next two shots both struck the windscreen, which promptly spider-webbed.

The leading police car went out of control, skidded across the road and slammed head-on into a Range Rover, the sickening crash audible even over the sound of the Harley's engine.

Neville smiled, aware that the Astra was still in pursuit. *Come on, you fuckers. Your turn.*

He guided the bike into Gray's Inn Road.

The police car followed.

12.06 a.m.

Doyle brought the Datsun to a halt and jumped out, heading towards the side entrance of Euston. Towards the two burly uniformed men who blocked the way.

'I've got to get inside,' Doyle said, reaching inside his jacket.

'No chance,' said the taller of the two constables.

Doyle produced a small leather wallet and flipped it open.

'Counter Terrorist Unit,' he said sharply, pushing past the policeman, sprinting up the short ramp towards the side door.

There was only one word to describe what he saw inside the station itself.

Pandemonium.

'Jesus Christ,' Doyle murmured under his breath, walking slowly past the left luggage area.

There were still a couple of hundred people on the concourse, all hurrying towards the exits. Mingled with them were uniformed staff from the station itself, workers from the shops and cafés. A seething mass of humanity all attempting to get out of the building as quickly as possible.

Doyle saw men and women running from the platforms to join the throng.

The announcement to evacuate the station was still booming from the loudspeakers.

Doyle saw policemen moving about amidst the confusion. The bright yellow helmet of a fireman bobbed into view. Then another.

He heard dogs barking.

Sniffer dogs, he assumed.

The announcement from the Tannoy blurted on, voices were raised, there were shouts, the sound of thousands of feet on the concourse. The dogs.

Bedlam.

More people were pouring up from the subway, scrambling awkwardly up escalators which hadn't been switched off and were still programmed to move downwards.

It looked like some bizarre fairground ride, but the faces on it showed anything but joy.

Doyle walked briskly across the concourse, glancing around.

Hoping Neville's left the bomb in plain sight?

A uniformed BR man ran past him.

Where the fuck is it?

There were so many places to hide a device.

Doyle heard footsteps close behind him and turned to see two uniformed men running in his direction.

He flipped open his wallet and showed his ID to the policemen, who nodded briskly and moved off in another direction.

As Doyle passed the counter of the Casey Jones stall he saw a cup of hot liquid standing on the counter, abandoned. Still steaming.

Lying close by the counter was a discarded ruck-sack.

Suitcases had been left on the concourse.

He even noticed a small plastic football, possibly dropped by a child. It was rolling across the concourse slowly, undisturbed by the many feet scuttling past it.

Doyle stood still, the noise echoing in his ears. The shouts, the Tannoy announcement, the dogs.

He looked down at his watch.

Twenty-five minutes to detonation.

'Shit,' he murmured under his breath.

'Doyle!'

The sound of his own name made him turn and he saw Calloway heading towards him, accompanied by two men dressed in black uniforms.

Bomb squad, Doyle thought.

'It's Neville,' the DI said. 'One of our mobile units has him in sight now. We've got a description of what he's wearing, we've even got the bike's reg number.'

'Bike?' Doyle said, looking puzzled.

'He's riding a motorbike. He shot a policeman here, two cars chased him, they're still on his tail now.'

'Where is he?' Doyle demanded.

'Christ knows but they've got him in sight,' Calloway said.

'You'd better make sure you take him alive or we'll never find those fucking bombs.'

'The station's nearly clear,' Calloway said, looking at the crowds still pouring through Euston's exits.

'Great,' Doyle murmured. 'That gives us less than half an hour before everything goes sky-high.' He looked at the men of the bomb squad. 'You'll never find it in time.'

'Let *us* worry about that,' the older of the two men said.

'If you don't we'll *all* be worrying about it,' Doyle snapped. Then he turned to Calloway again. 'The man Neville shot, is he dead?'

The DI shook his head.

'No,' he muttered. 'Not yet. The doctors don't hold out much hope though.'

Again Doyle looked at his watch.

Time was running out fast.

12.16 p.m.

There were three people on the pedestrian crossing ahead but Neville didn't slow down.

The pedestrians seemed oblivious to the approaching motorbike, even as its loud roar grew in their ears.

They heard sirens too.

A van sitting close to the crossing, engine idling, also presented an obstacle in the narrow road.

Neville twisted the throttle and the bike swung sharply to the right, hit the kerb, rose a foot or so into the air, then slammed down onto the pavement.

'Be careful,' screamed PC Garside as the Astra swept towards the crossing.

An elderly woman was on it, carrying what looked like a tatty shawl in her arms.

He realised as the car bore down on her that the object was a small dog.

The woman tried to scream as the police car roared past her on the crossing but she couldn't suck in enough air to produce the required sound.

The car missed her by inches.

'Christ,' roared Garside, peering out of the back window.

The old woman had collapsed in a heap, passers-by scurrying across towards her.

'I thought we'd hit her,' Garside said breathlessly.

His companion seemed more intent on keeping the fleeing Harley in sight, as Neville swung the bike back into the road.

The Astra scraped the side of a Peugeot as it turned a corner, the harsh shriek of metal on metal filling the air.

'Where the hell's the back-up?' Brenner rasped, struggling with the steering wheel. 'We're going to lose him.'

As if in answer to his entreaty, another police car pulled out from Harrison Street.

Ahead, a police bike nosed its way into traffic from Sidmouth Street.

'Block him off,' Brenner snarled, seeing the police bike heading towards the Harley.

'Puma three, come in, over,' a voice on the radio said, barely audible through the hiss of static.

'Puma three, go ahead, over,' Garside answered.

'This is Lima one. We have *you* and the suspect in sight. Over.'

Neville saw the newest of the pursuers join the chase.

The more the merrier.

The police bike was level with him, riding on the pavement, the occupant glancing across at him periodically.

The street had become a blur of moving vehicles, the smell of exhaust fumes and rubber hanging thickly in the air, the roar of powerful motors drowning out every other sound.

Traffic moving in the other direction swerved to avoid the oncoming procession.

Pedestrians tried to find cover, realising they weren't safe on either the road or the pavement.

There was a junction ahead.

More traffic lights.

Neville saw the glow of the red light.

A lorry was moving ponderously across the junction.

Neville even had time to read what was written on its large blue container.

He saw the words RIVER ISLAND as he sped across the front of the eighteen-wheeler, cutting yards ahead of the pursuing police bike.

As he cut across the path of the bike, Neville slid one hand inside his jacket and hauled out the .357.

He fired three shots, the weapon bucking fiercely in his hand.

The first shot missed.

The second struck the windscreen of the bike, shattered it and hit the left hand of the rider, blasting off two fingers.

The third struck the top box and tore a portion of it away.

Blood streaming from what was left of his fingers, the rider struggled to keep control of the bike, finally losing the battle.

The police bike went over, throwing the rider clear, the machine spinning across the Tarmac, slamming into the huge wheel of the lorry, which barely shuddered from the impact.

The bike exploded.

There was a sudden eruption of yellow and orange flame as the bike disappeared beneath a shrieking orb of fire.

'Jesus,' hissed Garside as the Astra sped through the aftermath of the explosion.

He could feel the heat through his open window, smell the stink of petrol which was spilling out across the road like fiery tentacles.

The motorcycle officer was lying flat on the road, blood spurting from his hand.

Thick black smoke was billowing upwards in a miniature mushroom cloud, hovering over the burning bike like a man-made storm cloud.

The second police car swept past in the Astra's wake.

'Officer down,' shouted Garside into the radio. 'Suspect

turning into Guildford Street. He's heading for Russell Square.'

12.18 p.m.

It reminded Doyle of a mausoleum.

Empty of people, apart from those in uniform, Euston was like some vast, futuristic sepulchre.

The virtual silence only added to the illusion.

Doyle could hear the sound of his own boot heels on the concourse as he walked.

Where to begin?

There were so many places Neville could have hidden the bomb. For a start they had no idea of its size or weight, no clue as to where the ex-para might have secreted it. What also worried Doyle was that they had no clue as to what *kind* of bomb it was.

Radio controlled. Mercury switch. Tremor activated.

Not a fucking clue.

The counter terrorist glanced at his watch.

All they did know was that it would be going off in under fifteen minutes.

The lower levels of the station had already been searched. The dogs had found nothing.

If the bomb was here, it was on the concourse somewhere.

There was a John Menzies shop to his left.

The counter terrorist stepped inside, glancing swiftly around at row after row of books and magazines. The bomb could be behind any of them.

Doyle stuck out a hand and swept the top shelf of books away, scattering them on the floor.

He did the same with the next. And the next.

Five rows of paperbacks ended up beneath his feet.

The shelves were empty. No bomb.

He repeated his actions with the other shelves.

Nothing.

As he turned to his right he saw two men hurrying up the ramp which led to the suburban platform. Both of them were leading sniffer dogs.

'Have you checked in here?' Doyle shouted, attracting their attention.

The two men let the dogs loose and they scuttled into the shop, snouts twitching.

Doyle moved on towards the café on the other side of the station.

There were uniformed men moving about inside it, some pausing every so often, kneeling to check under the tables.

Further along the concourse was a branch of Tie Rack. Doyle hurried towards it, past a coffee stall. The aroma of freshly roasted beans seemed pleasantly out of place amidst the confusion.

As he walked he glanced around him.

Neville could have planted this bomb weeks earlier. His actions weren't the hasty, desperate deeds of a madman. Everything he'd done so far had been planned. Methodical. There was a strategy at work here.

The other bombs had probably been planted around the same time.

Wherever the hell *they* might be?

Doyle reached Tie Rack and moved briskly through it, opening drawers, pulling out the contents, convinced, even as he searched, that he was looking in the wrong place.

But *where* to look?

Where could a bomb lie undiscovered for weeks, possibly even months, in a location so crammed with people every day?

He looked across at the toilets, vaulted the barrier and walked in.

There was water dripping somewhere, the steady plink, plink an accompaniment to the counter terrorist's footfalls.

The irony of the situation wasn't lost on Doyle and he almost managed a smile.

For years he'd cheated death at the hands of the IRA, terrorists, organised crime and Christ alone knew who else and yet now his life was threatened by one of his own.

By a British soldier.

What all his enemies had failed to do might be accomplished by a man he would have called an ally.

How side-splittingly, jaw-droppingly hilarious.

He pushed open the door of the first cubicle.

How ironic.

How fucking ironic.

Doyle took a step inside, ignoring the graffitti on the walls and door, the puddle of piss on the floor.

He flipped open the cistern and looked inside.

Empty.

He moved into the next cubicle.

The stench was appalling. So strong he almost retched.

'What's wrong with flushing it, you cunt,' he murmured, trying not to look into the clogged bowl.

He pushed off the lid of the second cistern.

Nothing.

He could still hear the sound of water dripping.

Doyle moved to the next cubicle.

Thirteen minutes until detonation.

Tick-tock. Tick-tock.

He pushed the lid of the third cistern away and looked in.

Fuck all.

You're clutching at straws but then what else is there to do?

One bomb an hour, Doyle mused.

When? Where?

He dug in his pocket for his cigarettes and lit one, sucking hard on it.

One an hour and you can't even find the first one.

He moved to the next cubicle.

12.21 p.m.

'Where the hell does he think he's going?' PC Garside mused aloud as the police car sped along in pursuit of the fleeing motorbike.

Brenner, still hunched over the wheel, didn't answer, his only concern being keeping Neville in sight.

The ex-para glanced over his shoulder and saw the pursuing vehicles, sirens blaring, lights flashing brightly.

Russell Square was just up ahead.

Neville smiled.

He eased up on the throttle slightly, the needle of the bike's speedo slipping towards forty.

Thirty-five.

'He's slowing down,' Brenner said triumphantly.

Thirty.

'We've got the fucker,' the driver snarled.

Twenty-five.

He saw Neville reach behind him, flip open one of the top boxes.

Brenner pressed down harder on the accelerator.

Behind him, the other police car was also drawing nearer.

Neville was coming up to a corner, guiding the bike almost gracefully around it into Southampton Row.

As he straightened up he pulled something from the top box.

'Oh Jesus,' gasped Garside.

He saw the Steyr gripped firmly in the ex-para's fist.

Brenner saw it too and all he could think to do was accelerate.

Ram the bastard.

Knock him off before he opens fire.

Before he . . .

The first fusillade drilled holes right across the front of the Astra, blasting out both headlights, puncturing the radiator grille in several places and smashing in the windscreen.

Glass flew back into the car and both men tried to shield their faces from the projectile shards.

Garside shouted in pain as one slit his left cheek to the bone.

Other fragments of the shattered crystal peppered his hands like translucent grapeshot, pieces sticking in the flesh.

Brenner struggled to control the car which skidded madly across the street.

The shriek of burning tyres was instantly eclipsed by the staccato rattle of a second burst from the sub-gun.

Bullets struck the car once more.

Brenner was slammed back in his chair as one of the 9mm slugs powered into his chest.

It felt as if he'd been struck by a hot hammer.

The bullet tore through him, burst from his back and lodged in the driver's seat.

He slumped forward over the wheel, still conscious, bleeding badly.

Garside grabbed for the wheel, trying to keep the spinning vehicle under control.

There was a terrifying impact from behind as the second police car rammed the first, the metal of its chassis simply buckling. The front bumper tore away in the impact.

Neville glanced once again over his shoulder and saw the two stricken emergency vehicles, the second ploughing into a parked car as the driver wrestled with the wheel.

In the Astra, Garside shouted in horror as he felt the car flip.

It struck the right-hand kerb doing thirty, its momentum causing the two offside wheels to rise off the ground.

In one manic second, the Astra was on its side.

Garside fell against his companion, looking down at Brenner who was bleeding badly from the bullet wound in his chest. Blood bubbled on his lips every time he tried to breathe through his mouth.

The driver of the second car, his head split from hairline to eyebrow, staggered from the vehicle clutching the wound, blood pouring through his fingers.

He stood in the centre of the road glancing around him. Shocked. Dazed.

Garside pushed his way through the shattered windscreen of the Astra and fell forward onto the pavement.

His head was spinning. He knew he was going to pass out.

People were walking towards him, as if in slow motion.

He could see the other wrecked police car, the driver now on his knees in the road, his head bloodied, his companion still slumped in the passenger seat, motionless.

Garside wondered if the man was dead.

He glanced back into the car and saw Brenner, head lolling uselessly on one side, blood dripping from his mouth.

And somewhere, it sounded like a million miles away, he heard the crackle of the radio.

'Puma three, come in, over.'

The world was spinning before him. His cheek hurt where the glass had cut it and, when he looked at his hands, he saw that they were like red gloves, pieces of glass sticking out of the flesh in many places.

'Puma three, come in, over.'

The voice on the radio was insistent.

Garside didn't care.

There was nothing he could do about it.

The people around him were still moving in slow motion but they seemed to be running now.

Some of them.

'Puma three.'

Fuck off, Garside thought.

He fell forward onto his face, the stink of burned rubber and petrol still strong in his nostrils.

We lost him, he thought, but the words wouldn't form on his lips.

We fucking lost him.

Garside blacked out.

Of Neville there was no sign.

12.26 p.m.

As Doyle emerged from the men's toilet on Euston station he caught sight of DI Calloway.

The policeman was standing talking to three uniformed men, one of whom was a fireman. As Doyle approached the little gathering the uniformed men scurried away towards the front of the building.

'We're not going to find it in time,' Calloway said flatly. 'I've given the order to get everyone off the station.'

Doyle nodded.

'Even if we did find it now there wouldn't be time to defuse it,' the DI continued. 'The fucker's won, hasn't he?'

'It's only the first round,' Doyle said quietly. 'There's a long way to go.'

Calloway allowed himself a sigh.

'No luck with the dogs?' Doyle asked, glancing first at his watch then at the clock high above them on the Arrivals/Departures board.

Calloway shook his head. 'We didn't have long enough.'

'I think we did,' Doyle said. 'Neville knew we'd come here. He knew we'd trace that call. It's all part of the game.'

'Some fucking game. What makes you so sure?'

'I told you before, I know how he thinks.'

'Well, it's a pity you can't read his fucking mind. Maybe we'd have found that bomb.'

'Maybe,' Doyle mused.

As he glanced around he saw more and more officers leaving the station. It seemed an orderly if somewhat speedy retreat.

121

'Doyle. What if the bomb *isn't* here?' Calloway said anxiously.

'Then we're in deep shit. Because if we can't find this one, chances are we won't be able to find the others either.'

'Could he be bluffing about the others?'

'What do *you* think?' Doyle began walking towards the exit. 'Come on, let's get out of here.'

They were among the last to leave the building, Doyle glancing around at the deserted station. At the shops, the ticket offices, the cafés.

'Where is it, you bastard?' he murmured under his breath.

As they stepped from the main doors, Doyle noticed that the gardens and concrete expanse which fronted the terminus were deserted, but the streets on either side and beyond the high hedge at the front were clogged with emergency vehicles of all kinds.

Fire engines. Ambulances. Police cars.

'We closed off all roads within a radius of half a mile,' Calloway briefed him. 'Just in case.'

'Any news on Neville?'

'He got away. We've got descriptions of him though, and the motorbike he was riding. We've even got the reg number. It's only a matter of time before we get him.'

'You sound very confident,' Doyle said, reaching for his cigarettes.

'He's put four of my fucking men in hospital, one of them is critical. We'll get him. He can't hide forever,' Calloway said angrily.

'He doesn't *want* to hide.'

The two men walked down the flight of stone steps that led into Eversholt Street.

'I thought you said *you'd* get him,' Calloway chided.

'I will. Whether I get him in time is another matter. He's got seven more bombs to play with after this one.' Doyle looked at his watch.

Almost time.

'Someone like Neville knows how to disappear in a big city,' he told the DI. 'Fifty *thousand* coppers couldn't find him if he doesn't want to be found.'

'But you *can*?'

Doyle didn't answer.

He glanced again at his watch.

Two minutes to detonation.

They waited.

12.31 p.m.

She realised that the smell was coming from the man beside her.

Cathy Cremer wrinkled her nose and glanced at the man who was flipping through the racks of compact discs.

He was in his late twenties, as she was, dressed in faded jeans which hung lower on his hips than they should. Especially when the T-shirt he wore was so short. Cathy glanced down and saw that more than the requisite amount of bum cleavage was on view.

It was all she could do to stop herself laughing.

However, the smell helped.

She tried to concentrate on the CDs which she herself was flipping through, but the overpowering stench of body odour finally became too much for her and she stepped away from the man, shooting him one final disgusted glance.

She pulled a handkerchief from the pocket of her jacket and wiped her nose, the smell of freshly laundered linen helping to dispel the stink of the individual now standing opposite her. She read the slogan printed on his T-shirt.

I'M TOO SEXY FOR THIS SHIRT it proclaimed in bright red letters.

Cathy finally managed a snigger.

She tried to concentrate on choosing more of the discs but found that a tall, blonde girl with a mountainous back-pack was blocking her path to the discs labelled POP AND ROCK – M.

Cathy moved further down the racks. She'd already selected four discs from the discount section of Tower Records in Piccadilly. That added up to about three hours of listening time, she mused. Scarcely enough to fill the time it would take to reach Singapore.

She shuddered even as she thought of the word, of the journey.

Singapore. Then on to Australia.

Her parents had moved there three years ago. This forthcoming trip would be the first time she'd seen them since they'd emigrated, intent on spending their retirement in sunnier climes.

They'd sent her half the fair. The rest she'd saved from her salary. It had been a struggle sometimes over the past three years but her present job paid well and the final instalment of cash for the trip had been easier to accumulate.

She'd worked on the switchboard of the Meridien Hotel in Piccadilly for just over ten months now. It was good pay and the work wasn't hard. She'd be sorry to leave but there was no way they were going to keep her job open for the two months she was away visiting her parents.

Her sister Joanne, who was to accompany her on the trip, didn't have the same problem with work. Two years older than Cathy, she worked in the A&R department of EMI Records. Personal assistant to the head of the department. The job was better paid and a damn sight more flexible. But Cathy had little doubt she'd find another job upon her return. At the moment that was the furthest thing from her mind. The trip was less than a week away. Everything it was possible to pack was already jammed into her two suitcases; she was now stocking up on items to kill time on the twenty-four-hour flight.

She picked up a couple more CDs, tapping her foot in time to the music that was playing inside the store.

She glanced at her purchases.

A pretty wide range. Something for all occasions, she thought, smiling to herself. Madonna. A compilation Country and Western album. Queen. Guns 'n Roses' first album and a Kate Bush compilation.

What else?

She moved as swiftly as she could between the racks. The shop was crowded as usual. Cathy remembered she needed a new set of headphones for her Discman so she headed towards the stairs leading down to the basement.

Her heels clicked loudly on the metal steps as she descended, almost dropping her purchases when she reached the bottom.

The music playing in the basement was different. Loud, abrasive. Jungle music.

It belonged in the jungle, thought Cathy as the simplistic racket filled her ears.

There was another section nearby boasting bargains, so she paused to flip through the array of discs, smiling as she found one marked 'Songs that Won the War'. She'd get it for her mum. A present.

Cathy glanced at her watch.

She should be getting back to work.

Just get the headphones, then head back.

She had no idea from which direction the blast came.

The ferocity of the explosion was so violent it seemed to fill the entire shop.

Cathy heard a loud bang then the world dissolved into a haze of red and yellow.

CDs, videos, racks and tapes were sent flying in all directions by the massive blast.

Cathy joined them, hurled across the shop like a rag doll, lifted as if on invisible strings. Suspended in the air for endless seconds before being slammed into a wall which was already ablaze.

It mattered little to her.

The initial blast had killed her instantly, ripping part of her clothing off as surely as it had torn away one of her arms and the lower part of her right leg.

The explosion funnelled up the stairs, a shrieking bolt of fire incinerating everything it touched. It melted flesh as easily as plastic.

Rolling clouds of smoke billowed out into Piccadilly Underground station, the shattering detonation reverberating off the walls and ceilings, deafening those nearby.

Screams began to fill the air, mingling with the cries of those dying or injured.

Many lay still, some hideously wounded.

The store was filled with the stench of smoke, the reeking

odour of burning plastic and the more pungent smell of scorched flesh.

Music was still playing.

Death had a tune.

12.38 p.m.

Doyle sipped his tea and looked around the mobile operations unit.

It was like an office on wheels. A massive white vehicle which resembled a motor-home, painted in police colours and equipped with everything from a fax machine to five phone lines. There was even a portable television hooked up to a VCR in one corner of the unit.

All the comforts of home.

A small desk had been placed at one end of the vehicle and it was behind this desk that DI Vic Calloway sat, ear pressed to a phone receiver, tracing patterns with a Biro as he talked.

Doyle got to his feet, lit up a cigarette and stood watching the policeman.

Calloway slammed down the phone.

'Jesus Christ,' he hissed through clenched teeth.

'How many?' Doyle asked.

'Fourteen dead, God knows how many injured.'

Doyle spat out a piece of tobacco.

'The media think it's terrorists,' the policeman continued.

Just like Neville wants them to think.

'There's a press conference in two hours back at the Yard,' Calloway added wearily.

'And two more bombs before it,' Doyle reminded him.

'Why tell us it was here?' snapped Calloway.

'He *didn't* tell us, I guessed. Looks like I was wrong, doesn't it?'

Calloway looked impassively at the counter terrorist.

'It's part of the game,' Doyle said.

'I'm sick of you calling it a fucking game. Fourteen people are dead because of Neville. This is no game, Doyle.'

'What are you going to tell the media?'

Calloway shook his head slowly.

'Who will you blame the bomb on?' Doyle persisted.

'We can put out a story it was a gas leak or something, buy some time.'

'A fucking gas leak? They might swallow that for the *first* explosion, but what about two, three, four, five, six, seven and eight? And forget about buying time, Calloway. You haven't got any time to buy. In less than an hour number two goes off. What excuse are you going to use then?'

Calloway had no answer. 'I might find this bloody maniac quicker if you gave me some help, Doyle,' the DI snapped. 'You know more than you're letting on.'

'Neville's *my* responsibility.'

'Bullshit!' shouted the policeman. 'Now you tell me what you know.'

'What are you going to do if I don't? Arrest me for obstruction?'

'I might just do that.'

'Arrest *me* and you'll never find Neville. I'm your only chance.'

'Then work *with* me, for Christ's sake.' There was desperation in Calloway's voice.

Doyle took a final drag on his cigarette then dropped it to the floor and stepped on the smouldering butt.

'Neville was in the army with a geezer called Kenneth Baxter,' he began. 'They were close, according to Neville's missus. Well, as close as *he* got to anyone. I checked up on Baxter with Army Intelligence, they gave me some details.'

Doyle explained briefly.

'And you think Baxter's involved?' Calloway said finally.

Doyle shook his head. 'I just want to talk to him,' he said. 'Find out what he knows about Neville.'

'What makes you think he'll tell you?'

'Why shouldn't he? He's got nothing to hide. Besides, I can be very persuasive.' The counter terrorist smiled thinly.

'Where's this firm he works for?'

'Cavendish Square.' Doyle looked at his watch. 'I can be there in half an hour.'

'How do I know you'll tell me what he said?'

'You don't. You'll have to trust me.'

Calloway eyed Doyle warily.

'If he knows anything, Doyle, I want to know,' the DI said, pointing a warning finger at the counter terrorist.

'Are Neville's wife and kid still at the hospital?'

'No. I had them moved to a safe house in Lambeth, until this is all over.'

'I'll need to talk to her again too. Let me have the address.'

'Don't you think she's been through enough?'

'She'll go through a bloody sight more if we can't find Neville quick and, at the moment, there's about as much chance of finding him as there is of Salman Rushdie turning up at a fucking Moslem wedding. Give me that address.'

Calloway scribbled something on a piece of paper and handed it to Doyle, who folded it up and pushed it into the back pocket of his jeans without even looking at it.

He headed for the door.

'If you need me you know where to contact me,' Calloway said.

'What about the bomb in Piccadilly?'

'The bomb squad is sorting through the wreckage now. As soon as they've got something they'll call. I'll let you know.'

Doyle looked at his watch. 'Let's hope they're quick,' he said wryly.

Calloway nodded slowly.

The door closed behind Doyle.

Calloway glanced at his watch.

They had just over fifty minutes before the next bomb went off.

12.49 p.m.

The multi-storey car park in Fetter Lane stunk of oil and petrol but Neville ignored the cloying odour.

As he pulled off the helmet he felt the perspiration running down both sides of his face, stinging his eyes as it dripped from his brows. He was breathing heavily, as if he'd just run a mile in the heat. He could feel his shirt sticking to his back. Sweat soaked into the material of his jeans around the crooks of his knees. But those damp patches would dry quickly, he thought, as he pulled off the heavy-duty motorcycle trousers, balling them up, stuffing them beneath the Volvo he was parked next to.

He knelt quickly and refastened one of his caterpillar

boots, tying the lace tightly then stamping his foot on the stained concrete floor.

He seemed to be the only occupant.

Row upon row of cars stretched to his left and right and he saw a blinking red light in one close by.

The LCD of an alarm.

It pulsed, blood red in the gloom of the car park, and Neville stared at it as if hypnotised by the rhythmic flickering.

He ran a hand through his hair, wiping sweat from his face, sucking in lungfuls of stale air.

On a level above him he heard a car engine being started, the sound amplified by the concrete walls and ceilings.

Neville waited a moment, watching as the car glided down the ramp to his right then disappeared from view.

He hung the leather jacket on one handlebar and stood motionless, hands on his hips, eyes closed, allowing the cool, rancid air inside the car park to wash over him. The sweat which was drying on him felt ice cold, but it was a welcome feeling and Neville enjoyed it for a few seconds longer before drawing in one final deep breath. He flipped open the top box of the Tour Glide.

The implement he sought was visible immediately and he picked up the screwdriver, kneeling, slotting the end into the head of the first screw that held the number plate in place.

It came free relatively easily. As did the second.

The third was more difficult.

He grunted irritably as he twisted the screwdriver, causing it to slip, scraping across the plate, gouging off some of the paint.

Neville hissed under his breath and continued working at it until it finally came free.

The fourth screw also came away with little effort.

It took him less than a minute to remove the front plate too.

Smiling to himself he slid the discarded plates together and strolled across to the waste bin which was positioned near to the lift.

Neville took one furtive look around then stuffed the plates into the bin, pulling a broken Domino's Pizza box over them. Then he walked back towards the bike, wiping his hands on his jeans.

The sweat on his body was dry now, the shirt no longer sticking to his back.

The damp patches on his jeans were almost dry.

He reached into the top box for the other set of number plates.

Then he heard footsteps.

Neville spun round, one hand touching the butt of the .357, aware of how ridiculously conspicuous he would have looked to any passer-by.

Who fucking cared?

If anyone stumbled upon him he'd kill them.

The footsteps, he realised, were coming from the level above him.

He heard the harsh clicking of high heels and realised it was a woman moving briskly across the concrete floor.

He waited a moment longer then heard the sound of a car door slamming, an engine being started.

He reached for his jacket and pulled it on, realising that she would pass by him on the way down.

Neville barely gave the Fiesta a second glance as it purred down the ramp, the driver glancing at him as she swept her long auburn hair away from her face.

He waited until the sound of the engine had died away

then quickly attached the new number plates, before dropping the screwdriver back into the top box.

Just like clockwork.

Neville mounted the bike and started it, the engine roaring loudly.

He pulled the helmet tightly over his head, wiping a little condensation from the visor before he rode down the ramps towards the exit.

The Fiesta was stopped at the barrier, the driver fumbling in her handbag for change while the attendant looked on intently, taking the opportunity to gaze at her knees.

He hastily averted his eyes when she pushed some coins into his hand and sat there, one hand propped out of the car waiting for her change. As she took it the exit barrier rose and she drove off.

The attendant barely looked at Neville as he took his money.

'Keep the change,' the ex-para said, smiling inside the helmet.

'Thanks,' the attendant grunted, gazing at the twenty pence he was left with.

As the barrier rose, Neville sped off.

1.06 p.m.

Number twenty-six Cavendish Square was an imposing-looking building but then again, thought Doyle, glancing round, every building in Cavendish Square was impressive.

Like so many properties adjacent to it, number twenty-six housed several occupants, several companies all operating behind its edifice of large Victorian town house complete with polished front door.

The intercom system arranged beside the brass-decorated door looked curiously incongruous. A twentieth-century imposition upon a more sedate age.

Very fucking philosophical. Ring the bell.

Doyle drew hard on his cigarette and ran appraising eyes over the list of occupants.

STRANGE AIR STUDIOS
MILLIGAN AND NYLES PR
MADAME OLENSKA (whoever the fuck she might be)
NEMESIS SECURITY

Doyle pressed the button beside the last name and stepped closer to the intercom.

'We're on the fourth floor, come up,' said an almost unbearably cheerful female voice and Doyle pushed the main door as he heard a buzzer sound.

A wide corridor led towards a small reception area with a desk but no receptionist. There was even a vase of fresh flowers set in the centre of the desk. A couple of leather sofas were pushed against the wall and a small table carried an assortment of magazines.

To his left, Doyle saw a lift. He pushed the Call button.

The reception area was suddenly filled with the sound of loud music and Doyle turned to see that another door behind the reception desk had opened.

A young woman in her mid-twenties emerged, smiled at him and flicked a strand of blonde hair away from her face. She was carrying a metal box which looked much too heavy for her.

'Can I take that for you?' Doyle offered, the cigarette

bouncing between his lips.

The young woman smiled again and nodded gratefully, handing him the box.

'It probably seems like an obvious statement but you work here, right?' Doyle said, gazing fixedly at her.

Shoulder-length blonde hair. Pale grey eyes.

She was wearing a baggy V-neck sweatshirt, leggings and a paid of black Reeboks which, he noticed, had bright yellow laces.

'I work for Strange Air,' she said, hooking a thumb over her shoulder. 'The recording studio.'

Doyle nodded, aware that she was assessing him.

They stepped into the lift when it arrived.

'Which floor?' she asked him, a well-manicured finger hovering over the buttons.

'Four.'

She pressed Four and Three.

The doors remained open.

She pushed again.

'It's temperamental,' she explained.

'I know how it feels.'

She giggled this time. An infectious sound.

The doors finally slid shut.

'This is a no smoking building.'

'I won't tell if you won't,' Doyle said.

'Only if I can have a drag?' she said, gazing lovingly at the cigarette.

He nodded and she took the cigarette from between his lips and sucked hard on it.

'Jesus,' she murmured. 'That's better.'

It was Doyle's turn to smile.

'Keep it,' he said, watching as she took another drag.

She shook her head, took the cigarette from her own

mouth and pushed it gently back between his lips. He licked at the filter and tasted her lipstick.

The lift continued to rise slowly.

'You're not Madame Olenska, are you?' Doyle said smiling.

The young woman laughed and shook her head.

'Who the hell is she?' he persisted.

'She's got a flat on the second floor, she's a mystic. Tarot cards, séances. That kind of thing. She gets a lot of business.'

'I wonder if she could tell me what's going to win the three-thirty at Kempton.'

Again the woman laughed, her gaze now riveted on Doyle. 'You don't look like one of her customers.'

'I'm not.'

The lift bumped to a halt at the third floor.

'This is me,' she said, holding out her arm for the metal box which Doyle handed to her. 'Thanks for your help. Nice to see the age of chivalry isn't dead.'

She stepped out of the lift, Doyle's eyes straying to her shapely legs and buttocks.

'I hope no one smells the smoke in the lift,' she said as she walked off down the corridor.

'I'll tell them it was you,' he called after her, and he heard that infectious laugh once more as the lift doors slid shut.

Doyle took one last drag on the cigarette, then dropped it to the floor and ground it out beneath his boot as the lift reached four.

He stepped out on to polished wood floors.

There was another reception area opposite him, the woman behind it looking up with concern on her face as he strode towards her.

'Can I help you?' she said, forcing a smile.

'Yeah, you buzzed me in,' he told her, reaching inside his jacket for his ID which he flipped open before her. 'Sean Doyle, Counter Terrorist Unit. I'm looking for Kenneth Baxter.'

1.10 p.m.

The contents of the plastic tray didn't look like much.

A few blackened, twisted pieces of plastic, some wire, a portion of battery, fragments of glass and other items which resembled little more than drops of solidified wax.

Detective Sergeant Colin Mason leaned on the work top, peering at the stuff in the tray, occasionally sucking in a deep breath. Sometimes peering at the other two men in the room.

John Fenton and Peter Draper were members of the bomb squad. Both in their late thirties, both dressed in black uniforms, they even looked alike. The same full features, same slim build. The only difference immediately apparent was that Fenton was much taller than his companion. A good six inches, Mason guessed.

Draper was chewing gum, rolling the balled-up silver foil which the stick had been wrapped in beneath his finger as if he was trying to shape it into a perfect sphere.

'It was Semtex all right,' Fenton said finally. 'I'd say about ten pounds, maybe less.'

'Are you sure?' Mason demanded.

'About the explosive or the weight?' Fenton asked.

'It was definitely C4,' Draper added. 'We ran acetone tests on the debris. The spectrometry confirmed it.'

'Hidden inside a video cassette case as far as we can tell,' Fenton informed the policeman.

'How the hell did Neville manage that?' Mason wanted to know.

'Easy,' Fenton said. 'He took the cassette out and put the Semtex in the box instead.'

'You know what I mean,' Mason snapped. 'How long could it have been there?'

'Two hours, two days, two weeks. It's impossible to say,' Draper said. 'He'd have needed to be sure it was in a case that wouldn't be removed before he wanted to detonate it. Something he was sure no one would buy.'

Fenton just shrugged.

'And how was it detonated?' Mason persisted.

'Battery,' Fenton said, pointing to a portion of a Duracell with the end of his pencil. 'We found this at the scene. All high explosives need to be started by a separate detonating blast. With portable bombs like this one Neville used, it's nearly always batteries.'

'Some use low explosives as the detonator,' Draper added.

'What the fuck are *low* explosives?' Mason enquired.

'Stuff like black powder or smokeless,' Draper explained, still chewing. 'The kind of powder used in cartridges. Natural gas is a low explosive. Mixtures of air, even petrol. Low explosive just burns unless it's activated and when it is, the explosion created is totally different from blasts caused by high explosive. The low stuff creates a sort of throwing action. High explosive shatters its target. Mind you, it does detonate at a rate of up to five thousand feet a second, so you can see the difference.' He smiled smugly.

'How would Neville have set it off?' Mason asked.

'I told you, the detonator was a battery,' Fenton began.

'I mean, by remote control. What?'

The two bomb squad men looked at each other.

'An electronic signal of some kind, I'd say,' Fenton offered.

His companion nodded in agreement.

'It must have had a fair old range on it,' Fenton continued.

'And been attuned to that device specifically,' Draper added.

'Keep it simple, will you?' Mason snapped.

'With an electronic detonator, if the bomber isn't quite sure what he's doing, the bomb could be set off prematurely by any kind of electronic emission. A TV remote control. The signal from a radio. Even too much neon.'

'Neville obviously know his stuff,' Draper said.

'Like we didn't already know,' Mason grunted. 'What about the other bombs he's planted or that he intends to detonate. Could they be the same?'

'It's very likely,' Draper explained. 'Most bombers tend to stick to the same kind of device. They stick to what they know. Chances are, Neville's other bombs are the same.'

'All seven of them,' Mason muttered.

'When's the next one due?' Draper wanted to know.

Mason looked at his watch and sucked in a deep breath.

'About twenty minutes,' he said quietly. 'Christ alone knows where.'

1.13 p.m.

Doyle watched as the receptionist picked up the phone on her desk and pressed one digit, her eyes still fixed on him.

'Would you like to take a seat, Mr Doyle?' she said, motioning towards some canvas chairs arranged opposite the desk. A couple of potted plants and a small table bearing magazines completed the illusion and made the waiting area of Nemesis Security look more like a dentist's reception area.

Doyle sauntered across to the table and picked up the top magazine, flipping through it disinterestedly, turning to glance back at the receptionist every now and then.

He looked down at the other magazines. *GQ. Empire. Elle. Cosmopolitan.*

Very eclectic. What kind of fucking customers did Nemesis get?

Doyle reached into his pocket and pulled out his cigarettes, lighting up, aware of the frown creasing the receptionist's brow as she watched him.

He blew out a stream of smoke and smiled at her.

A door to his right opened and a tall man with glasses and a goatee beard emerged, looking first at the receptionist then at Doyle. His expression was one of bewilderment.

'Mr Doyle?' he said falteringly, extending his right hand, which Doyle shook firmly, feeling the strength in it. 'My name is Michael Andrews. I own Nemesis Security.'

Doyle flashed his ID.

'If you'd like to come through into my office,' said Andrews, ushering Doyle towards the door from which he'd just appeared.

'No calls,' said Andrews as he shut the door behind them.

'I'm not going to waste your time,' Doyle said. 'And *I'm* in a hurry too.'

He glanced around the office.

It was immaculate. Neat, tidy. More potted plants.

There were photographs on the walls to his left and right.

Doyle wandered across and looked at them.

Andrews pictured with Elton John.

Another of him with Sharon Stone.

With Tom Cruise.

There was even a Gold Disc mounted on one wall. The inscription read: *To Mike. May Your Rock Always Roll. Presented by AC/DC.*

Andrews watched as Doyle scanned the photos and other memorabilia.

'We've looked after all of them at one time or another,' he said smugly, pulling at his goatee.

'It's not your clients I'm interested in, it's one of your employees,' Doyle told him, turning to face him. 'Kenneth Baxter.' Doyle sat down opposite the other man. 'I need to speak to him.'

'Can I ask what it's to do with?'

'How much do you know about him?'

'I'm his employer, not his brother,' said Andrews and Doyle wasn't slow to catch the note of sarcasm in his voice. 'I know he's good at his job. He wouldn't be working for *me* if he wasn't. As for personal details, it depends what you want to know.'

'I'm not asking for his inside leg measurement,' Doyle snarled. 'What do you know about his record?'

'What record?'

'Don't fuck me about, Andrews. His record before he joined your company.'

'I know he was in the paras and—'

'So you know he was dishonourably discharged for flogging army explosives and weapons to the IRA *and* the UVF?'

141

Andrews was silent for a moment. 'It was never con-clusively proved,' he said quietly.

'Bollocks. Who told you that? Baxter?'

'Even if it *was* true, his military record was exemplary. His training and experience made him a perfect choice for personal security.'

'How many of your other employees have got criminal records?'

'Look, who the bloody hell do you think you are? Who I do or don't employ is my concern. This is my business.'

'I couldn't give two fucks about your business. I just want to talk to Kenneth Baxter.'

'He's working.'

'Where?'

'Upper Brook Street. He's with two other men. They're taking care of some members of the Saudi Royal family.'

'I need an address.'

'I can't just pull him off a job on your say so. I need to know more details.'

'That's classified information. Just give me the address.'

'Number eight,' Andrews muttered.

'Can I use your phone?' Doyle asked, pulling the object towards him.

'Be my guest. Anything else you'd like while you're here?' Andrews said scathingly.

Doyle ignored him and dialled.

The voice at the other end of the line was Calloway's.

'Send some men to number eight Upper Brook Street,' Doyle instructed. 'Pick up Kenneth Baxter for question-ing.'

Calloway asked what Doyle intended doing next.

'I'm going to see Julie Neville again.'

Calloway asked what for.

'A chat,' Doyle said and hung up.

He got to his feet.

'You've got no right to harass my employees,' Andrews said menacingly. 'I could lose money over this.'

'Send me the fucking bill,' chided Doyle, heading for the door.

Andrews rose in his chair but Doyle gestured for him to sit down, pulling open the door.

'I'll see myself out,' he said quietly. 'I know you're a busy man.'

And he was gone.

He strode across to the lift, aware that the secretary was watching him, his boot heels clacking loudly on the polished floor.

The lift arrived and Doyle stepped in, rode it to the ground floor and made his way out.

He looked at his watch.

Next stop Lambeth. The safe house.

He slid behind the wheel of the Datsun, pulled the orange disabled sticker from the front windscreen and pushed it into the glove compartment.

Fuck it. He had to get a parking space somehow.

Doyle switched on the cassette, music filling the car.

'. . . If that's the only thing that's stopping war, then thank God for the bomb . . .'

He switched it off again.

Another glance at his watch.

Tick-tock. Tick-tock.

As he drove he looked around. At the cars. The buildings.

So many places to hide an explosive device.

He drove on.

1.23 p.m.

'I want to talk to Doyle.'

DS Colin Mason recognised the voice immediately.

He reached for a pen on his desk and scribbled the time on the corner of a pad then, with the end of the Biro, he pressed another digit on the phone.

'Doyle's not here, Neville. Can't you talk to me?' Mason asked.

'I want the mechanic, not the fucking oily rag,' Neville growled.

Mason gripped the receiver more tightly, trying to control his anger.

Fuck you, you psychotic bastard.

'I know you're tracing this call by the way,' Neville continued. 'You're wasting your time. Just like you were at Euston.'

'Round one to you, eh?' Mason said, barely able to contain his fury.

'Not just the round, the whole fucking fight, shithead. Now let me talk to Doyle.'

'I told you, Doyle's not here.'

'Well, fucking find him.'

'Look, I'm going to patch you through to my superior, *he* might know where Doyle is.'

Mason hit another couple of buttons.

As he did so the office door opened and a uniformed man stuck his head through.

'Get this fucking call traced. Quick,' the DS snapped.

'I told that other cunt, I want to speak to Doyle,' Neville rasped.

Inside the Mobile Operations Vehicle, Calloway

144

glanced at his watch as he listened to Neville.

'Listen to me, Neville,' the DI implored.

'I don't want to listen to you. Besides, you're not the one to start giving ultimatums, are you?'

'I'm not giving you ultimatums, I'm *asking* you to listen.'

There was a second's silence at the other end of the phone.

'Neville?'

'Yeah, go on, I'm listening.'

'This can stop now, before anyone else is killed.'

'Fuck you. It stops when *I* get what I want, and I think the quicker you give me what I want, the better for everyone. The next bomb goes off in less than ten minutes.'

'Why are you killing innocent people? Your own people?'

'They're not *my* people. They couldn't give a fuck about me now. As far as they're concerned, I did my bit when the fighting in Ireland was going on. They don't want to know me now. *My* people were in Ulster with me. Other soldiers. Men like Doyle.

'Do you know Doyle?'

'I know what he did.'

'You know he wants to kill you?'

Neville chuckled.

'He'll try. What the fuck do I care? Do you think that frightens me?' Neville snarled. 'Do you think I'm frightened of dying?'

'No, I don't, I just don't understand why so many other people have to die too.'

'Don't try to understand. Besides, if you give me what I want nobody else *has* to die, do they? The quicker you give me my daughter, the quicker this is all over.'

'Where's the next bomb, Neville? At least give us a *chance* to find it.'

'Fuck you. Put Doyle on.'

A light flashed on the console in front of Neville and he pressed the button to switch the other phone to speaker.

'We've got the trace,' Mason informed him. 'Leicester Square.'

'I'm waiting for Doyle,' Neville said again.

Calloway gripped the receiver more tightly.

'You've got to give me time to contact him, I—'

Neville cut him short. 'Time's up. I'll speak to you after the next bomb.' He laughed.

'Go to hell!' roared Calloway.

'Already been,' Neville said and hung up.

1.30 p.m.

There was a loud rumble followed closely by a thunderous crash.

Clouds of dust billowed upwards in a choking cloud.

Stephen Casey stood on the corner of Lower John Street, one corner of Golden Square, and watched as the rubble tumbled down the chute before clattering to rest on the pile already gathered in the large skip to his left.

Casey could see that a Mercedes parked close by had been covered with a thin sheen of brick dust. The vehicle looked as if it was beginning to rust.

The car was legally parked. He knew, he'd already checked it, his inspection of the vehicle accompanied by one or two jeers from the workmen toiling high above him on the scaffolding of the building. Two of them had leaned over the edge of the parapet and called out something to him as he'd checked the meter beside which the Mercedes was parked. He'd also checked the tax disc, which was valid too.

He hadn't heard clearly what the men had shouted, the sound of crashing rubble had drowned their words. He'd only managed to catch the odd word here and there. Something about a ticket. He'd heard the word Hitler. He was sure he had.

He'd been a traffic warden for the last seven years, so it wouldn't have been the first time.

Casey readjusted his cap and crossed to his right, glancing back once again at the building with the skeletal framework of scaffolding before it.

As he reached the other side of Golden Square there was another loud crash as more rubble hurtled down the chute into the skip. More brick dust rose.

A despatch rider cruised into view from the northern end of the square.

He glanced at Casey as he slowed down, wondered whether to leave the bike on the yellow lines outside the building he was delivering to and decided to take the chance.

As he entered the building he held up one gloved finger in the traffic warden's direction, indicating how long he was going to be.

Casey waved back and smiled to himself.

He wouldn't have booked the rider. He wouldn't and neither would any of his colleagues. They weren't *that* bad, despite what the public thought.

Casey moved across the square, glancing around him.

People were moving through it on either side of the central grass rectangle. Surrounded by iron railings and flower beds, it was a pleasant enough setting. A little piece of greenery enclosed by the vast expanses of concrete and steel which seemed to have sprung up around it.

Casey often sat in the square on one of the benches and ate his sandwiches when he found time for lunch. He'd usually try and work his patrol so that he ended up there when it was time to eat. Workers from nearby offices did likewise in the summer. Some even sunbathed on the grass in hot weather. It was a pleasing little oasis.

There was another almighty crash as more rubble was despatched down the chute.

He glanced in the window of a design shop as he passed, gazing at the two or three mannequins there. They were all dressed in the garish, brightly coloured creations of the shop. Crop tops, wrap-around skirts in multicoloured patterns, box jackets with unusually large shoulder pads.

He could see two young women towards the back of the showroom chatting animatedly. Both of them were dressed in black mini-skirts. One wore thick grey tights beneath. It seemed to defeat the object, Casey thought, noticing that they both gazed at him as he passed.

The Metro to his left was illegally parked.

He hurried his pace as he headed towards it, noting that it stood on double yellow lines outside the Ear, Nose and Throat Hospital.

There was nothing remarkable about the car. Pale green, about four years old, bodywork immaculately clean. As he drew level with it he gently placed one hand on the bonnet, which was cool.

The car had obviously been there some time.

He peered through the window into the vehicle.

There was an *A–Z* open on the passenger seat, bent back and dog-eared through use.

A fresh-air strip was hanging from the rear-view mirror. Casey tried the door.

Locked.

He glanced at the back seats,

There were a couple of books there. Kids' books. Some balled-up sweet papers had been scattered over the upholstery. A half-eaten bag of wine gums also lay there.

A furry Garfield was stuck to the side window by four suction cups attached to its feet.

Casey walked around the car and saw a sticker in the back window.

A heart and the simple message: *I Love Life.*

Casey smiled and reached for his book of tickets.

The explosion was so ferocious that it lifted him several feet into the air.

All he heard was a sound like a paper bag bursting. A very, very large paper bag. Then nothing.

He was dead before he hit the pavement.

The skip had exploded with the force of a small warhead, the metal it was constructed from joining with the shattered bricks it held to form a blanket of lethal shrapnel.

Like some enormous hand-grenade, the shattered skip erupted, sending metal and pieces of stone in all directions.

The concussion blast was strong enough to overturn the Mercedes parked close by, the bodywork already shredded by the flying debris.

The back window of the Metro was smashed in by a piece of stone the size of a football.

The scaffolding in front of the building merely crumbled, pieces of metal piping and wooden gangways collapsing like a house of cards.

Two of the workmen toppled earthward with the ruins, one of them managing a scream of terror before he landed on the concrete below. His head burst like an overripe melon.

The second fell into what was left of the skip, his spine snapping in several places as he struck the riven container and what was left of its load.

Several of the cars parked close to the skip burst into flames, petrol tanks holed by lumps of flying stone or metal.

The fires seemed to start a chain reaction, each successive vehicle catching fire, burning for a few minutes then exploding, adding more thick black smoke to the heaving pall already settling over the square.

A combination of the concussion blast and the flying debris had blasted in almost every window of the buildings which made up the square.

Stephen Casey lay on his face, his back torn open by a piece of metal, his spine exposed, blood pouring from a dozen wounds.

The blast had ripped off one arm at the elbow, shredded his trousers, blown him out of his shoes.

It had all happened so quickly.

The blast, the deafening explosion, the flying debris.

An uneasy silence descended over Golden Square, as dense as the cloud of black smoke which hovered above it like an ethereal shroud.

1.38 p.m.

As Doyle pulled the Datsun to a halt he fumbled in his pocket for the piece of paper which Calloway had given him.

Number fifty-nine Mitre Road, Lambeth.

He glanced at the door of the building before him.

This was the place.

He locked the car, lit a cigarette and strolled up to the door, ringing the bell twice.

The WPC who answered the door was in her early twenties and she looked quizzically at Doyle, who flipped open the slim leather wallet which held his ID.

She'd barely had time to glance at the small photo inside and compare it with the craggy-featured individual before her when he shut it and slid it back inside his jacket.

As the coat parted she saw the butt of the Beretta beneath his left arm.

'I want to speak to Julie Neville.'

'I hadn't been told she was going to be questioned again,' the WPC said warily.

'What's your name?' Doyle demanded.

'WPC Robertson, sir.'

'Did they give you a first name, WPC, and you don't have to call *me* sir.'

Doyle was looking around as he spoke. The house was small. Clean and immaculately decorated. He could smell coffee from the kitchen to the rear of the building. From a room to his right he could hear a television.

'Lucy,' the policewoman told him.

'Well, Lucy, I want to talk to Julie Neville. If you don't trust me, ring Detective Inspector Calloway, he'll clear it.'

'Would you mind?'

Doyle frowned.

'Right, you've proved you're efficient,' he said. 'Now let me see Mrs Neville, I haven't got all bloody day.' He pushed past the policewoman and into the sitting room.

Julie Neville was seated on the sofa in the room, slender legs drawn up beneath her, both hands cradling a mug of coffee.

'What do *you* want?' she said, looking at Doyle dismissively.

'A chat.'

'Another one?' she said, sipping her coffee.

Doyle looked at the WPC.

'If that coffee's fresh I'd love a cup, please, Lucy.' He smiled.

He sat down beside Julie Neville who pulled her bare feet closer to her, away from the counter terrorist.

He ran his finger along the sole of her right foot.

She glared at him.

The WPC was still hesitating in the doorway.

'White, one sugar,' Doyle said, staring at her, his steely grey eyes narrowing. 'Now, please, Lucy.'

The policewoman glanced at Julie who nodded slowly.

'I'll be all right,' she said softly.

'Call if you need me,' said the WPC and stepped outside the room.

'Very cosy,' Doyle said. 'They seem to be looking after you.'

'What do you care, Doyle?'

'I think you read me wrong, Julie. I *do* care. Where's your daughter?'

'Lisa's upstairs. Lucy's been keeping her entertained. They seem to be getting on pretty well.'

'So, not *all* coppers are bastards then?'

'I didn't say they were.'

She took the cigarette he offered, sucking hard on it as he lit it for her.

Julie blew a stream of smoke in Doyle's direction as she exhaled.

152

'I heard about the bombs,' she said quietly.

Doyle nodded.

'How many people has he killed?'

The counter terrorist shrugged. 'Including the second bomb, it must be over twenty now.'

'Oh, Christ,' she murmured, running a hand through her hair. 'How are you going to stop him?'

'I'll get him, don't worry about it,' Doyle assured her.

'You seem very certain of that, Doyle.'

'I am. But I need your help.'

She looked quizzically at him.

'He's not going to stop until he gets what he wants,' Doyle told her. 'And he wants his daughter.'

Julie sat up, her eyes fixed on Doyle.

'It's the only way, Julie,' he told her. 'That's why I'm here. I *need* your daughter.'

1.46 p.m.

As Calloway and Mason stepped inside the interview room at New Scotland Yard, Kenneth Baxter hesitated.

He stood motionless at the threshold, gazing around the room which was empty but for a table, four chairs and a tape recorder, which Calloway sat down next to.

Mason leaned against the wall behind his superior.

Baxter finally followed them in, eyeing both policemen warily, pausing again when Calloway gestured towards one of the chairs on the other side of the table.

'You haven't told me what the charge is,' said Baxter.

'There *is* no charge, Mr Baxter,' the DI told him, watching as the other man finally sat down.

'What do you think we *should* be charging you with?' Mason enquired.

Baxter smiled and leaned back in his chair, clasping his fingers together on his stomach. He wore a large Gold Sovereign ring on the middle finger of his right hand and the light from the fluorescents in the ceiling glinted on the metal as he rocked gently back and forth.

'We need your help,' Calloway said. 'You know a man called Robert Neville, we need some information about him.'

'They said that when they arrested me,' Baxter murmured.

'You're *not* under arrest,' Calloway assured him. 'We just need some help.'

'Why pick on me?'

'As I said, you know Neville.'

'What makes you think that?'

'You were in the army together,' Calloway said, as if he needed to refresh Baxter's memory.

'I was in the army with a lot of blokes, it doesn't mean I can remember all of them,' Baxter said dismissively.

Calloway regarded Baxter carefully.

Why so aggressive?

Baxter was still rocking back and forth on his chair.

Something bothering you?

'What *can* you remember about him?' the DI asked.

Baxter shrugged. 'He was pretty quiet, kept himself to himself. What do you want to know?'

'We want to know what *you* know,' Mason interjected irritably.

Calloway shot him a warning glance.

Baxter smiled mockingly again.

'Was Neville still in your unit when you were thrown out of the army?' the DS persisted.

Baxter stopped rocking on his chair and allowed it to drop forward. 'What the fuck are you talking about?'

'We know about the court martial, Mason said gleefully.

'It was never proved. None of the charges were,' Baxter growled.

'They proved enough to throw you out,' Mason chided.

'Who's on fucking trial here, anyway?' rasped Baxter. 'I thought you wanted to know about Neville.'

'We do. Why don't you tell us what you know,' Calloway added. 'Have you seen him since you left the army?'

'No,' Baxter said flatly.

'He hasn't rung you?' the DI continued. 'Hasn't tried to contact you at work?'

'No.'

Baxter began turning the Sovereign ring gently on his finger, his gaze wavering slightly.

Calloway leaned forward in his seat, both hands clasped on the table before him. 'Did Neville know why you were thrown out of the army?'

'Everybody knew,' Baxter sneered. 'When the fucking army stitch you up, they make a good job of it.'

'Why do it?' Calloway enquired. 'Why would the army do it if there was no truth in the charges?'

'No smoke without fire, eh?' Mason smiled.

'I never sold guns to anyone,' Baxter told the policemen. 'And, even if I did, that's got fuck all to do with you. I'm not under arrest, you said that.' He pointed an accusing finger in Calloway's direction.

'Did Neville have anything to do with it?' Calloway persisted.

'I thought this was about Neville.'

'It is, but you're not telling us much,' the DI said.

'We heard you were close,' Mason pressed.

'And who the hell told you that?' Baxter demanded.

'Come on, Mr Baxter. You served together, in the same unit, for how long? Seven years? Eight years?' Calloway said. 'The Paras are supposed to be different, aren't they? A team? Everyone counting on everyone else? Neville must have spoken about the way he felt, about what was going on in Ireland. Did he tell you about his family?'

'He was married with a kid, I know that.'

'Did you ever meet his family?'

'No.'

'How long have you worked for Nemesis Security?' Mason asked.

'Eighteen months.'

'Do you enjoy your work?' the DS continued.

'It's better than drawing the bloody dole.'

'It must be dangerous sometimes though,' Mason insisted.

Baxter chuckled.

'So is being a copper, isn't it?' he said, grinning. 'Especially when you've got some nutter letting off bombs.'

Baxter leaned back on the two rear legs of his chair and began rocking once more.

'What do you know about the bombs?' the DI asked.

'Only what I heard on the news,' Baxter said. 'When's the next one?'

Calloway looked at his watch.

'In about forty-five minutes,' he said quietly.

Baxter got to his feet.

'Well, I hope you find it,' he said, smiling. 'Now, if there's nothing else, I've got work to do.'

156

'Sit down, Mr Baxter,' Calloway said.

'Why? You said I wasn't under arrest. If that's true I must be free to go. I came here of my own free will and now I want to leave.'

'Before you do, there's someone else I'd like you to speak to,' said Calloway softly.

1.53 p.m.

'You're crazy,' said Julie Neville, a note of incredulity in her voice.

Doyle took another drag on his cigarette and held her gaze.

'You want to use *my* daughter as bait to catch Bob?' she said, shaking her head. 'I can't believe that.'

'It's Lisa he wants,' Doyle said. 'That's *all* he wants. Not money. Not some political bullshit and no plane to fucking Cuba. He wants his daughter, pure and simple.'

'No wonder they sent you after him. You're crazier than he is. Do you honestly believe I'd let you give Lisa to *him*?'

'I'm not talking about giving her to him, I'm talking about using her to tempt him out into the open.'

'You're talking about using her as bait. You can call it what you like but that's what you want to do.'

'A lot of people are going to die if I don't get him soon. All I want is a little help. She wouldn't be in any danger. I'd be there.'

'And that's supposed to make me feel better? Forget it.'

'He's not going to hurt her, is he? Be logical. She's the only thing he wants. He won't harm her.'

'Doyle, she's my daughter too.'

'I'm not going to *give* her to him.'

'So what are you going to do?'

'Tell him he can have her. When he turns up to get her, I'll kill him.'

Julie swallowed hard.

'Just like that?' she said softly.

Doyle nodded.

'And if something goes wrong? What if *he* kills *you*? What happens to Lisa then?'

The sitting-room door opened and Doyle looked up to see WPC Robertson standing there.

'There's a phone call for you, Mr Doyle,' she said. 'It's DI Calloway. He says it's important.'

Doyle nodded and got to his feet, following the policewoman out into the hall and through to the kitchen where she nodded towards the phone.

In the sitting room, Julie Neville got to her feet and crossed to the TV set. She stood staring blankly at the screen for a moment then switched the set off. She could see her own reflection in the blank eye of the television.

She moved to the sitting-room window and peered out. A number of cars were parked in the street, but only one of them had an occupant.

A uniformed policeman was sitting in an Astra about fifteen yards from the front door of number fifty-nine Mitre Road. He was yawning, she noticed, shuffling uncomfortably in his seat, occasionally glancing around at the few people who passed by.

Julie watched him for a few seconds longer, then made her way out to the hall and up the stairs.

As she climbed she could hear Doyle's voice coming from the kitchen but she took no notice of what he was saying.

She reached the landing and headed for the first door on her left.

Lisa Neville didn't look up as her mother entered, she seemed more concerned with the dolls which were scattered around her. Julie watched as the little girl carefully dressed one in a red swimsuit, using a tiny plastic comb to untangle the knotted synthetic hair.

Julie felt an almost uncontrollable urge to rush across to her daughter and sweep her up in her arms. Anything just to feel the warmth of her body, but instead she knelt down on the floor beside her child and reached out one hand, stroking the little girl's hair.

'Mum, do you think Cindy is beautiful?' Lisa held up the swimsuit-clad doll for inspection.

'Nearly as beautiful as you,' Julie said, smiling.

'I think I like Barbi better but she hasn't got as many clothes,' Lisa observed, reaching for another of the dolls. 'That's a shame, isn't it?'

Julie nodded and manoeuvred herself into a cross-legged position beside her daughter.

'How much longer do we have to stay here, Mum?'

'Not long, darling,' Julie said, none too convincingly.

'Is Daddy coming here to see us?'

I hope not.

'No, darling, he's not,' Julie told her daughter. 'I don't know where Daddy is.'

'When will we see him again?'

Julie could only shake her head.

She reached for one of the dolls and held it before her, smoothing the long hair into place.

'Use this,' Lisa advised, handing her the tiny plastic comb.

Julie did as she was instructed, getting to her feet when she heard voices in the hallway downstairs.

She wandered out onto the landing and saw Doyle standing down there, one hand on the front door handle.

He looked up at her.

'Got to go,' he said.

'What a shame,' Julie answered.

'Think about what I said,' Doyle repeated. 'She wouldn't be harmed. I'd see to that.'

'I'm supposed to trust you?'

'Who else have you got?' He opened the door. 'Well, think about it anyway. Because if that's the only way I can get him, then the next time I come back, I'm not asking. I'm *taking* your daughter.'

And he was gone.

2.17 p.m.

Calloway was standing in the corridor outside the interview room when Doyle stepped out of the lift.

The counter terrorist headed towards the DI, dropping his cigarette butt on to the polished floor, swiftly grinding it out beneath his boot.

'Well?' Doyle said. 'Has he said much?'

'Nothing worth a toss,' Calloway told him.

'How did he take to being pulled in?'

'How do *you* think? He's pissed off. He wants to know what's going on.'

As Doyle put his hand on the doorknob, Calloway gripped his arm, holding him back.

'For what it's worth, I think you could be right,' the DI said. 'I think he knows something. I'm fucked if I know what, but he's hiding something.'

'What makes you say that?'

'Copper's instinct?'

Doyle smiled.

As he entered the room both Mason and Baxter looked up.

'Mr Baxter, this is Sean Doyle,' Calloway said. 'He'd like to ask you some questions too.'

'Who's next? The fucking tea lady?' snapped Baxter, turning his back on Doyle, who moved around to sit opposite him, reaching inside his jacket for his ID. He flipped open the wallet and pushed it across the table towards Baxter.

'Counter Terrorist Unit,' he mumbled then leaned back on his chair, a smile hovering on his lips. 'I've heard of your lot.'

'Only good things I hope,' said Doyle mockingly, retrieving the ID.

'The *real* tough guys. Harder than the SAS.' Baxter chuckled.

'I thought the Paras were the *real* glory boys,' Doyle prompted.

'We did what we had to do in uniforms. We didn't have to hide.'

'Is that what Neville thought?'

'How the fuck do *I* know?'

'You were in his unit. You knew him.'

'I've already answered these questions,' Baxter protested.

'Not for *me* you haven't,' Doyle reminded him sharply.

The two men regarded each other coldly for a moment then Doyle looked up at Calloway. 'I'll speak to Mr Baxter alone if that's all right?'

Calloway hesitated a second then nodded, gesturing to Mason to follow him out of the room.

The DS followed reluctantly, closing the door.

Doyle pulled out his cigarettes, lit one then offered the pack to Baxter who declined.

'Look, I'm not going to bullshit you, Baxter,' Doyle said. 'I know you served with Neville, I know you and he were close, I know you've been in contact with him since you left the army.'

Don't push it too early.

Baxter looked surprised.

'I don't give a fuck about you; Neville's the one I'm interested in and I'm going to find him with or without your help, but I want to know if he got his equipment from you. The equipment he's using now.'

Careful. One step at a time.

'I don't know what you're talking about,' Baxter said dismissively but not too convincingly.

'Neville's got enough weapons and explosives to fight a fucking war, I just want to know if he got them from you.'

Baxter cracked out laughing.

'Did I say something funny?' Doyle hissed.

'The army said I supplied weapons to the IRA and the UVF,' Baxter said, smiling.

'And *did* you?'

'Maybe I did. Who fucking cares? It's all over now, isn't it? In ten years nobody's even going to remember anything that happened in Ireland. It's history already.'

'Tell me about it, I was there too, you know,' Doyle snapped.

'Yeah, you were there,' Baxter murmured, his tone lower but still venomous. 'Not on the fucking streets you weren't. Not being gobbed at by women and kids. The people we were supposed to be out there helping.

162

No. Not the fucking Counter Terrorist Unit, creeping around *undercover* somewhere. We were the ones out in the open. Target practice for any cunt with an Armalite. One day they'd talk to you, the next they'd be throwing fucking bricks. None of us knew who was on our side.'

'And Neville felt the same way.' It came out as a statement, not a question.

'Fucking right he did. We *all* did. We knew we could rely on each other, nobody else.'

'And it's still like that, isn't it?' Doyle mused. 'Neville told me he missed it.'

'When did you speak to him?' Baxter blurted, genuinely surprised.

'Earlier today.'

'Why did they send you, Doyle? Who sent you?'

'After Neville? The army.'

'Why?'

'Why the fuck do you think? They want him dead.'

'And you're going to do it?'

Doyle nodded slowly.

'You'd kill one of your own for *them*?' Baxter said quietly.

'Do you think I want to?'

'Do *you* miss it, Doyle?'

The counter terrorist took a long drag on his cigarette.

'Every fucking day,' he said finally. 'But it's over. All that's left is Neville.'

'We were important then. Neville, me. You. Our lives *meant* something.'

'We all sing the same fucking song, Baxter. But you know what, you're right, nobody gives a fuck and Neville knows that and that's why he's doing what he's doing now. I just want to know if he's doing what he's doing with stuff that he got from you.'

The door opened and Mason peered in, his face flushed.

'Doyle,' he said breathlessly. 'Phone call.'

'Not now,' he hissed.

The DS remained where he was. 'It's Neville.'

2.23 p.m.

'That's the deal. If you let me see Lisa, I won't activate the next bomb.'

Doyle perched on the edge of the desk, eyes fixed on the speaker-phone.

Calloway watched the face of the counter terrorist. If there were any thoughts flickering away behind those steel grey eyes then they didn't show in his expression.

Mason looked anxiously at the speaker-phone and then at his superior.

'Did you hear what I said, Doyle?' Neville repeated finally, his voice even. 'It's a fair deal. It's more lives saved. How many have died so far? Twenty? Thirty?'

'Why? Are you keeping a scorecard?' Doyle growled.

Calloway shot him an anxious glance.

'This isn't about your daughter, Neville. I know that,' Doyle said.

'I want her back.'

'And you know you'll never get her, so why don't you stop the bullshit now.'

Calloway shot out a hand and grabbed Doyle's arm. 'What the hell are you trying to do?' he demanded. 'Provoke him?'

164

Doyle pulled away angrily, glaring at the DI.

'It's over, Neville,' Doyle said with an air of finality. 'Set the fucking bomb off. And the next, and the next.'

'That's a lot of lives, Doyle,' Neville told him. 'How many do you want on your conscience?'

'I haven't got a fucking conscience.'

'Make the deal,' Calloway snapped angrily.

Doyle fixed him in a withering stare.

'We've got a friend of yours here, Neville,' the counter terrorist said. 'Kenneth Baxter. Remember?'

There was a moment's silence at the other end of the line.

'You got the gear from Baxter, didn't you? The guns, the explosives.'

A few more seconds of silence then Neville chuckled. 'Is that what he told you?'

'Yeah. Dropped you right in it. Up to your fucking neck.'

'You're a fucking liar, Doyle,' Neville laughed.

'Blew the gaff on you without even thinking about it,' Doyle continued. 'You see, *he* know it's over too. He knows, *I* know. It doesn't matter what you do, Neville. Things are different now. Times have changed. The fighting in Ireland is over. You should have died in Belfast. Perhaps we all should.'

'What the hell are you talking about?' hissed Calloway. 'Just make the deal, for Christ's sake.'

'Who's there with you?' Neville wanted to know.

'The police,' Doyle informed him.

'Are they listening to me?'

'Hanging on your every word,' Doyle chided.

'Neville, listen to me,' Calloway said, moving closer to the speaker-phone.

Doyle swung himself off the table, digging out his cigarettes.

'Are you serious about making a deal?' Calloway continued.

'You let me see Lisa and I won't detonate the next bomb,' Neville repeated.

'OK,' Calloway said. 'Where do you want us to bring her to?'

'Hyde Park,' Neville said. 'The corner by Marble Arch. I want her there by three-thirty. One minute later and I'll detonate the next bomb.'

'She'll be there, I give you my word.'

'Fuck your word. I want my daughter.'

'How do we know we can trust you?' Calloway insisted.

'You don't,' Neville said flatly.

He hung up.

Calloway spun round and glared at Doyle.

'I'm trying to buy us more time and you're antagonising him,' the DI snarled. 'What the fuck are you playing at?'

'You play your way, I'll play mine,' Doyle snarled.

'What about Baxter?' Mason interjected.

'Let him go,' Doyle said. 'But put a tail on him.'

Mason looked at his superior, who hesitated a second then nodded.

The DS slipped out of the room.

'He's got to be stopped, Doyle,' Calloway said.

'You did the right thing,' the counter terrorist told him.

'Then what the hell was that bullshit with Neville?' the DI said angrily. 'What's going on between you and him?'

Doyle smiled. 'You'd never understand,' he said softly. Then he glanced at his watch. 'Who's going to tell Julie

Neville you're using her daughter as bait because I don't think she'd want to hear it from me.'

'I'll take care of it. I'll send somebody to pick her up.'

'Half three, he said, didn't he?' Doyle mused.

Calloway nodded. 'Let's hope to God he shows up.'

'He'll be there,' said Doyle, sucking gently on his cigarette.

He slipped a hand inside his jacket and patted the butt of the automatic.

Neville replaced the phone and stepped away from the booth.

The woman who had been waiting for him to finish pushed forward immediately, practically bumping into him.

Neville looked at her sternly for a second until she turned her back on him and began jabbering into the phone in a language he didn't recognise.

Foreign bitch.

Across the road the magnificent edifice of St Paul's Cathedral rose up before him, the dome pushing upwards towards the cloud-filled sky.

Hundreds of sightseers were milling around the building, some sitting on the step which led up to its main entrance. He saw several people eating sandwiches on the stone stairway. A young man dressed in a long black T-shirt and shorts was swigging from a can of Coke, pointing towards the dome.

Neville could hear him as he swung his leg over the seat of the Harley Davidson.

Another fucking foreigner.

Neville started his engine, revved it hard for a second. 'I'm coming, Lisa,' he said to himself, then he pulled out into the traffic.

2.27 p.m.

Julie Neville regarded her reflection in the full-length mirror then sighed heavily and turned towards the small suitcase on the bed behind her.

She took out a clean T-shirt and slipped it on, tucking it into her jeans, then she pulled on a pair of white socks and stepped into her Reeboks, one foot perched on the end of the bed as she fastened the laces.

She hadn't had much time to gather clothes from the remains of the house after the explosion. There hadn't been much left to gather. A handful of things for herself and Lisa. That had been it.

Lisa.

She could hear sounds of movement from the bedroom across the landing of the safe house where her daughter still played happily, oblivious it seemed to what had already happened and what might still occur.

Julie crossed to the front window of the house and looked out.

The Astra with its solitary uniformed occupant was still parked across the street, the policeman slumped down in the driving seat, head tilted back.

She wondered if he was sleeping.

Julie fastened the zip around the small suitcase and felt its weight.

All she had was in that one small bag.

All that and Lisa.

She crossed to the other room, directly opposite, and stood for a second, gazing down at her daughter who was chattering quietly to one of her dolls.

If the little girl saw her she said nothing and, after a moment, Julie turned and stepped back onto the landing, peering over the banister down into the hall.

'Lucy,' she called, her voice reverberating in the narrow confines of the stairwell.

WPC Robertson appeared at the bottom of the steps and smiled up at her.

'Kettle's just boiled,' said the policewoman.

'Could you come up for a minute?' Julie asked, trying to control the quiver in her voice.

'Are you all right?'

Julie nodded and stepped back, watching as the policewoman began climbing the stairs.

The steps creaked protestingly as she reached the top.

'Is anything wrong, Julie?' the policewoman asked, wondering why the other woman's expression had suddenly hardened.

Julie grabbed for the small suitcase, gripping the handle, swinging it with as much power as she could muster.

It struck the policewoman in the face, split her bottom lip and knocked her off balance.

She clutched at empty air for a second then toppled backwards, trying to break her fall, flailing arms smacking against the wall and balustrade.

Julie stood watching as the WPC tumbled over and over down the stairs, each step bringing a renewed grunt of pain from her.

As she reached the bottom her head cracked savagely against the floor.

She tried to rise, blood streaming from her mouth but, with a despairing groan, she fell on to her back, eyes closed.

Julie dashed into the other bedroom.

'Come on, darling,' she said urgently, gathering up her daughter's dolls, unzipping the case and shoving them in.

'What are you doing, Mum?' Lisa protested

'We've got to go, quickly. Come on.' There was desperation in Julie's voice now.

'But, Mum—'

Julie yanked the little girl upright, gripping her arm tightly.

'Come on,' she said, barely able to prevent herself shouting.

As she pushed the last of the dolls into the case she noticed that there were specks of blood on the material.

The two of them emerged on to the landing, Julie practically dragging her daughter.

At the bottom of the stairs, WPC Lucy Robertson still lay unconscious, blood running from the wound in her lip. A ribbon of crimson was also flowing from one nostril.

Lisa gaped at the immobile form as they passed, almost tripping over the outstretched legs.

Julie headed through into the kitchen and unlocked the back door.

At the rear of the house there was a small garden, surrounded on three sides by a high wooden fence. Julie headed for the gate at the end.

She tugged at the latch.

It was locked.

'Stay here,' she told Lisa and bolted back inside the house.

There had to be a key somewhere.

She glanced at the figure of the policewoman and then scuttled across to her, sliding her hands into the pockets of Lucy's skirt.

Nothing.

She tried the blouse which was also flecked with blood.

There were two keys inside one of the breast pockets.

Julie took them both and hurried back outside, pushing first one then the other into the lock which secured the gate.

The second turned easily.

She pulled open the gate and peered out.

There was a path leading along the back of the houses. It looked clear.

As she pushed the gate shut behind her, from inside the house Julie heard the phone ringing.

'Come on, darling,' she said, looking down at Lisa.

'Where are we going, Mum?'

'Away. Just away.'

They began walking.

Waterloo was only a couple of streets away.

Inside the house the phone continued to ring.

2.34 p.m.

Doyle glanced around the room and guessed that there were fifty or more journalists inside.

Four rows of plastic seats had been hastily arranged before a long table, itself raised on a small plinth. There were notepads on the table, pens, glasses and a jug of water.

He counted three camera crews, their powerful lights trained on the raised table.

Microphones had been propped up close to the desk, a maze of cables running from them.

Every now and then a flash would burst into life, adding even more light to the room. Photographers checked their cameras, reporters scribbled on pads.

Others stood around talking loudly, many checking their watches.

Doyle did the same.

Three minutes past the deadline.

It looked as if Neville had kept his word and not detonated the next bomb.

Not *yet* anyway.

Units of armed police had been despatched to Hyde
Park and its surrounding areas, all with orders not to
shoot even if Neville put in an appearance.

If they killed him, no one would be able to find the
other bombs.

'The big one goes up at eight.'

Doyle could still hear Neville's words ringing in his
ears.

How big?

And where?

Doyle looked anxiously at his watch, his eyes scanning
the assembled throng of media.

Like flies round shit.

They smelled blood on this one. And if Neville kept up
the way he'd been going, they'd do more than fucking
smell it.

A door to the left of the room opened and Doyle
watched as Calloway and Mason strode inside in the
wake of a powerfully built man with hands like ham
hocks.

Commissioner Frank O'Connor sat down and poured
himself a glass of water.

'Ladies and Gentlemen,' he began, his voice heavily
tinged with a Scots accent. 'I would ask you to be brief
with your questions after I've read our official statement. Time is the most important factor in this case.'
He gestured towards his two subordinates. 'Detective
Inspector Calloway and Detective Sergeant Mason are

heading the investigation, you may wish to address some points to them when they're ready. As I said, the most important thing about this press conference is that it is kept brief.'

The room was filled with blinding light as a dozen camera flashes lit up.

'Two bombs have exploded in the centre of London today,' O'Connor began. 'One at 12.31 p.m. in Piccadilly and a second at 1.31 p.m. in Golden Square. Casualties so far are twenty-one dead and forty-seven injured.'

'What about the explosion in London Road this morning?' a voice from the back asked.

O'Connor looked up irritably.

'There were no casualties caused by that blast,' he snapped. 'Returning to the statement.' He scratched his chin with his finger. 'An investigation is in progress.' The big Scot put down the statement and sipped from his glass.

A cacophony of shouts filled the room.

More camera flashes.

Doyle saw a television cameraman move closer to the table behind which the three policemen sat.

'Is it terrorists?' someone shouted

'No,' O'Connor said flatly.

'How can you be sure? What if it's the IRA?' another voice echoed.

'We have evidence to suggest that it is definitely *not* a terrorist group,' the Commissioner said.

'Who is responsible? Do you have a suspect?' a voice close to Doyle called.

'Yes, we do. As far as we know one man is responsible for these bombings.'

'What's his name?' someone else called.

'I'm not prepared to release that information yet,' O'Connor announced.

'Why is he doing it? Is he a psycho or are the bombings politically motivated?' another journalist enquired.

'We haven't sufficient information yet,' O'Connor said, blinking hard as another barrage of flashes went off before him.

'What steps have you taken to capture the bomber?'

'There are patrols in most parts of the city,' O'Connor explained. 'We have aerial surveillance in operation too. Rest assured, we *will* find this man.'

Doyle smiled to himself.

You fucking hope.

'Is he armed?' another journalist asked.

O'Connor looked at Calloway.

'He is armed,' the DI said, leaning a little too close to the microphones. There was a momentary piercing whine of feedback. The DI tapped the microphone nearest to him almost apologetically.

'Are you using armed police to get him?' the same journalist persisted.

Calloway looked at his superior as if for confirmation before answering.

The big Scot merely nodded almost imperceptibly.

'We have armed units in the field,' Calloway said.

'An armed suspect, armed police too, this could be dangerous for the public.'

'It'll be more dangerous if we don't catch him,' Calloway replied irritably to the journalist's question.

'Are you sure he's working alone?' a TV interviewer asked.

'Yes,' Calloway answered.

'And there are no political motives behind the bombings?'

174

the TV interviewer continued. 'Has he made any other demands?'

'We're not releasing that information yet,' O'Connor interjected.

'So he *has* made demands of some kind?' the interviewer pressed. 'What does he want? Money? Is this bomber holding the city to ransom?'

'It's nothing as melodramatic as that,' O'Connor said dismissively.

'Two bombs have already been detonated, can you assure us there won't be more?'

'We are confident that the suspect will be apprehended within the hour,' O'Connor responded.

Doyle raised his eyebrows.

Very fucking optimistic.

'Will there be more bombs?' the same voice echoed.

O'Connor got to his feet. 'This press conference is now officially closed,' he said.

Calloway and Mason also stood up.

Another volley of flashes accompanied their movement towards the door.

Doyle slipped out of another door, leaving the journalists to shout more questions at the retreating policemen.

He found the trio of men in a corridor beyond.

'Who the hell are you?' O'Connor demanded, casting a distasteful glance at Doyle.

'Doyle. Counter Terrorist Unit. Army Intelligence sent me after Neville.'

The big Scot eyed Doyle warily, taking in the long hair, unshaven face, the battered leather jacket, grubby jeans and polish-starved cowboy boots.

'Why?' the Commissioner wanted to know.

'He's an ex-para, isn't he?' Doyle said.

'He's a civilian now, he's nothing to do with the bloody army,' O'Connor snapped.

'He's been making big fucking bangs with army explosives, shooting your boys with army weapons and he's using his army training to make you look like cunts. I'd say the army had an interest, wouldn't you?' Doyle said quietly.

O'Connor turned to his officers.

'Listen, you get this bastard Neville,' he hissed. 'And you get him fast. If those bloody newspaper people start digging, Christ alone knows what they'll come up with. They could have the whole city in panic by four o'clock. Now you take care of this.'

'We've had a bit of a set-back, sir,' Calloway said.

O'Connor narrowed his eyes.

'We were going to meet with Neville, bargain with him,' the DI said. 'He says all he wants is his daughter. The only problem is, we don't have his daughter any more.'

'Where the hell is she?' O'Connor snarled.

'We had her and her mother in a safe house in Lambeth,' Calloway explained. 'I was told, just before we went into the press conference, that his wife had fled from there and taken the girl with her.'

'Jesus Christ, what the hell is going on around here? Why did she run?'

'I told her we might use the kid as a bargaining tool to get Neville,' said Doyle. 'It must have frightened her.'

'So it's your fault?' O'Connor snapped. 'Keep your bloody nose out, Doyle. This is police business.'

'Fuck you,' the counter terrorist retorted. 'I was sent to get Neville and that's what I'm going to do. I don't care how.'

'So now we've got to find his wife and kid as well as him,' Mason interjected.

'How the hell are you going to do a deal with Neville when there's no kid to bargain with?' O'Connor demanded.

'*Neville* doesn't know that,' Doyle explained. 'He has no idea he's been set up.'

'And when he does?' O'Connor challenged. 'How many more bombs does he have?'

Doyle took a drag on his cigarette.

'When he finds out he's been fucked over,' he said quietly, 'I think we're going to find out *exactly* how many he's got left.'

3.12 p.m.

The cross-threads of the telescopic sight wavered for a second before settling on the woman's head.

She was over five hundred yards away but the powerful scope made it seem as if she were no more than a foot or so ahead.

The cross-threads matched perfectly on her forehead.

'Bang,' murmured Doyle.

He handed the Heckler and Koch HK81 rifle back to the uniformed man next to him, amused at the look of bewilderment on the policeman's face.

The man was part of an armed unit perched atop the Cumberland Hotel like so many blue-clad crows. From their vantage point high above Marble Arch they could see virtually the full length of Oxford Street, Park Lane and the Bayswater Road.

From whichever direction Neville decided to approach, they'd spot him with ease.

If the bastard even showed up, Doyle mused, crossing to the parapet of the hotel and looking down.

It was a straight drop.

Over four hundred feet to the pavement below.

Doyle peered down at the pedestrians beneath, jostling along the heaving thoroughfares.

Two pigeons were sitting unconcernedly on the parapet, heads bobbing back and forth.

'Wondering which one to shit on?' Doyle mused and turned again to look at the six armed men he shared the rooftop with.

All were lying prone on the roof, four of them already with the stocks of their weapons pressed to their shoulders. Another was feeding rounds into the magazine of his rifle. The HK81s were designed to take either five-, twenty- or thirty-round mags, Doyle remembered.

Nice guns.

He slid the Beretta from its holster, worked the slide then flicked on the safety.

Ready.

The pistol would do sweet FA from this range but then Doyle didn't expect to have to use it from four hundred yards away. He planned on being much closer to Neville when he emptied it into him.

The remaining officer was tightening the wing nut which held the bipod at the end of the barrel in place.

Doyle knew that there were six more armed officers on the roof of the building opposite.

Six more on the roof of the Odeon Marble Arch.

Christ alone knew how many plain-clothed and

uniformed coppers were down there amongst the tourists and shoppers, workers and sightseers.

They were all armed.

Neville would expect that.

That was one of the reasons *he* was armed.

If the shooting started, Doyle thought, how many body bags would they need?

He carefully surveyed the faces of the policemen around him.

Older men. Mostly in their forties.

Experienced?

How many of them had ever shot at anything other than a target?

Doyle peered down at the throngs of shoppers and shook his head.

All it would take would be one nervous finger. One shot.

Shit.

He didn't even want to think about it.

Calloway glanced at the dashboard clock of the Peugeot 405 then at his own watch.

He sucked in a worried breath, held it for a moment then let it out as a sigh.

Even with the windows wound up, the noise of the traffic passing was loud. The sheer volume of traffic was quite awesome. He saw one of the London sightseeing buses pass, the guide standing at the front of the upper deck, gesturing towards Marble Arch as the heads of the three occupants of the bus turned in that general direction.

The Peugeot was parked close to the mouth of the underground car park just off North Ride. The vehicle was hidden from the view of anyone approaching from either Oxford Street or Park Lane, stationed, as it was, on the exit ramp of the car park.

Other police cars, marked and unmarked, were inside the underground area itself.

Waiting.

Calloway reached for the radio and thought about checking in with the groups of armed men stationed up on the buildings nearby but then he decided against it.

He'd already checked five minutes earlier.

Nervous?

He pulled at the vanity mirror on the passenger side of the Peugeot and swiftly inspected his reflection.

You look like shit.

He slapped the sun visor back into place and sat back in his seat.

'Where are you, Neville?' he whispered, glancing again at his watch.

'Daylight fucking robbery.'

He looked to his right as Mason clambered back behind the wheel.

The smell of fried onions filled the car.

The DS took a bite of the huge hot-dog he was clutching, wiping away with a paper napkin the tomato sauce which dribbled down his chin.

'There's some geezer selling these.' He brandished the hot-dog like a trophy. 'He's got one of those mobile stalls, probably bloody filthy anyway, just round the corner in the park. Two and a half quid for a fucking hot dog and a Coke. Fifty pence extra for the onions. Daylight fucking robbery.' He pushed more of the food into his mouth.

'I thought most of those stalls had been closed down,' the DI said. 'An environmental health officer found flies' eggs inside a hamburger from one of them last week. No maggots. Just the eggs.'

'Ha, bloody, ha,' said Mason through a mouthful of food.

Calloway's stomach rumbled.

'Want some?' Mason asked, pushing the hot-dog towards him.

Calloway raised one eyebrow and shook his head in horror.

Instead he reached for the can of Coke which Mason had propped on the dashboard. The DI took a sip, belched loudly then reached for the two-way.

'What are you doing?' Mason asked.

'Checking.'

'Vic, if they spot Neville, they'll let us know quick enough.'

'I'll check anyway.'

Robert Neville could see the police car approaching in his wing mirror.

Just take it easy.

There were two people at the pedestrian crossing and the police car, like Neville, slowed down to let them pass.

The driver of the car glanced at Neville.

They're looking for a man in a black leather outfit.

The ex-para turned and looked directly at the uniformed man.

Not even the same number plates, are they, shithead?

Neville thought how easy it would be to lean back and flip up the top box lid. Snake a hand in and pull the Steyr free.

The driver was watching as a young woman in a particularly short skirt crossed in front of them.

Neville grinned inside the helmet, looking first at the girl then at the police car.

Do you know how close to death you are?

The police car pulled off.

Neville followed.

He was less than thirty seconds from Park Lane.

As he rode he slid his left hand into the pocket of his jacket and ran his finger over the small object there.

The detonator had a single red switch on it.

Neville slowed his speed slightly, checked behind him then swung the bike into Audley Street.

They would be waiting. He'd known that all along.

Another right and he was heading down Hill Street back in the direction of Berkeley Square.

There was another way.

3.21 p.m.

The sound reminded her of a dog in pain.

Julie Neville gritted her teeth as the escalator rose, the sound seemingly rising in volume with it.

A loud, grating wail reverberated around the vaulted ceiling and pounded her eardrums.

The inner workings of the moving stairs needed attention. She didn't have to be a mechanic to realise that.

Lisa had asked her what the noise was as soon as they'd stepped from the train at Tottenham Court Road.

'They should do something about it,' she'd added indignantly.

Julie had to agree. She glanced at the procession of faces being ferried downwards on the opposite escalator.

Some smiling, some chatting to friends, most as blank and expressionless as her own.

She and Lisa stepped off the moving staircase and Julie pushed their tickets into the machine, ushering her daughter through as the automatic bars swung open, then hurrying through herself before they slammed shut.

They took the first exit ahead of them, climbing the steps, Julie gripping her daughter's hand tightly so they didn't become separated in the crowd of people both entering and leaving the Underground station.

When they finally emerged at street level, Julie wiped her face with the back of one hand.

The early morning chill had given way to sunshine and, as they walked, the small suitcase which she carried seemed to have mysteriously increased in weight. Julie could feel a single bead of perspiration trickling down the middle of her back. Above her, the sky was filled with bloated cloud which occasionally blotted out the sun, but the warmth was still there, wrapping itself around her like an unwelcome blanket.

Jesus. What a difference from the early morning.

The day had stretched into an eternity. Each hour elongated and protracted.

She was beginning to wonder if this particular day was ever going to end.

She noticed the policeman on the opposite side of the road.

Was he looking for her?

They would have discovered she'd fled by now, that much she was certain of.

They would be looking for her and Lisa.

The policeman crossed the street and headed off up New Oxford Street.

Julie breathed an audible sigh of relief as she watched him go.

'Mum, I'm hungry,' Lisa said, kicking at a crushed Pepsi can. It skidded across the pavement and struck the foot of a suited man who shot her an irritated glance.

Julie could feel her own stomach churning but she was unsure whether it was hunger or anxiety.

The police were looking for her. Her husband was still out there somewhere. He'd let off two bombs already, Christ alone knew what he had in mind next.

'Mum,' Lisa persisted.

Julie smiled down at her and they moved through the crowd into Oxford Street, to the McDonald's opposite the entrance to the tube station they'd just left.

As Julie pushed open the door the smell of frying food enveloped them and they joined one of the queues.

Lisa looked up excitedly, as Julie flipped open her purse and saw about twenty pounds in there.

Is that it? Your total possessions? The sum of your life?

Twenty quid. A small suitcase and a daughter.

In front of her, two youths were comparing purchases from the Virgin Mega-Store next door, pulling CDs from plastic bags and glancing at the covers.

Julie looked at them enviously. They have no worries, she thought.

She looked to her left, saw that one of the other queues had disappeared so she hurried across to the counter, Lisa scurrying beside her.

They ordered and Lisa carried the cardboard tray downstairs, where an employee was mopping the floor. Julie had to skirt around him as she followed Lisa to a table in the corner, finally dumping the suitcase on the bench beside her.

Lisa was already pulling fries and burgers from the brown bag, prising milkshakes from the cardboard tray.

Julie took a bite of her cheeseburger and glanced around.

She had to find a phone.

3.27 p.m.

'What the fuck is he playing at?'

Doyle held the two-way to one ear while he scanned Park Lane and Marble Arch with the binoculars.

'Doyle? Can you hear me?' Calloway said, more agitatedly. 'I said—'

'I heard you,' the counter terrorist interrupted. Still he swept the powerful glasses back and forth.

Searching.

'Where the hell is Neville?' Calloway's angry voice demanded.

'He could already be here,' Doyle said flatly. '*He's* probably watching *us*.'

'How could he be?'

'Come on, Calloway, he'll be expecting a fucking trap, he's not stupid.'

'So why agree to the meeting?'

'He's testing us.'

The cunning bastard.

Doyle walked to the parapet and glanced first to his left and then to his right, peering through the magnifying lenses.

Come out, come out, wherever you are.

One of the armed policemen shifted position, still trying to keep his eye pressed to the telescopic sight of the HK81.

'I wouldn't worry about it,' Doyle said quietly as he passed the man. 'This bastard's not going to show,' he said into the two-way.

'How can you be sure?' Calloway asked urgently.

'Call it a gut feeling. Give it another ten minutes then pull your men out.'

'You're not going to listen to him, are you, Vic?' snapped Mason, glaring at his superior.

Inside the Peugeot, Calloway held the two-way tightly, his mind spinning.

Why hadn't Neville shown up?

Was Doyle right? Was the ex-para wise to their plan?

How could he be?

'Doyle,' the DI said. 'Why *wouldn't* Neville show up? If he wants his daughter that badly, surely—'

'Just trust me on this,' Doyle interrupted.

'Why the hell *should* we trust him?' Mason barked.

'He hasn't been wrong so far,' Calloway said.

'No, he hasn't, has he? Not *once*.'

'Meaning?'

'He says he knows how Neville thinks, how his mind works. Isn't that convenient?' the DS said angrily. 'What if they're in this together?'

Calloway shook his head.

'He was so anxious for us to pull in Kenneth Baxter for questioning,' Mason persisted. 'What if that was just a fucking smokescreen? To take the suspicion away from Doyle himself.'

Calloway looked at his companion and held his gaze. 'You think Doyle is involved in these bombings?'

Mason didn't answer.

The two-way crackled again.

'Calloway. What's your answer?' Doyle's voice was breaking up slightly.

'I wouldn't trust him as far as I could throw him,' Mason said.

'Ten minutes,' Calloway said into the two-way.

Mason shook his head dismissively. 'You're crazier than he is, Vic.'

'And what the hell would *you* do?'

'Wait until the bastard shows up then let those fucking snipers loose on him.'

'And if they kill him, what about the other bombs?'

'If he's dead he can't detonate them, can he?'

Calloway shook his head.

'It's Doyle's call this time,' he said quietly. '*This* time.'

3.37 p.m.

She had to get away.

Julie knew that she had to get out of London.

Away from her husband, away from the police.

Away from the memories.

Could you run from memories?

She picked up a french fry and dipped it into a puddle of tomato sauce, nibbling on the end, watching as Lisa pushed another piece of hamburger into her mouth.

She reached out a hand and smoothed down the little girl's hair.

She had to get Lisa away.

Julie sat back in her seat and took a sip of her milkshake.

All the memories weren't bad, she thought. Not everything she was running from was so terrible.

And what are you running to?

A better life?

She smiled bitterly to herself.

Her life with Neville hadn't always been so intolerable. Most of the time he'd been away. The army.

The army always came first for him. Even after Lisa was born.

But in the beginning it had been different. She had loved him. She was sure she had. She'd felt a depth of feeling but never been certain that it was the all-embracing, enveloping sensation of true love.

She'd told him she loved him. Usually in times of passion and, at the beginning, there'd been plenty of those too but, as the years had worn on, the words had begun to sound more empty to her. Their meaning less valid.

So, why did you marry him in the first place?

Her father had died when she was twelve, her mother two years later. Julie had moved in with her elder sister who'd provided the roof over her head more from duty than philanthropy. It had been an uneventful adolescence for her, apart from what her sister had described as an avalanche of blokes.

Julie smiled to herself as she remembered the older girl's words.

It was true. There had been many boyfriends. *Too* many perhaps.

The boyfriends appeared and disappeared as quickly as her jobs in those days.

Barmaid. Shop assistant. Supermarket cashier.

Men and work in quick succession.

And what did she want out of it all?

Some security? Some love?

Some hope?

She'd been twenty-five when she met Neville.

There had been a fire inside him. And it had burned in his eyes. That was what she remembered most about meeting him for the first time. His eyes. So hypnotic, so piercing.

She'd looked into those eyes on that first night they'd shared his bed, she'd listened to him talk about the army, about his own background, which was not unlike hers. He too was without family.

He was a way out for her.

Her sister had welcomed Neville's arrival. The prospect of their marriage had been even more welcome.

A little over a year later they did the deed at a register office in Tower Hamlets. Two weeks later, her sister emigrated to Canada.

Julie had spoken to her twice during the intervening eight years.

When Lisa had been born, she hadn't even sent her a congratulations card.

Julie looked at her daughter who was prodding the piece of green gherkin she'd taken from her burger with a chip, as if it were some kind of loathsome fungus.

'Have you finished?'

Lisa nodded.

'We'd better go.'

'Where are we going, Mum?'

Julie wished she could tell her.

3.56 p.m.

Doyle took a drag on his cigarette and regarded the photo on Calloway's desk blankly.

The DI, his wife and two children.

He guessed the older one was in her teens.

Pretty kid.

Her finely chiselled features were obviously inherited from her mother, he mused, glancing at Calloway's grizzled visage.

If he and Georgie had had kids, what . . .

He tried to brush the thought from his mind.

Forget it.

Tried to wipe her image from his memory.

Not a chance.

He put the photo back and glanced around the office at the other men.

Calloway was seated behind his desk studying a map of central London.

Mason stood behind him, looking down at the map, occasionally sipping from a cup of coffee.

Two other men, who had been introduced to Doyle as John Fenton and Peter Draper, members of the bomb squad, were seated across from him. Fenton kept glancing at his watch. A nervous gesture, Doyle decided.

Draper was chewing thoughtfully on a piece of gum.

'So,' said Doyle finally, gaze fixed on the policemen.

'So, what?' Calloway asked.

'Four hours until the big one goes off and we're no closer to finding Neville,' Doyle reminded them.

'Or his wife and kid,' Calloway said quietly.

'So why haven't you found him, Doyle?' Mason snapped. 'You're the fucking expert.'

Doyle ignored him. 'How many men have you got on the streets?'

'Two hundred,' Calloway answered. 'We've got mobile units patrolling, men walking the streets, we've even got three helicopters in use. And we still can't find him.'

Calloway got to his feet and crossed to the window of his office. 'I don't know what more we can do.'

'Give him what he wants,' Doyle said flatly.

'What guarantee have we got he won't detonate the rest of the bombs, even if we *do* give him what he wants?' Calloway said. 'Assuming of course that we *had* what he wants.'

'Just be grateful Neville doesn't know you haven't got the kid,' Doyle added.

'The policewoman who was injured during the escape seems to be improving,' Mason said. 'If you hadn't told Julie Neville we were going to use her child as a bargaining tool this would never have happened.'

'Fuck you,' Doyle said dismissively.

'Why aren't you out there looking for Neville?' Mason persisted. 'You claim to know how he thinks. Why can't *you* find him?'

'I'm not a fucking mind-reader, fatso,' Doyle snapped. 'I understand what he's thinking *about*, not what he's thinking. Prick.'

Mason took a step around the table.

Doyle rose to meet him.

Come on then, fuckhead.

Mason stopped and held Doyle's gaze for a moment longer.

'Just shut it, both of you,' Calloway interjected. 'We all know what we have to do. Julie Neville and her daughter have to be found, Robert Neville has to be stopped and the rest of those bombs must be located.'

'Just like that,' Doyle said.

He turned to look at the members of the bomb squad. 'You say the bombs were constructed the same way?'

Fenton nodded.

'Electronically activated,' Doyle added.

'So there's every reason to believe the others are the same?' Calloway said.

'It's highly likely,' Fenton told him. 'But we can't be certain.'

'So if we find Neville and blow him away, the bombs could still go off?' Mason clarified.

Doyle clapped mockingly.

Mason shot him an angry glance.

'What about Kenneth Baxter?' Doyle asked.

'We've got his place under surveillance, just in case you're right about him and Neville,' Calloway said.

Doyle lit up a cigarette and began pacing the office slowly.

'Neville still thinks we've got his daughter,' he said. 'As long as he believes that we're OK. If he finds out she's missing we're fucked.'

There was a knock on the office door.

'Come in,' Calloway called and a uniformed officer entered the room.

He crossed to the desk and handed something to the DI.

It was an envelope.

'This was handed into reception just now, sir,' the officer said. 'Some kid brought it in, early teens. He said a bloke stopped him on the street and promised him a tenner if he delivered it here.'

'Where is the kid now?'

'We've got him downstairs,' the officer replied. 'I thought it best to hold him until you'd seen the note.'

Calloway opened it, unfolded the paper inside and smoothed it out on his desk.

The other men gathered round.

I WILL CALL AT FIVE.

I WANT TO SPEAK TO MY DAUGHTER THEN. I NEED TO KNOW SHE IS ALL RIGHT.

IF I DO NOT TALK TO HER I WILL DETONATE ANOTHER BOMB.

NEVILLE

Doyle looked at his watch.

'Unless we find that kid in the next hour,' he murmured, 'you'd better make sure you've got a good supply of fucking body bags.'

4.03 p.m.

Neville spooned sugar into his cappuccino, watching as it sank slowly through the froth.

As he stirred, he glanced out of the café window.

The Harley Davidson was parked directly outside the building, wedged between two cars.

A couple of dispatch riders were leaning against their bikes, sipping from Styrofoam cups and talking, both of them dressed from head to foot in leathers.

Neville took a sip of his coffee, decided it wasn't sweet enough and added more sugar.

Like so many of the other cafés in Dean Street, this one was barely large enough to accommodate four tables, a counter and some stools. Visitors came and went with great rapidity, taking drinks and sandwiches with them or occasionally sitting if there was an empty seat.

Apart from himself, there were four American tourists inside the café, seated around one table.

At another, two young women talked and shared a cigarette, much to the consternation of the man at the table next to them. Every time one of them exhaled he wrinkled his nose and glared disdainfully at them.

At the other table a man a little younger than himself was consulting one of the daily papers while his wife fed their baby using a plastic spoon.

Neville gazed intently at the woman.

Perhaps a little *too* intently.

It was as if she felt his gaze upon her and finally looked in his direction.

He continued to stare, watching her over the rim of his cup as he drank.

She tried to ignore him, concentrating on feeding the baby.

There was a roar outside as one of the dispatch riders revved his engine and pulled away, a sound which seemed to distract both Neville and the woman.

The child would take no more food and began to cry softly until it was lifted on to its mother's shoulder for winding.

Neville watched again, his fascination with the woman and her child restored.

He couldn't remember much about Lisa's childhood.

Not surprising really, he'd hardly been there.

He only ever saw her on leave visits. Months apart.

She seemed so different to him every time he saw her.

All those years lost.

He'd been in Londonderry when she was born.

The first he'd known of her arrival was a phone call from Julie that night when he'd returned to barracks after a patrol. It had been another two weeks after that before he'd finally seen her.

And when he had?

Neville had wondered if he was supposed to cry, supposed to feel some massive upswell of emotion at the sight of his first born.

He remembered how carefully he'd held her, as if she were formed from fine porcelain instead of flesh and bone. The tenderness required had been alien to him.

He'd loved her. He still did, more than anything in the world, but in the beginning her fragility had frightened him. He couldn't cope.

Tenderness was not his way. It never had been.

He'd been on road-block duty near the border on her first birthday.

Riding a convoy of trucks through Strabane on her second.

Whenever he came home he brought her presents. He came loaded with toys and sweets like some ill-timed Santa Claus. But all the time he was with Lisa, he wanted to be back in Northern Ireland.

She was the most important *part* of his life, the army *was* his life.

Had been.

There was nothing for him any more. Not there.

No army. No life.

No point?

He drained what was left in his cup and got to his feet, glancing at the young woman and her baby for the final time before heading out on to the pavement where he slipped on his helmet and climbed aboard the Harley.

He flicked on the ignition and the bike roared into life.

Neville swung left into Old Compton Street, and he

turned right into Moor Street. He slowed down slightly as he emerged into Cambridge Circus.

The phone box was to his left.

Neville smiled.

4.14 p.m.

Kenneth Baxter stood with the phone pressed to his ear.

Despite the fact that the line had gone dead he still kept the receiver there, as if the dormant device was suddenly going to spring into life once again.

Then finally, slowly, he dropped it back on to the cradle.

As he did so he checked his watch.

The clock on the mantelpiece showed a different hour.

The same hour it always showed.

It had belonged to his mother. One of the few things he'd claimed when she died. The clock hadn't worked since. Baxter wasn't even sure if it had ever worked. It was what was affectionately known in families as an heirloom. In other words it was a piece of old junk which successive generations had tried to sell, found out was worthless and clung to because they had nowhere else to hide it away.

So it was with the clock.

It looked strangely incongruous on the mantelpiece. A relic of a bygone age. At odds with the more modern furniture and decoration in the rest of the place.

Antique clocks didn't usually sit well with Ikea and MFI furniture.

Baxter made his way to the bathroom, spun the cold tap and splashed his face with water, gazing at his reflection as he straightened up.

He looked dark beneath the eyes, as if he were in need of some sleep.

He'd napped for an hour or so earlier in the day, not long after returning from New Scotland Yard, and it had revived him somewhat. The cold water against his flesh seemed to complete the job.

Through the open window he heard a train.

His home in Newham was close to West Ham station, and on the still air, he could hear the rumble of another tube as it passed through.

The sound competed with some noise coming from the recreation ground close by.

Kids probably, Baxter thought. Skiving.

He checked his watch again.

No. School was closed for the day. They were entitled to be there.

He remembered where he should be and pulled on a denim shirt, slipping it over his T-shirt, the tails flapping as he walked.

Baxter dropped a packet of cigarettes into one top pocket and his front door key into the other as he headed out.

The voice he'd heard on the other end of the phone still seemed to linger in his ear and he paused momentarily, glancing at the phone as if expecting it to ring once again

It didn't.

'Not bad,' said PC Mark Hagan, studying the photo of Julie Neville approvingly.

It was a monochrome snap. Taken on holiday, he guessed.

Julie was smiling into the camera, seated on a blanket spread out on the ground, slender legs drawn up beneath her.

Beside him in the passenger seat his companion, younger by a year, PC Rob Wells glanced across at the photo then back at the two which he himself held.

One was of Neville.

The other of Lisa.

The two policemen had already studied the pictures Christ alone knew how many times that day.

Mind you, it gave them something to do while they sat in the unmarked car about twenty yards from Kenneth Baxter's house.

Both men were dressed in jeans, Hagan wore a faded blue shirt, Wells a T-shirt which bore the legend: ALL THIS AND MONEY TOO.

He put one foot up on the dashboard and started flicking idly at the laces of his trainers.

Around his feet lay a couple of discarded Styrofoam cups and a McDonald's bag stuffed with empty quarter-pounder cartons and soiled napkins.

The car could do with a good clean on the outside too, Hagan mused, noticing the thin layer of grime covering the bonnet. Also there was a huge streak of bird shit on the windscreen. He thought about flicking on the wipers to dislodge it but then decided against it.

'It's a pity we're not watching some bird, isn't it?' Wells said.

'What?' Hagan murmured.

'This stakeout stuff.'

Hagan smiled.

'You've been watching too many bloody American cop shows,' he said, flipping open the glove compartment and pulling out the packet of wine gums inside. 'Stakeout.' He grunted.

'Well, that's what it is, isn't it?' Wells protested. 'We've been sitting watching Baxter's place for the last three hours.'

'It's not a stakeout, it's surveillance,' Hagan reminded him.

'Stakeout sounds better though, doesn't it? It sounds more exciting.'

'I suppose so,' Hagan said, offering the wine gums to his companion, who took a red one.

'Claret,' he said, reading what was printed on the confection. 'That's a load of bollocks, isn't it? I mean, they call them wine gums but they've got no wine in them. At least liqueurs have got real booze in them. I used to eat them when I was a kid. The sherry ones. I used to bite the ends off, suck out the sherry then chuck the chocolate away.'

Both men laughed.

'My gran always used to have this big box of them,' Wells continued. 'Me and my brother bought them for her every Christmas then ate the lot.'

Hagan pushed another wine gum into his mouth and chuckled, glancing out of the side window.

He was the first to see Baxter emerge.

'Rob,' he said, still chewing.

Wells looked over.

'You call in, I'll follow him,' the younger man said.

He watched as Baxter strode down the road, long legs eating up the ground.

Wells snatched a two-way from the back seat, jammed it into the pocket of his jeans then climbed slowly out of the car. He leaned against the vehicle for a moment, glancing to his left and right, hoping his act of nonchalance was working

'Don't lose him, for fuck's sake,' Hagan said, watching

Baxter in the wing mirror. 'It looks as if he's heading towards the cemetery.'

Wells ran a hand through his hair then set off.

He was about thirty yards behind his quarry on the opposite side of the road.

Hagan waited a moment longer then reached for the radio.

4.27 p.m.

This is bullshit and you know it.

Doyle guided the Datsun over Blackfriars Bridge, glancing to either side swiftly, seeing the grimy water of the Thames snaking through the city like a long, parched reptilian tongue.

Fucking bullshit.

The car ahead stalled and Doyle muttered under his breath, glancing again at the pedestrians nearest him.

In a city of nine million people you think you're just going to spot them?

He waited for the car ahead to start moving again.

Julie Neville and her daughter and, oh, wait a minute, there's Robert Neville too. What a stroke of quite amazing fucking luck.

Doyle shook his head.

The words needle and haystack sprang to mind.

Drive around London, spot the three people you need to find just like that.

Piece of piss.

The car in front moved off, Doyle drove on, cranking up the volume on his cassette.

'. . . *Living in the fast lane is easy, 'til you run out of road . . .*'

He tapped a finger on the wheel in time to the thumping beat of the music.

'. . . Friends will turn to strangers when you're out of control . . .'

As he brought the car to a halt at traffic lights, the counter terrorist scanned those who walked before him.

Will the Neville family please step forward?

Again he looked at his watch. It was becoming a habit. One which he seemed to have acquired the longer the day went on. And with good reason.

In just over thirty minutes, if Neville didn't speak to his daughter, he would detonate another bomb.

God alone knew where, and God had fuck all to do with it.

Bomb.

Doyle suppressed a smile.

Just like old times, eh?

Belfast. Londonderry.

London.

What was the difference?

People *had* died, more *would* die.

Trying to find an armed and dangerous man. It had a ring of familiarity to it, didn't it?

Welcome familiarity?

The lights changed to green and Doyle turned left, guiding the car along the Victoria Embankment, the river and the pedestrians to his left-hand side now.

He sucked one last lungful of smoke from the cigarette and jammed it into the already badly overflowing ashtray.

Immediately he lit another.

'. . . It's a hard life to love . . .' thundered the cassette.

Doyle shook his head.

They weren't going to do it.

It was as simple as that.

Barring a miracle, there would be another explosion at five.

A miracle.

Julie and Lisa Neville were probably out of the city by now.

Long gone.

Doyle slowed down for the next set of lights.

Come on, think. Where would Neville go? You're supposed to know how he works. After all, he's not that different to you, is he?

Finding Neville was one thing. Finding his wife and kid was another.

Doyle looked at his watch again.

'Shit,' he murmured under his breath.

Tick-tock. Tick-tock.

He'd known when he climbed into the Datsun that he'd been clutching at straws. That cruising the streets of the capital in search of a missing woman and her child smacked of desperation, but what the hell else was there to do? Besides, he needed to be alone for a while. He'd been around others too long already today.

He needed the solitude which had been so much a part of his life for so long. He needed no company.

Not even Georgie?

Her image flashed fleetingly through his mind and he blinked hard to drive it away.

It persisted stubbornly for a few seconds longer than he would have liked, then was gone.

He sucked hard on the cigarette.

The traffic moved on.

So did time.

4.32 p.m.

The East London Cemetery stretched for roughly half a mile towards all compass points, one of many resting places that seemed like green oases within the desert of concrete, brick and glass that comprised the capital.

Separated from the memorial recreation ground alongside it by a high privet hedge, the cemetery was the usual clutter of headstones, some old, some new, of well-kept and uncared-for graves. Of resting places for those admirably old and some pitifully young.

At its centre was the crematorium. The hub of an unmoving wheel.

A network of paths, some gravel, some Tarmac, wound through the cemetery like arteries. Elsewhere, walkways had been fashioned across grass by the passage of so many feet.

So many mourners.

There was a number of wooden benches too, most of them placed close to the taps which also dotted the necropolis.

Kenneth Baxter walked slowly past one of these taps, glancing at it as it dripped water on to the gravel below.

A slight breeze was blowing now and it brought with it the scent of flowers.

He glanced at the graves flanking the path as he walked, hands dug into the pockets of his jeans. Many had flowers on them, some still wrapped in Cellophane, which crackled whenever the breeze blew too strongly.

He saw some rose petals skitter across the path ahead of him, propelled by a gust of wind.

A middle-aged woman was filling a plastic watering can from one of the taps.

Baxter watched her as she lugged the heavy article back towards a nearby grave and filled the metal vase on the plinth. Then she carefully began arranging carnations in the vase.

The tap continued to drip.

One droplet for each tear shed in this place?

Baxter continued walking, his pace slow and even. But his pace didn't match the expression on his face.

As he walked he looked constantly back and forth, eyes scanning the cemetery.

Searching.

Had he looked behind him he wouldn't have found anything too unusual about the young man in the jeans and T-shirt who had just entered the graveyard.

PC Rob Wells saw Baxter ahead of him but, instead of following, he turned off on one of the gravel paths at his right-hand side and made his way slowly along it, his trainers crunching on the bed of loose stone.

He walked slowly, apparently unconcerned by anything, convinced that Baxter hadn't spotted him but, more importantly, that his quarry hadn't realised he was a plainclothes policeman.

Wells saw Baxter turn off on to one of the secondary paths and the policeman cut across some grass to ensure he didn't lose sight of the older man.

As he stepped on a grave, Wells apologised under his breath to the occupant, feeling stupid but also sorry to have disturbed the reverence he felt was due to the deceased.

The graves in this part of the cemetery were older, many of them untended and overgrown. He glanced at a number of the headstones, many of which were cracked, moss having crept into the rents like gangrene into an open wound.

DIED 1923 proclaimed what little was readable of the inscription on one headstone.

The stone was mottled, the pot which stood on the plinth rusted.

Beside it was another which sported only the rotting stems of long-dead flowers and, as Wells passed, he could smell the cloying stench of rotting plants and stagnant water.

Baxter sat down on one of the benches, legs stretched out, fingers intertwined on his stomach.

Wells walked on, wondering if he should find a better vantage point, somewhere more secluded. He could always make out he was visiting a grave if he was spotted.

But why the hell should he be spotted?

He walked on, aware that his heart was beating a little faster.

Wells saw Baxter rise.

Saw him take two or three paces towards the newcomer.

'Jesus,' he murmured under his breath, trying to avoid staring at Baxter.

There were some trees up ahead to his left. Wells knew he had to reach them, use them as cover while he spoke into the two-way.

Don't hurry, just stay calm.

Baxter stood still and waited for the newcomer to approach *him*.

From behind the cover of the largest tree, Wells pulled the two-way from his pocket and switched it on, his eyes still fixed on Baxter.

'Mark, come in, it's me,' Wells said, keeping his voice low. 'You're not going to believe this.'

4.46 p.m.

'Are you sure?' said PC Mark Hagan, gripping the radio more tightly.

'Come and have a look yourself if you don't believe me,' Wells snapped back. 'I'm standing here looking at them now. Baxter and Julie Neville. They're thirty feet away from me, for Christ's sake. Now call in. Quick.'

'What about the kid?'

'She's here too.'

Hagan ran a hand through his hair, sucking in a deep breath.

'Stay close to them, Rob,' he said into the two-way.

'I wasn't planning on going anywhere,' Wells assured him.

'Bingo.'

Calloway spun round to face his companion, a smile stretched across his face.

'What is it?' Mason enquired.

'Julie *and* Lisa Neville. We've got them,' the DI said triumphantly, still holding the phone to his ear. 'The East London Cemetery in Newham. One of the surveillance units watching Baxter just spotted them.'

'What the hell is Julie Neville doing with Baxter?'

'We'll find that out later. Right now we've got to get to the kid, she's got to be able to speak to Neville when he calls at five.'

Mason looked at his watch.

'We'll never do it in time,' he said, his breath coming in short gasps.

'We've got to,' Calloway told him.

*

206

'You'll never get her back to New Scotland Yard in time for Neville's call,' said Doyle, his eyes now fixed on the vehicles ahead of him. He was no longer interested in the pedestrians on either side. 'Is there some way you can patch his call through to one of your cars at the scene?'

'We'll try,' Calloway answered.

'Don't *try*. Fucking *do* it,' Doyle almost shouted, glancing at his watch.

'There are more mobile units closing in on the cemetery now. They can't escape.'

'You mean Julie Neville and her daughter aren't in custody yet?' Doyle said incredulously. 'How the fuck is the kid supposed to talk to her father if you haven't even grabbed her yet?'

'If we move in too fast they could run for it. Julie Neville could escape again.'

'And if you don't move fast enough Neville's going to detonate that bomb. Grab them, Calloway, for Christ's sake. Them *and* Baxter.'

Doyle hit his horn as the car ahead of him hesitated at a green light.

'Where are you now?'

'Coming up to Westminster Bridge,' Doyle told Calloway. 'I'll be with you in about ten minutes. If I'm lucky.'

He hit the horn again, almost nudging the Fiesta in front to one side in his haste.

Kenneth Baxter and Julie Neville.

What the fuck was going on?

Doyle pressed down on the accelerator when he could, constantly striking the horn in an effort to move the traffic which clogged the road ahead of him.

Again he looked at his watch.

'No fucking way,' Doyle hissed, his tone edged.

With frustration?

With defeat?

With the certainty that, this time, they were too late.

4.51 p.m.

They all heard the sirens.

The strident wail seemed to converge from all directions, shattering the solitude of the cemetery.

Julie Neville looked helplessly at Baxter, her eyes wide, almost imploring.

Baxter himself had already turned and was heading towards the main entrance of the graveyard.

Lisa grabbed her mother's hand, wondering what the noise signified.

'What the hell's going on?' Wells hissed into the two-way, glancing at Baxter, then Julie and the child.

'Arrest them, Rob, now,' Hagan told him. 'That's direct from the guv'nor. Take them.'

Wells swallowed hard and advanced towards the trio who were moving rapidly along one of the Tarmac paths.

'Stop,' Wells shouted, fumbling in his pocket for his ID. 'Police.'

He brandished the wallet above his head and took a step towards the trio before him.

Lisa moved closer to her mother.

Baxter merely slowed his pace and looked at the young man in the jeans and T-shirt.

Julie pulled her daughter tightly to her, a protective arm around her shoulder.

'Just stay where you are,' Wells called, trying to hide

208

the quiver in his voice. 'We just need to talk to you, Mrs Neville. You and your daughter.'

'You keep away from my daughter,' Julie hissed at him.

Baxter stepped up to join her.

The sound of sirens was almost deafening now. They could all hear car doors being slammed and the thudding of many feet moving across the road outside the cemetery. There were shouts.

Wells was still advancing, still waving his ID.

'Nobody's going to hurt either of you,' he said, trying to inject as much reassurance as possible into his tone.

Baxter looked towards the cemetery gates and saw uniformed policemen outside.

'We need your daughter,' Wells said.

'You're not giving her to *him*,' Julie said defiantly.

Wells looked puzzled.

'My husband wants her,' Julie continued. 'He's not going to get her and you're not going to help him.'

The two-way in Wells' back pocket crackled urgently.

'*We* haven't done anything wrong,' Julie told him. '*We're* not the criminals.'

'I know that,' Wells told her.

'What about them?' Baxter said, indicating the uniformed men now moving towards the cemetery gates. 'Do *they* know?'

The radio crackled again.

Wells swallowed hard.

What now? Grab the kid?

He licked his lips nervously.

'We don't want to hurt you or your daughter,' he said. 'But we need your help. It's very important.'

Lisa was holding tightly to Julie's leg, her eyes fixed on the young man moving steadily towards them.

'Mum,' she said softly.

'We need your help, that's all,' Wells repeated.

'And if I refuse?'

'There's nowhere for you to run now, Mrs Neville.' Wells held her gaze.

Julie looked at him then down at her daughter.

'No one's going to hurt you,' Wells repeated. 'I promise you.'

The radio hissed like an angry snake.

'Please,' the policeman pleaded.

Julie nodded.

Thank Christ, Wells thought.

'We've got to hurry,' he said anxiously.

4.57 p.m.

There were beads of perspiration on Doyle's forehead as he pushed open the door of Detective Inspector Calloway's office.

He looked at the DI then at Detective Sergeant Mason who was standing staring at the phone, as if his persistent gaze would cause it to ring. Or perhaps prevent it.

Doyle ran a hand through his hair, brushing sweat with it.

'Have you set up the link to the car in Newham?' Doyle wanted to know.

'We're having problems with it,' Calloway said, his face pale. 'The girl will be able to hear Neville but he won't be able to hear her.'

'Oh, fucking great.'

'We *tried*, Doyle,' Calloway snapped angrily. 'We're still trying.'

'Well try harder,' Doyle rasped.

Mason looked at the counter terrorist, who was pulling a cigarette from the packet.

'What else can we do?' the DS barked. 'You couldn't find Neville, could you? The fucking expert.'

'Shut it, fatso,' Doyle said, lighting his cigarette. 'You couldn't find your oversized arse with two hands and a fucking map.'

Mason took a step towards Doyle who merely glared at him and blew a stream of smoke across the office.

The phone on Calloway's desk rang.

The three men looked at each other, the room silent but for the high-pitched signal.

Two rings.

Calloway looked at the phone.

Three rings.

Doyle sucked hard on his cigarette.

The DI picked up the receiver.

Doyle moved closer to the desk, his eyes never leaving the policeman's face. He saw him frown.

'Not this one,' Calloway said. 'I said to keep this line clear.'

He slammed down the receiver.

'Jesus Christ,' hissed the DI. 'Someone put an internal call through here.'

Doyle shook his head.

Mason checked his watch.

'What about the link?' Doyle asked.

'They can't have managed it,' Calloway told him. 'We would have been notified.'

'Then we're fucked. If Neville finds out we haven't got

his kid, that's it. That's all, folks.' He made a fist of his right hand then flicked his fingers upwards. 'Bang.'

The phone rang again.

Calloway waited.

Two rings.

Three.

He picked it up. 'Detective Inspector Calloway.'

Both Mason and Doyle saw him nod almost imperceptibly.

The DI reached forward and pressed a switch on the console beside the phone, replacing the receiver on its cradle.

Through the speaker-phone they could hear Robert Neville's voice echoing around the office.

'It's time,' he said. 'I want to speak to my daughter.'

'We know, we got your note,' Calloway told him.

Neville chuckled. 'I was going to deliver it personally but I decided against it,' he said jovially.

'Gutless bastard,' Doyle called.

'Hello, Doyle,' said Neville. 'I thought you'd still be there.'

'I'm here until the end, Neville,' the counter terrorist told him. '*Your* end.'

'Don't hold your breath,' Neville retorted. 'Now let me speak to Lisa.'

Calloway gripped the receiver more tightly.

'I want your assurance that you won't let off any more bombs—' the DI began, but Neville cut him short.

'You're in no position to make fucking deals. Put her on. Now!'

Silence.

'Don't fuck me around,' Neville continued, his voice growing in volume. 'Let me speak to her *now*.'

'Neville, I—'

'I warned you what would happen. How many more lives do you want on your conscience?'

The phone went dead.

5.03 p.m.

The plane was going down.

Flames were pouring from its tail and one wing, smoke trailing behind it.

Paul Mortimer raked it with machine-gun fire once more and grinned as the stricken craft finally hit the ground, exploding in a great yellow fireball.

GAME OVER flashed up on the screen and he chuckled to himself as his score appeared on the top right-hand corner of the screen.

On either side of him similar sounds joined together to form one discordant cacophony.

The punches and kicks from the combat games, the explosions emanating from the *shoot-em-up's*. And through it all, the shouts and joyful exclamations of those playing the games.

The bank of arcade games was on the first floor of the Trocadero complex between Leicester Square and Piccadilly Circus. The building itself housed shops, the Guinness Book of Records exhibition, places to eat and a twelve-screen cinema.

It was towards the main entrance that Mortimer briefly glanced.

Penny was in there now with their two children, wedged in with the masses of others who had flocked to see the newest Batman film on its first day of release. The queues had been massive. Paul had bought the tickets himself a week earlier as a birthday treat for Jake, their elder child.

Mortimer had wanted to see the film himself but, as ever, something had come up at the last minute and he'd been forced to pack his wife and the children off together, arranging to meet them outside when the performance ended.

When the work was there he had to take it.

He'd run his own photographic business for the last eighteen months and things were going well. Better than even he'd dared to hope. It had been a tough decision to take in the first place, striking out alone. The photographic firm he'd worked for since leaving college eight years earlier had provided steady and well-paid work, but Mortimer had wanted to escape the shackles of being an employee. Besides, he felt his talents could be better used in fields other than taking pictures for the Next and Top Man catalogues.

Mind you, the work had been pleasant, he had to admit that and, while shooting part of the lingerie section for a Freemans catalogue, he'd met Penny.

The attraction had been instant.

They'd married seven months later. Two years on she was pregnant with Jake.

Kelly followed eighteen months after.

When he'd first suggested going it alone Penny had been her usual practical self, sitting down and working out, to the last copper, how much he would need to earn to maintain the comfortable life-style which they had built for themselves. It wouldn't be easy, they'd both realised that, but Mortimer had many contacts in the business and Penny herself had been asked to return to modelling on a part-time basis. Just hands, face and feet (even a body as well preserved and cared for as hers hadn't quite recovered sufficiently from producing two children to allow her back into the lingerie business). But the offers coming her way were good too.

They had decided they could make a go of things and the best way to prove it was to do it.

Mortimer had worked steadily, sometimes frenziedly, Penny thought, since forming his own company.

He'd received the phone call from the Athenaeum Hotel that morning, asking him if he would come in and speak to them. Discuss the possibility of him taking on a long-term contract to photograph their promotional material.

They had agreed to his price on the spot.

Mortimer smiled, spun round in the seat and fed more coins into the video game.

One more go before he met his family.

Two teenagers stood watching him as he gleefully racked up another huge score. Perhaps they wondered why this man in his early thirties was so engrossed in the game they were waiting to play. He looked old enough to be their father, they thought.

Nevertheless they watched intently.

He was pretty good for an older bloke.

The explosion which killed all three of them was enormous.

A sudden screaming eruption of fire and smoke seemed to fill the entire building as it roared outwards from its source.

Before the screen they were watching dissolved, Mortimer and the two youths saw just two words before them.

GAME OVER.

5.14 p.m.

'That bloody maniac,' roared DS Colin Mason. He held both hands to his head, fingers clasped at the back of his skull. 'Christ. How many more?'

'How many dead?' Doyle asked. He stood at one of the large picture windows of Calloway's office gazing out over the city.

The DI glanced at the piece of paper before him and shook his head.

'It's difficult to tell so early,' He said wearily. 'But initial estimates put the death toll at twelve. More than three times that injured, some of them critical.'

'Any idea how big the device was?'

'Too early to say,' Calloway informed Doyle. 'The bomb squad is at the Trocadero now checking it out. It'll be another couple of hours before they come up with a full report.'

'Two bombs within half a mile of each other,' Mason said. 'We're going to have to close off central London at this rate.'

'How can we close off the entire centre of a city?' Calloway snapped. 'Besides, we don't know if the next bomb will be in the centre or further out.' He slammed the table with the flat of his hand. 'Maybe we should evacuate the whole damn place until we catch Neville.'

'I want to know how he's managed to keep clear of our patrols for so long,' Mason added.

'If he's riding a motorbike then he's wearing a helmet, isn't he, Sherlock?' Doyle chided. 'Chances are he's changed bikes or at least changed clothes since this morning. What are you going to do, pull in every bike rider in the city for questioning?'

'So let's hear *your* suggestions, Doyle,' Mason barked.

'Do what he says,' the counter terrorist said quietly. 'If he wants his daughter, then fucking give her to him.'

'Give in to him?' Mason said scornfully. 'Never.'

Doyle shrugged. 'You've got another option,' he said, sucking on his cigarette.

'Which is?' Calloway demanded.

'Let him use up the rest of the explosive. By my calculations, he should have about a hundred and twenty pounds left.'

'Let him use it?' Mason gasped incredulously. 'You mean let him detonate more bombs?'

'Then give him his daughter,' Doyle rasped. 'It's the only way you're going to stop him. *You* can't handle a man like Neville. He's not some dickhead with a sawn-off shotgun or a nigger purse snatcher. He's a professional. And he's right out of your league.' He pointed an accusatory finger towards the DS.

'You sound as if you admire him,' Calloway murmured.

'I don't admire him, I understand him,' Doyle said. 'I've been fighting men like him for longer than I can remember.'

The phone rang.

Calloway picked it up.

Doyle watched the expression on his face change.

'Neville,' the DI said. He pressed the button on the console to switch the phone to speaker.

'I warned you what would happen if I didn't speak to my daughter,' Neville said, his voice echoing from the speakers.

'Twelve more people killed,' Mason shouted. 'I hope you're happy, you mad bastard.'

'Is Doyle there?' Neville wanted to know, ignoring the outburst.

'Yeah, I'm here.'

'I need your help.'

'Fuck you,' Doyle called back.

'I want my daughter, and this time *you're* going to make sure I get her.'

'How?'

'You're going to bring her to me personally.'

5.16 p.m.

Silence fell upon the room.

Both Mason and Calloway looked at Doyle, who took the cigarette from his lips and stubbed it out, watching the plume of smoke rise lazily into the air.

'Did you hear what I said?' Neville asked.

Doyle didn't answer.

'We heard,' Calloway responded.

'Forget it, Neville, I'm not playing your fucking games,' Doyle told him.

'Then a lot more people are going to die, aren't they?' Neville reminded him.

'What do you want Doyle to do?' Calloway said.

Doyle shot him an angry glance, but the DI held up a restraining hand.

'Like I said, I want him to bring me my daughter,' Neville continued. 'No tricks, no double-cross. If he tries to pull anything I'll let off another bomb.'

'You'll do it anyway,' Doyle said dismissively.

'You'll have to trust me not to,' Neville chuckled.

'I wouldn't trust you to tell me what day of the week it was,' Doyle snarled.

'Here's the deal,' Neville began. 'Doyle brings Lisa to me and I won't detonate the other bombs. Any fucking about and I'll let *all* of them blow and that includes the big one.'

'I thought you were saving that one until eight o'clock,' Doyle said mockingly.

'Only if I don't get what I want.'

'If you blow them all you've got nothing to bargain with,' Doyle pointed out.

'Maybe, but you've got an awful lot of dead bodies on your hands if I do.'

'He'll do it,' Mason interjected.

'Don't *you* tell *me* what I will or won't do,' Doyle hissed.

'Come on, Doyle,' Neville continued. 'You wanted to find me, didn't you? I'm giving you the chance. Bring Lisa to me and you'll find me.'

'Yeah, pointing a fucking gun at my head.'

'That's a possibility,' Neville sniggered. 'So, what do you say?'

'I want to know what your game is, Neville. What's all this about? Or don't *you* even know any more? Is it about your daughter or is it about what went on in Ireland? You can't change it now. You can't change the past, *or* the future. It's over out there.'

'Maybe not.'

'What's that supposed to mean?'

'Bombs in London, bombs in Belfast, bombs in Dublin. One city's the same as another.'

Doyle stroked his chin thoughtfully.

Bombs in Dublin.

'What the hell's he talking about?' Calloway demanded.

219

'He's bluffing,' Doyle said.

'Can you take that chance, Doyle?' Neville teased.

The counter terrorist was pacing the office, head bowed slightly. He swept one hand through his long hair and sucked in a deep breath.

'London today, Dublin or Belfast tomorrow,' Neville continued. 'Unless I get what I want. Unless you *bring* me what I want. Is it a deal?'

Take the kid. Get close to Neville. Kill the cunt.

'I'm not going to wait all fucking night, Doyle. Yes or no?'

Do it. How else are you going to find him?

'Tell me the deal.'

'Is that a yes?' Neville pressed.

'You *know* it is,' Doyle growled.

I'm coming to get you, shithead.

'I knew I could count on you, Doyle,' Neville laughed. 'We're two of a kind. I'm going to send you and Lisa on a little journey first, before I meet you. I'll tell you where to go and when. Just make sure you listen carefully to what I say. I'll call back with the first set of instructions.'

He hung up.

'Bastard!' Doyle shouted, then, turning to Calloway, 'I've got to talk to Julie Neville. Where is she?'

'A car is bringing her, Kenneth Baxter and the little girl here.'

'Well, let me know as soon as they get here,' Doyle instructed, heading for the door. 'Someone's got to tell Julie Neville what we're going to do with her daughter.'

'Where are *you* going?' Calloway asked.

'There's something I've got to do,' Doyle told him.

5.23 p.m.

Doyle paused outside the interview room for a moment, as if to compose himself, then he pushed open the door and walked in.

Julie Neville was seated on one side of a small table with a mug of hot tea cradled between her hands.

She was watching the rising steam, as if fascinated by it.

Only when the door closed did she look up, eyes narrowing as she caught sight of Doyle.

The WPC who was seated in the room with her got to her feet as Doyle nodded towards her.

She left him and Julie alone.

'We're going to have to stop meeting like this,' he said quietly.

'Am I under arrest?' Julie demanded. 'Because if I'm not, then I'd like to see my daughter.'

Doyle perched on a corner of the table and lit a cigarette.

'Your daughter's fine,' he reassured her. 'I've just seen her. She's happy enough. She's playing Snap with two coppers. I reckon she'll beat them.'

'Cut the bullshit, Doyle. You're no good at it. Why am I here?'

'OK. No bullshit. I need your kid.'

'We've had this conversation before. No way. You're not giving her to Bob and that's the end of it. I don't care how many bombs he lets off.'

'You don't care how many people die because of him?'

'The only person I care about is Lisa and I'm not letting you use her like some kind of bloody prize for Bob. Now, if I'm not under arrest I'd like to go.' She got to her feet.

'I think the police call it protective custody,' Doyle told her. 'Like that house in Lambeth you ran away from. They're trying to look after you and your daughter, not hurt you.'

'And you, what are you trying to do?'

'My job,' he said simply.

They locked stares for a moment then Julie sat down again.

'We've had new instructions from your husband,' Doyle updated her. 'He wants me to deliver your daughter to him. If I don't, he'll set off the rest of the bombs. I need your help, Julie. I'll give it to you straight. If I agree to do what your husband wants, take your daughter to him, then that'll be the end of it.'

'How do you know?'

'Because when I get close enough I'll kill him.'

'He might kill *you*.'

'He'll try.'

'And if he does? What happens to Lisa then? I daren't take that chance, Doyle.'

'If he doesn't get what he wants and he detonates all the bombs, he might just come looking for her himself when he's got nothing left to lose. Do you trust the police to stop him? You know him better than I do. You know he won't stop until either he's got his daughter or she's dead, because you can bet your arse if *he* can't have her he'll make fucking sure *you* can't. Now that's your choice. Trust me or the police.'

'I don't trust anyone.'

'What about Kenneth Baxter?'

Julie held his gaze.

'Where does he fit into all this, Julie? Why did you go to him?'

Still she didn't answer.

'You could have got out of London,' Doyle continued. 'Jumped on a train anywhere and just stayed on it until you'd put enough distance between you and your husband, the police *and* me. But you didn't. You went to Baxter. Why?'

'I couldn't think of anyone else,' she said, tracing a slender finger around the rim of the mug.

'No family? No friends?' Doyle challenged.

'He *is* a friend.'

'How long have you known him?'

'Nine or ten years. Almost as long as I've known Bob. Bob brought him home one time when he was on leave. All three of us were friends. He was about the only person Bob ever trusted.'

'Apart from you?' Doyle said, a hint of sarcasm in his voice.

She either failed to notice the tone or chose to ignore it, and simply nodded slowly.

'Where is he now?' she asked.

'Baxter? He's in the next room, as far as I know.'

She sighed.

'Then perhaps you owe it to him to tell him what you just told me,' Julie said wearily. 'About taking Lisa to Bob.'

'Why?'

'He has a right to know.'

'It's got fuck all to do with Baxter.'

'It's got *everything* to do with him. Lisa's his daughter.'

5.25 p.m.

Doyle shook his head and smiled mirthlessly.

'Neville obviously doesn't know that Lisa isn't *his*.' It came out more like a statement than a question.

223

Julie shook her head. 'If he did he'd have killed me *and* Ken by now. I'm the only one who knows, and now you. Lisa thinks Bob is her father. I want it to stay that way, Doyle.'

'How long has this been going on?'

'Almost nine years. On and off.'

'And Neville never suspected?'

Julie shook her head.

'No, I suppose he wouldn't, would he?' Doyle chided. 'His best friend and his wife.' He grunted. 'Fucking hell, and you worry about not trusting *him*.'

'I don't need a lecture on morality, Doyle.'

'I'm not giving one. I don't care if you were getting fucked by Baxter or the entire band of the Coldstream Guards. The only thing that bothers me is getting Neville and to do that I need your help. Or, more to the point, your daughter's help.'

'Are you asking for my permission?'

'You could say that.'

'Promise me no harm will come to her.'

'I'll look after her. I don't make promises.'

'You have to kill him?'

'That was what I was planning to do from the beginning. I'd have thought you'd be glad to see the back of him too. It'll protect your little secret, won't it?'

'Fuck you, Doyle.'

'If that's what you want. Shall I get in the queue behind Baxter?'

'You bastard.' She lunged forward, slapping at Doyle's face.

He caught her wrist in one powerful hand and pushed her back on to her seat, finally releasing her, stepping back a pace.

224

'Did you love him?' he asked, his voice low.

'Who?'

'Baxter.'

'I don't think so. It wasn't like that. It wasn't some big love affair. We just—'

'Fucked,' Doyle interjected. 'Are you sure Lisa's Baxter's?'

'Yes. I hadn't known Ken very long. Bob was on duty when it happened.'

'That was convenient. And he never suspected?'

'Why should he? Besides, I can be discreet when I have to be.'

'I bet you can.'

'I didn't want it to happen that way, Doyle. If it hadn't been Ken, it would have been someone else. I just didn't want Lisa hurt.'

'Why didn't you just leave Neville?'

'I don't know. I loved him at the beginning.'

'Is that why you were fucking his best mate?'

'I wouldn't expect you to understand, Doyle. What do you know about love or emotion?'

'Nothing any more,' he said quietly, averting his eyes.

A vision flashed into his mind.

Georgie. Laughing.

Dying.

He tried to drive the image away.

But it didn't want to leave.

They were together. Kissing. Making love.

Jesus, it still hurt to be without her.

So much pain. When would it end?

He sucked in a deep breath.

'You're going to have to talk to your daughter,' he said. 'Tell her what's going on.'

'I can't,' Julie said falteringly. 'How can I tell her what I just told you? That her father isn't really her father? Jesus Christ, Ken doesn't even know she's his.'

Doyle shook his head slowly.

'Look,' he began. 'I'm not asking you to tell her – or Ken – what you told me, or anything else about this whole fucking mess. Just tell Lisa she's going to see her father . . . At least the geezer she *thinks* is her father.'

Julie eyed him furiously.

'Tell her I've got to take her,' Doyle continued. 'Tell her she's going to have to do what I say.' He smiled. 'You can even tell her to trust me.'

5.46 p.m.

'This is crazy,' said DS Colin Mason, pacing the office. 'There must be something else we can do instead of just sitting here and waiting for that fucking headcase to ring.'

'Such as?' Calloway enquired.

'All this sitting around,' Mason continued irritably. 'The waiting. He's doing it on purpose. Neville's playing fucking games with us.'

The harsh metallic sound of an automatic being cocked caused him to spin round.

Doyle held the 92F burst-fire in his hands, examining the sleek lines of the pistol before pushing it back into its shoulder holster.

'If he frisks you, he'll find that,' Calloway pointed out.

'If he gets that close,' Mason added. 'He might just blow your head off from a distance and then take the kid.'

In answer, Doyle pushed down the top of his cowboy boot slightly to reveal the ankle holster.

He tapped the butt of the PD Star then pulled the boot back up.

'He won't find *that*,' Doyle said with an air of certainty.

'Proper Secret Agent, aren't you, Doyle?' Mason chided.

The counter terrorist fixed Mason in an unwavering stare until the policeman finally turned away and continued pacing.

'All this waiting about,' the DS said. 'It's like—'

'Waiting for a bomb to go off?' Doyle offered.

'That's not funny, Doyle,' Mason growled.

'Did he say what time he was ringing back – he didn't, did he?' Doyle mused.

Calloway shook his head.

'He could keep us sitting here for the next three or four hours if he wanted to,' the DI said.

Doyle glanced at his watch.

'I don't think so,' he murmured. 'He says he's going to let the big one off at eight and I reckon he will.'

'Even if he gets his daughter back?' Calloway said.

'He's stalling,' Doyle continued. 'He could set it off anyway, even if he does get her. We don't know how big the thing is. A hundred, a hundred and fifty pounds. It'd be one hell of a fucking diversion.'

Doyle had said nothing to the two policemen about his talk with Julie Neville. At least she'd agreed to allow her daughter to be taken along by Doyle, but that was all.

They also knew nothing of the counter terrorist's attempts to contact Major John Wetherby.

Twice Doyle had attempted to ring the Army Intelligence officer but, on both occasions, Wetherby had been unavailable, not at his desk or some other bullshit excuse.

Doyle had slammed down the phone the second time.

Wetherby needed to know what was happening. It was as simple as that.

Doyle had decided to check in.

Old habits died hard.

Besides, Doyle had wanted to tell Wetherby that he was closing in on Neville and also warn him that there might well be some more civilian casualties. In particular, an eight-year-old girl.

The phone rang and Calloway grabbed it.

'You took your time, Neville,' he said, switching the phone to speaker.

'Right, just listen,' Neville began. 'Doyle, can you hear me?'

'Get on with it,' the counter terrorist called back.

'I'll keep it simple,' Neville said. 'When I said I wanted Doyle to bring Lisa to me, I meant Doyle and Doyle alone. No back-up. No plain-clothes coppers following at a discreet distance. If I even smell a copper there'll be another explosion. Got it? Now this is how we play the game. Doyle, I'm going to give you locations. Each one is a phone box. I'm going to bounce you all over London to make sure you're not being followed. First one phone box, then another, then another, until I'm satisfied. When I am, I'll give you the location to bring Lisa to me. This is how it works. I tell you which phone box to get to, the phone rings five times. If it isn't answered after five rings I'll detonate a bomb. If anyone else other than you answers it I'll detonate a bomb. Got that?'

'Got it.'

'Right, here goes then and, Doyle, you take good care of

my little girl,' Neville rasped. 'First phone box is an easy one. Get to the public phones at St James's tube station. Move it. You've got eight minutes.'

The line went dead.

5.51 p.m.

I don't fucking need this.

Doyle slowed his pace slightly, glancing round to see that the little girl was having trouble keeping up with him.

Playing Neville's game alone would be bad enough, but I can do without the kid.

'Come on,' he said, trying to sound as cheerful as possible.

That was how you were supposed to sound when you were talking to kids, wasn't it?

Lisa scuttled along beside him, bumping into him when he stopped hurriedly at a corner.

She almost overbalanced but Doyle shot out a hand and pulled her along with him.

'Where are we going?' she asked.

'Didn't your mum tell you? We're going to see your dad.'

The bloke you think is your dad, at any rate.

'Mum said I had to do what you told me.'

'That's right.'

They reached the entrance to St James's tube station.

There were a number of people climbing the steps from below and more than one glanced inquisitively at the man with the long brown hair and the stubble-covered face as he pulled the little girl in the jeans and blue cardigan along with him.

Perhaps a little too roughly sometimes.

Doyle hurried down the steps, Lisa struggling along behind.

Come on, come on.

He helped her down the last two stairs, eyes scanning the concourse for the phones.

To his left.

He strode towards them, Lisa in tow.

Two phones. One was out of order.

Doyle leaned against the working one and pulled cigarettes from his jacket, jamming one between his lips but not lighting it.

'You'll get a cough,' said Lisa, looking up at him.

Doyle looked puzzled.

'If you smoke, you get a cough,' she continued. 'They told us that at school. I told Mum she should give up.'

'Did your teacher tell you that smoking was bad for you?'

Lisa nodded.

'Well, you tell your teacher from me that non-smokers die every day.' He smiled crookedly.

The phone rang.

Doyle snatched it up and pressed the receiver to his ear.

'Yeah,' he said.

'Doyle?'

'You know bloody well it is.'

'Is Lisa with you?' Neville demanded.

'Yes.'

'Let me speak to her.'

'This wasn't part of the plan.'

'Who's making the fucking rules, Doyle? Let me speak to her,' Neville barked.

Doyle pushed the phone towards the child, who had trouble reaching it because the cord was so short.

Doyle lifted her up.

'Is that my princess?' Neville said.

'Dad. Where are you?' Lisa said excitedly.

'I'm waiting for you,' he told her. 'Let me speak to the man who's with you and we'll talk later.'

She handed the phone to Doyle, who put her down once more.

'Satisfied?' Doyle snapped into the phone.

'Listen to me. The next stop is Oxford Circus, there's a phone box outside Top Shop. It should take twenty minutes by tube. It means your friends won't be able to hear you while you're in the tunnels though.'

'What the fuck are you talking about?' Doyle hissed.

'Watch your language in front of my daughter, Doyle,' Neville said reproachfully. 'I know you're in contact with the police, I wouldn't have expected anything else. I thought you might wear a wire but that's a bit primitive, isn't it? What have you got? A mobile?'

Doyle exhaled deeply. 'Yeah, full marks, Sherlock.'

'Well, just make sure they don't get over-eager. Like I said, if I see a copper, Bang! Now move it, you've got twenty minutes to get to the next phone box.'

5.57 p.m.

The train from St James's to Victoria had been crowded. The walkways and platform leading to the Victoria line had been busy too, but the train which was now heading towards Oxford Circus was so jam-packed with people Doyle found it hard to breathe.

231

Beside him, Lisa clung to his belt, fascinated it seemed by the large man who was seated opposite her, his bald head gleaming beneath the lights inside the tube.

He was wearing a dark suit and he was clearly hot. Beads of perspiration were forming on his hairless pate and Lisa watched as one droplet edged its way slowly past his temple and began a slow journey down his cheek towards his jaw.

As the train slid to a halt, Doyle turned, trying to duck slightly to read the station name on the plate on the tunnel wall. Green Park.

One more stop.

No one moved as the doors opened.

No one got off.

Instead, the crush inside the train became even more uncomfortable as those at Green Park pushed and shoved their way into the already tightly packed mass inside the carriage.

Lisa was nearly knocked off her feet by a tall man in faded black jeans and a T-shirt. He seemed not to notice her and she moved closer to Doyle, who was gripping one of the overhead bars as tightly as he could.

The man in the black jeans was wearing a Walkman and the irritating rattle of the music he was listening to seemed to fill the carriage.

Behind Doyle stood a woman in her mid-forties. Her hair was impossibly immobile, as if the coiffure had been moulded then welded to her head. She was wearing trousers and a pair of trainers which looked dazzlingly white. She was holding a number of shopping bags, one of which was digging uncomfortably into Doyle's back.

He looked irritably at her, gazing into her eyes through her glasses.

She stared back for a moment then turned to the man standing with her.

He was wearing a baseball cap with NIKE emblazoned across the front, wisps of white hair poking out from either side.

'Are you OK, honey?' he said, in a loud accented voice, which attracted a number of stares from other passengers.

Fucking Yanks, Doyle thought.

The doors slid shut and the train moved off.

The carriage smelled of perspiration and perfume. Conflicting odours. There was a hint of garlic in the musty air too. Doyle looked around at his fellow passengers as if seeking the culprit.

Further down the carriage a young woman wearing leggings and a polo-neck sweater was sweeping a hand through her long auburn hair, trying to readjust her position as the train moved away. Doyle studied her face briefly then found his gaze straying to her breasts. Beneath the sweater they were unfettered by a bra. He could see the outline of her nipples pushing against the material.

Typical. I'm wedged up against some fat Yank and a bastard who smells of garlic. Why not her?

He held the woman in his gaze for a few seconds longer. The train lurched to one side and Lisa gripped more tightly to Doyle to prevent herself overbalancing. Not that she would have fallen anyway, the other travellers were too tightly wedged in the carriage to allow her to overbalance.

Christ, he hated crowds. Hated being so close to other people.

He rarely travelled by tube and, if he did, he tried to make sure it was after rush-hour.

233

Not like now. Right in the middle of it.

Doyle glanced at his watch.

The train slowed down.

Approaching the station.

It stopped in the tunnel.

What the fuck was going on?

There were a number of groans from inside the carriage.

The American woman with the shopping bags dug him in the back once more and this time Doyle spun round and glared at her.

'Why have we stopped?' Lisa asked.

Doyle didn't answer.

'Why have we stopped?' she persisted.

'I don't know,' he snapped back, the vehemence of his reply causing a number of people to look in his direction.

The train bumped forward a few yards, stopped again then continued on its way.

As it slid into Oxford Circus station, Doyle was already pushing his way towards the door, pulling Lisa along with him.

The doors opened and Doyle barged out, through the passengers waiting to board.

Lisa felt his hand gripping hers tightly. A little too tightly.

It hurt.

She tried to twist her hand inside his but the sweat on his palm made his skin slippery.

As he pulled at her in an attempt to rush her through the heaving throng on the platform, her hand slipped free of his.

Someone bumped into her, buffeted her away from him.

Doyle felt her hand slide from his.

He spun round.

The passengers both embarking and alighting seemed to swell into one huge amorphous mass. Faces passed before him as he scanned the crowd frantically for Lisa.

6.08 p.m.

'Shit,' he snarled, pushing past a woman with a baby who was climbing on.

He scanned the faces around him, then lowered his gaze.

Where the hell was she?

Doyle pushed a youth in an REM sweatshirt aside and heard the boy mutter something under his breath.

The walkway which led across to the Bakerloo line platform was a few feet ahead of him.

What if Lisa had wandered up there?

He shoved uncaringly through the passengers, finally catching sight of her.

She had backed up against the wall and was standing still, looking up with wide-eyed bewilderment at the sea of people surrounding her.

But she didn't move.

Sensible kid.

Doyle reached her and swept her up in his arms, unsure how he should hold her. He heard her grunt in discomfort as he squeezed her a little too hard.

'A man bumped into me,' she said almost apologetically. 'I couldn't hold on to your hand.'

Doyle lifted her on to his shoulders and began striding through the crowd.

Lisa smiled now, perched on those powerful shoulders, happy with her vantage point. She could see over the heads of the other people on the platform.

'Hold on to my jacket,' he told her and she gripped the leather collar, smiling as Doyle hurried through the crowd.

When they reached the escalators he lifted her down again and she stood beside him as the moving stairs rose upwards.

Doyle looked at his watch.

No time to stand still.

He grabbed Lisa's hand and they began climbing, watched by a number of people, one or two of whom were a little concerned at how difficult the child in the jeans was finding it to keep up with the long-haired man in the leather jacket and the cowboy boots.

Doyle reached the top of the escalator and headed for the exit, pausing only briefly to ensure that Lisa was still with him. He ushered her through the automatic gates and squeezed through behind her.

'There,' he said, pointing to the flight of steps which led up towards Oxford Street and, with the little girl still struggling to stay with him, he began to climb.

Lisa paused halfway up, stopping to look at a man who was sitting cross-legged and shoeless on the steps.

His hair was long, so dirty it looked as if it was matted into dreadlocks. He wore a filthy grey overcoat which was open, revealing a body just weeks away from almost complete emaciation.

A dirty jumper was lying in front of him, folded to form a kind of hollow at its centre. In that hole lay a few coins.

'Come on,' Doyle said, seeing Lisa staring at the tramp as if hypnotised.

He smiled at her, his teeth whiter than they should have been for one so dirty.

She remained gazing at the man.

'Lisa, for Christ's sake, come on,' Doyle snapped, ignoring the disapproving glance of a woman who passed him on the stairs.

Finally Lisa dug one tiny hand into the pocket of her jeans and produced two coins.

Doyle watched as she dropped them on to the reeking jumper.

Lisa bounded up the steps and joined him, slipping her hand into his. Together they emerged into Oxford Street.

Top Shop was directly opposite.

Doyle could see the phone box.

He urged Lisa to the roadside, waited for a gap in the traffic, then swept her up into his arms once more and darted across.

She giggled as he put her down, trying to grip his hand again but Doyle pulled away, moving towards the phone box.

There was a woman standing close to it, pulling a phone card from her purse.

The phone began to ring.

6.15 p.m.

Doyle stepped in front of the woman who shot him an angry glance.

'Excuse *me*,' she said, reproachfully, standing and watching as he snatched up the receiver.

'Doyle,' he said.

Silence at the other end.

'Neville, can you hear me?'

'I can hear you.' Neville's voice came down the line. 'Well done. I want to speak to Lisa.'

'I was here first, you know,' the woman continued from behind Doyle.

Still he ignored her, instead pulling Lisa to him, handing her the receiver.

'Hello, sweetheart,' Neville said to her, his tone lightening.

'Dad, I just saw this man and he had no money,' Lisa babbled. 'So I gave him some of my pocket money.'

'You're a good girl.'

'I said, "*I* was here first",' the woman persisted, tapping Doyle on the shoulder.

He turned and looked her squarely in the eye, the ferocity of his stare causing her to take a step back.

'I think he was hungry, Dad,' Lisa continued. 'Perhaps he can get something to eat now.'

'Good girl. Let me speak to the man with you again,' Neville instructed, waiting while Lisa handed the receiver back to Doyle.

'You make sure you keep her safe, Doyle,' the ex-para warned.

'She's fine. Now get on with it.'

'Bedford Square, just off Tottenham Court Road,' Neville instructed. 'There're public phones on the eastern side. Five minutes.'

'Don't be fucking ridiculous,' Doyle snarled. 'I can't make that in five minutes.'

'I've told you before, watch your language in front of my little girl,' Neville rebuked. 'Bedford Square, five minutes or more people die.'

'You bastard, I'll—'

'Doyle, if you're worried about getting there on time, do you want some advice? Try running.'

Neville hung up.

Doyle looked around, as if hoping to find some kind of divine inspiration in the crowds thronging the pavement or the vehicles clogging the road.

What to do?

On his own he might be able to make the run to Bedford Square in time.

Maybe.

With the kid as company he didn't have a chance.

They could take the tube to Tottenham Court Road then run like hell the last few hundred yards, but if the train was delayed he was fucked.

Taxi?

Forget it. The traffic was bumper to bumper. It would take longer by road than any other alternative.

Come on, think.

He glanced to his right and left.

'Where are we going?' Lisa asked.

Come on, time's running out.

The little girl was pulling at the bottom of his jacket now. 'I want to see my dad.'

Doyle pulled away from her.

Jesus Christ. There it was. Fifty yards from him.

Salvation.

The Kawasaki KR-1S had stopped at the traffic lights in Oxford Circus, its engine idling, its rider adjusting the strap on his helmet.

'Don't move,' Doyle said, dropping to one knee so that his face was directly in front of Lisa. 'Promise me you won't move.'

She nodded.

He leaped to his feet and sprinted off down the street, bumping into people, knocking them aside in his desperation to reach the bike.

The lights were still on red.

Doyle reached the railings at the end of the pavement and hurdled them, ignoring the curious looks from passers-by.

He ran across to the motor-cyclist and gripped his arm.

The man pulled away irritably.

'I need your bike,' Doyle said breathlessly.

'Fuck off,' the rider said, eyeing Doyle as if he were some kind of lunatic. He revved the engine, as if to force Doyle away.

Doyle slid one hand inside his jacket and pulled out the Beretta. He pressed the barrel to the rider's head.

'Get off the fucking bike now,' he snarled.

The rider did as he was told.

No argument. No hesitation.

Doyle holstered the weapon, swung his leg over the seat of the Kawasaki and twisted the handlebars, guiding the bike up onto the pavement.

The roar of the engine mingled with the screams of pedestrians as they scattered, anxious to escape this maniac who was roaring along the walkway on such a powerful machine.

He hit the brakes as he reached Lisa who was still standing obediently by the phone box.

He shot out a hand to her.

'Get on,' he said.

Lisa looked at the bike with a combination of fascination and fear.

'Now you hold on to my belt as tightly as you can and don't let go, right?' he instructed, almost lifting her up on to the pillion with one hand.

He worked the throttle then rode on down the pavement, finally swinging the bike on to the road.

He reached behind him and gently touched Lisa's back in an attempt to reassure her and also to prevent her from toppling off the bike, which was now speeding up Oxford Street, cutting alongside the gridlocked traffic.

He gunned the throttle once more, wondering, even now, if there would be time.

6.19 p.m.

Calloway put down the phone, waited a second then pressed the receiver to his ear and pressed 'Redial'.

Julie Neville watched anxiously as the DI waited for an answer, fingers drumming slowly on the desk-top.

'No answer,' he said quietly.

'What the hell is Doyle playing at?' Mason snapped.

'It's ringing. He's just not answering it,' the DI elaborated.

Julie got to her feet.

'Can't you find out where he is?' she demanded.

'Not unless he contacts us,' Calloway said.

'What if Bob's already killed him, taken my daughter?' she said, panic in her voice.

'Doyle knows what he's doing,' the DI said, trying to sound as reassuring as possible.

The mobile continued to ring.

Doyle heard the phone.

Or at least he was aware of it, jammed into the back pocket of his jeans. The roar of the Kawasaki's engine relegated it to little more than a burble on the periphery of his hearing.

They were heading up Tottenham Court Road now.

Minutes away.

He glanced down at his watch.

The lights ahead were on red.

He pulled up alongside a Range Rover, the driver glancing at him then at Lisa, still perched precariously on the back of the powerful machine, her hands laced into Doyle's belt.

'Are you all right?' Doyle asked her, glancing back over his shoulder.

She could only nod, her face drained of colour.

The lights changed to green and Doyle sped off, swinging right into Bayley Street and then again into Bedford Square, easing off the throttle, eyes scanning the square for the phones Neville had spoken of.

There was a large, white building directly opposite him, much of its frontage formed from tinted glass. It also bore a huge clock.

Doyle looked up at the hands crawling round.

The phones were in front of this building.

He sped across the cobbled square, narrowly avoiding two men who were crossing in front of him.

One of them shouted something which he didn't catch.

Doyle hit the brakes, bringing one foot down to further slow the Kawasaki.

A woman in her early twenties was emerging from the glass-fronted building, a man a little older beside her. They were chatting animatedly, the woman laughing loudly.

She was the first to hear the phone ring.

Doyle saw her look towards it, saw her say something to her companion.

Saw her begin walking towards it.

'Oh shit,' he muttered, lifting Lisa clear of the bike, his eyes on the woman.

The phone had rung twice already.

'Leave it,' he roared at her.

She looked at him, as did her companion, but both offered only dismissive glances.

Doyle ran towards the phone as it rang for the third time.

'Get away from it,' he bellowed at the woman who now seemed intent on picking it up.

Her companion, a tall, thin man in a linen suit, his hair slicked back into a pony tail, stepped forward as if to frighten Doyle off.

The counter terrorist barged the woman aside and picked up the phone just before it could ring for the fifth time.

'Doyle,' he gasped into it.

'I'm impressed,' Neville told him.

'Hey,' said the tall man in the linen suit. 'What do you think you're playing at?'

Doyle felt a hand on his shoulder.

'I'm talking to *you*,' the tall man insisted.

'What's going on?' Neville demanded.

'You could have hurt her,' the tall man said, his hand still on Doyle's shoulder.

'Hang on,' Doyle said into the phone.

He pulled the Beretta from its holster and jammed the barrel against the tip of the tall man's nose.

'I'll hurt *you* if you don't take your fucking hand off my shoulder,' Doyle snarled, thumbing back the hammer.

The colour drained from the man's face until his flesh was the same colour as his cream jacket.

Doyle heard a low rumbling sound as the tall man's bowels loosened.

'Fuck off, you ponce,' Doyle snarled, the gun still aimed at the man's head.

'Oh my God,' the woman stammered, backing away, tripping on the kerb.

'Go on, move it. Get away from here,' Doyle continued.

The man was frozen to the spot. It was as if every muscle in his body had locked. Apart from his sphincter which seemed to be working quite freely.

'What's happening?' Neville persisted. 'If you're trying to set me up I'll—'

'Some stupid bitch was going to answer the phone,' Doyle told him. 'Her boyfriend decided to be a fucking hero.'

'You'd better not be fucking me about, Doyle.'

'I made it, didn't I? Just talk.'

Doyle looked round and saw that the man and the woman had fled back inside the glass-fronted building.

He eased the trigger forward and reholstered the automatic.

'Is Lisa still with you?' Neville demanded.

Doyle beckoned her over, handing her the phone.

'Are you all right, darling?' Neville asked her. 'Is the man looking after you?'

'Yes, Dad,' she said. 'I didn't like the motorbike though. I thought I was going to fall off.'

Doyle rolled his eyes irritably.

'I'll see you soon, sweetheart,' Neville told her. 'Give the phone back to the other man.'

Lisa did as she was told.

'What fucking motorbike, Doyle?' Neville hissed. 'I told you only public transport.'

'You never said that,' Doyle reminded him. 'Besides, how else was I going to get here on time? Or didn't you want me to? Looking forward to letting off another bomb, are you?'

'Get rid of the bike. Understand? You use public transport or you fucking walk, that's one of the rules. You put my daughter's life in danger, you bastard.'

'Just give me the next set of instructions,' Doyle demanded angrily.

Silence.

'Neville. Are you listening?' Doyle snapped. He thought he could hear chuckling on the other end of the line.

'I knew I picked the right bloke,' said Neville finally.

Doyle's knuckles turned white as his grip tightened.

'Phone box in Cambridge Circus,' Neville instructed. 'It's a straight run, Doyle. You've got ten minutes.'

6.28 p.m.

Doyle felt as if his lungs were going to burst.

He was running with his mouth open, sucking in huge breaths which seemed to sear his throat as he gulped them down.

Even Lisa was breathing heavily and he was carrying her.

The child had been light, as he'd expected, but running down Tottenham Court Road and then Charing Cross Road clutching her like some kind of oversized doll was proving too much.

Sweat was coursing down his face and he could feel his T-shirt sticking to his back.

His heart was thumping so hard against his ribs he feared it might bruise.

And for the entire journey he was met with curious glances from those he passed. Some even stopped and looked at him, watching him as he sprinted down the thoroughfare clutching the child.

Some assumed it was his daughter.

One or two entertained darker thoughts.

A middle-aged man leaving Foyles with a bagful of books saw Doyle running with Lisa and wondered whether or not to phone the police.

Was this an abduction?

He watched as the leather-jacketed man ran on through the crowds, his mind turning one way then the other like some kind of revolving door.

When Doyle disappeared into a crowd outside the Marquee, the man walked on but the vision remained in his mind.

The unshaven, long-haired man, his face sheathed in perspiration, bumping uncaringly past pedestrians while he held tightly to the little girl, who looked pale and tired and who clung to the man's shoulders almost reluctantly.

Doyle saw the flashing blue lights as he passed the Marquee.

The ambulance was parked on the corner of Old Compton Street, lights turning silently.

A crowd had gathered, five deep in places, around the emergency vehicle.

Doyle glanced into the road and saw the twisted frame of a racing bike lying against the kerb.

There was some broken glass.

Some blood.

The car which had hit the cyclist was standing immobile a few yards from the junction, the driver leaning against his vehicle, head bowed. The policemen were talking to the man, one offering a comforting hand on the shoulder.

The cyclist was lying still on the road, ambulancemen gathered around him.

Only his legs were visible, the skin having been ripped from his knees and calves. One leg was twisted beneath him and Doyle could see something white protruding from the mass of crimson which covered his shins.

He guessed that the car must have run over the unfortunate cyclist's legs but, right now, all that concerned him was that the road was blocked.

The road was blocked. The pavement was clogged with morbid fuckers trying to get a look at the victim.

Doyle had to get around this diversion.

He hurried across the road, Lisa now gazing across at the crowd, who reminded Doyle of carrion birds, waiting around for anything interesting. Waiting to pick over the road-kill.

Maybe a bomb in amongst *those* rubber-necking bastards wouldn't be a bad idea.

He tried to suck in more stale air but couldn't. He put Lisa down and stood still for a second, head spinning, hair plastered to the back of his neck. He coughed, hawked and propelled a lump of mucus on to the pavement.

Lisa looked at him as if he'd just breathed fire.

'Come on,' Doyle said breathlessly, grabbing her hand. 'Show me how fast you can run.'

She managed a smile and they set off, her little legs keeping pace with his longer ones.

They were practically at Cambridge Circus. He could see the phone boxes across the road but the traffic coming from their right was swift and heavy.

Doyle stood with his hands on his hips, waiting for a gap in the endless stream of vehicles.

He managed a glance at his watch.

'Come on, for Christ's sake,' he whispered anxiously, the breath catching in his throat.

Time was almost up.

He coughed again.

The lights at the Circus were changing.

Amber.

He picked Lisa up once more.

Red.

Doyle ran across the road with as much speed as he could muster, put Lisa down and headed straight for the phones.

There were three of them.

One was already ringing.

Had it just started?

And ringing.

He reached the first one and picked it up.

Dead line.

The ringing continued.

How many fucking rings is that?

He snatched at the second.

'Doyle,' he gasped into it but then realised that there was only buzzing at the other end.

Then the ringing stopped.

'Oh Christ!' he gasped, slumping against the phone box.

The third phone rang.

Doyle grabbed the receiver and pressed it to his ear.

'Neville, listen to me,' he panted.

'Five rings, Doyle,' Neville said. 'I said five.'

'You were early,' Doyle rasped, wiping his mouth with the back of his hand.

'No. *You* were *late*. Firework time.'

'No, Neville, you bastard, don't—' Doyle bellowed into the handset.

The line was dead.

6.29 p.m.

Doyle stood still, hands on thighs, bent forward at the waist, sucking in lungfuls of air.

Lisa watched him, her eyes drawn to the scar on his left cheek.

She took a step towards him, mesmerised by the old wound, wanting to touch it, to trace the outline of the mark which ran from his eye to his jaw.

'Does that hurt?'

'What?' Doyle managed, perspiration dripping from his chin, splashing on the pavement at his feet.

'*That*,' Lisa persisted and touched the scar.

Doyle gripped her wrist gently and held her, looking into her eyes.

Lisa looked fearful, then Doyle released her, even managed a small smile.

'It doesn't hurt,' he said softly.

It did when it first happened.

'It happened a long time ago,' he continued.

How long? Five years? Ten?

249

He straightened up.

Who fucking cared?

As Doyle pulled the mobile phone from the back pocket of his jeans it rang.

'Doyle, are you OK?' said the voice and he recognised it immediately as belonging to Calloway.

'I didn't make it in time.'

'We know that. Another bomb went off about thirty seconds ago.'

'Oh Christ. Where?'

'Baker Street, close to Madame Tussauds. We don't know the extent of the damage or the casualties yet.'

'Shit,' Doyle hissed.

'What happened?' Calloway asked. 'How come you didn't get to the phone in time?'

Doyle thought about hurling the phone away then decided against it.

'Do *you* want to come and do this? You're lucky it didn't happen earlier.'

'What about the next set of instructions?'

'I haven't had them. He hung up, then detonated the bomb.'

'Where are you now?'

'Cambridge Circus, outside the Palace Theatre.'

The third phone rang again.

Doyle snatched it up and pressed it to his ear.

'You're still there,' said Neville. 'I had a feeling you might be, waiting for your next set of orders.'

'You don't give me orders, Neville. Nobody does,' Doyle snarled.

'As long as I've got the Semtex, *I* give the orders, Mister Counter Terrorist.' Neville chuckled. 'It is ironic, isn't it? All those years chasing the IRA, while I was chasing them too. Now you're chasing *me*. Makes you laugh, doesn't it?'

'I'm pissing myself.'

Holding the mobile phone away from him, Doyle could still hear Calloway's voice but it sounded so distant now, swallowed up by the din of traffic. He switched off the mobile and returned his attention to Neville.

'Whatever the fuck you want, get on with it,' he said irritably.

'You *know* what I want.'

'Yeah, and I'm getting sick of hearing about it.'

'Tough. This game goes on for as long as I want it to.'

'Until eight o'clock, you mean. The *big* one,' said Doyle. 'Or are you full of shit?'

'What do *you* think, Doyle?'

'I think you're fucking dead when I find you.'

'Shut up and listen. Liverpool Street station, public phones on the concourse close to WH Smith. You've got thirty minutes. Don't fuck it up again, Doyle.'

Doyle pressed the required digits on the mobile and the call was answered immediately.

'Neville called back.'

Calloway wanted to know the next location.

Doyle told him.

'Keep away, Calloway,' Doyle ordered. 'And you make sure none of your boys get involved. You know Neville's not fucking about. *I'll* take care of him.'

'Doyle, Mrs Neville wants to talk to you,' the DI said.

'No time,' Doyle told him and switched off the mobile.

DS Colin Mason had sat listening to the conversation with Doyle over the speaker-phone in Calloway's office. Now he made his way down the corridor to his own office and slipped inside, almost furtively.

The two-way was lying on his desk. It took him seconds to find the frequency he sought, a deafening blast of static signalling its discovery.

This had gone on too long.

Neville was making them look like idiots, the fucking maniac.

Something had to be done, Mason knew that. He also knew his superior was not the man to do it.

Nor was Doyle.

The arrogant bastard.

Neville had to be stopped and, as far as Mason was concerned, there was only one way to do it. More bombs or not.

'Osprey One, come in, over,' he said into the two-way.

Then he waited for the police helicopter to reply.

6.43 p.m.

'Why do you hate my dad?'

The question seemed to come from the very air itself.

Doyle had his eyes closed as the Underground train pulled out of the station. He was grateful that it was so much quieter than earlier. There weren't above a dozen people in the entire carriage and most of those were seated at the far end.

He opened his eyes and looked down at Lisa, who was seated beside him, pulling at a loose thread on one sleeve of her cardigan.

'I don't hate him.'

Which was true.

'Then why do you shout at him on the phone?' Lisa persisted.

Doyle sucked in a deep breath.

I really fucking need this now. Some deep, meaningful conversation with an eight-year-old kid about a man she thinks is her father. A man I'm going to kill.

'Because he gets me mad,' Doyle answered eventually.

Lisa continued playing with the loose thread.

'He's ill,' she explained.

'Who says so?'

'My mum. She said that Dad isn't well, that he should see a doctor or something.' She looked up at him. 'Is he going to die?'

He is when I get hold of him.

Doyle thought about saying yes. It would have been the easiest option. It might even have shut her up.

He looked into her wide, questioning eyes.

Christ, they were so blue. So perfectly, flawlessly blue. Like sapphires lit from behind.

'What else did your mum say about him?'

'She didn't talk much about him. I sometimes heard them shouting when he came home. I used to listen at the top of the stairs. They thought I was asleep but I used to creep out of my room and listen to them.'

'What happened when your dad came home *this* time?'

'Mum was surprised to see him.'

'Yeah, I bet she was.'

'They argued a lot this time.'

'Did your dad ever hurt her?'

'No. He wouldn't do that.'

'Did he ever hurt *you*?'

'He loves me. He always tells me that. He wouldn't hurt me.'

Doyle slid his hand inside his jacket and pulled out the Beretta, keeping it low, away from any prying gazes he might attract from the other passengers. The metal gleamed dully beneath the fluorescents inside the carriage.

'Do you know what that is, Lisa?' he asked her.

'It's a gun.'

'Have you ever seen your dad with one?'

She nodded.

'He pointed one at my mum once,' she said, swallowing hard. 'I think they were playing because my dad was laughing.'

'What about your mum?'

'She just told me to go to my room. They didn't shout at each other that night.'

Doyle holstered the automatic, noticing that his movements had attracted the attention of a man sitting a few seats away.

Doyle glared at him and the man returned to reading his newspaper.

'When will I see my dad?' Lisa asked.

'Soon,' Doyle reassured her.

'And what will happen then?'

I'll kill him.

'I want my mum and dad to be together again. I don't like it when they shout at each other. I miss my dad.'

Again Doyle found himself looking into those blue eyes. Eyes that were now moist at the corners. She sniffed back a tear.

'Are *you* married?'

Doyle smiled.

'No,' he told her.

'Do you love anybody?'

He closed his eyes briefly.

She was there in his memory.

Georgie.

He could see her laughing. Such an infectious laugh.

The memories were still so strong. He saw her sitting opposite him in a restaurant, long blonde hair cascading over her shoulders, her gloriously slim body hugged by the tight, short black dress she wore.

Perfection.

He gritted his teeth, the knot of muscles at the side of his jaw pulsing.

'Do you love anybody?'

He looked down at Lisa.

'No,' he said. 'I don't love anybody.'

He tried to force the image to the back of his mind but it clung stubbornly.

The train was leaving the station.

Liverpool Street was the next stop.

Doyle checked his watch.

6.48 p.m.

'He won't hurt her, Julie, calm down,' Kenneth Baxter said, rising from his seat and attempting to slide one arm around Julie Neville's waist.

She shook loose angrily.

'How do you *know* that?'

'I know Bob.'

She laughed humourlessly.

'Do you, Ken? Do you know him? Does Doyle? I'm not even sure I do. I don't think anyone knows what's going on inside his mind. He's unpredictable. He's dangerous. I think he's insane.'

'He's not going to hurt his own daughter, is he?' Baxter argued.

Julie looked at him.

But she's not HIS *daughter. She's* YOUR *daughter.*

She let out a weary breath.

Should she tell him the truth, let him know that his own flesh and blood was in danger?

She reached for the packet of Superkings on the table and lit one, blowing out a long stream of smoke.

'When the hell are they going to release us?' Baxter looked around at the bare walls of the room inside New Scotland Yard.

'They said we can leave when we want to, we're not under arrest,' she reminded him. 'Why? Are you getting nervous, Ken?'

'What the hell is *that* supposed to mean?'

'The weapons that Bob's using, he got them from you, didn't he? *And* the explosives?'

'You're starting to sound like one of those coppers,' he snapped. 'Don't *you* trust me either?'

'I don't know *who* to trust any more.' She looked at him pleadingly. 'Just tell me the truth. Did Bob get those weapons from you?'

'Yes,' said Baxter, unfalteringly. 'He came to me nearly two years ago, he knew I was selling to both sides. He knew I had access to the Quartermaster's stores, he knew I could get what he wanted.'

'But why did he want it?'

Baxter could only shrug.

'At the time I didn't know. I didn't care either,' he said, flatly. 'He was a friend. He asked me to do something for him, I did it. That's how friendship works, isn't it?'

'If he'd known about you and me he'd have killed us both.'

'But he *didn't* know, did he? Why, what's wrong? Is your conscience pricking you after eight years?'

She fixed him with an angry stare.

'Did he get the explosive from you too?'

Baxter nodded.

'He contacted me about that a lot later,' he told her. 'After I'd left the army. I still had the contacts though, on both sides.'

'And you didn't ask him why he wanted that either?'

'It wasn't my business.'

'He's killing people with those explosives, Ken. Isn't that your business either?'

'Don't preach to me, Julie. It's a bit late for lectures. Anyway, what do *you* care? Once Doyle finds him he'll kill him and it'll all be over. We won't have to hide any more.' He slipped his arm around her shoulders, feeling her pull away but less vehemently this time. When he looked into her eyes he saw tears there.

'Isn't that what you want?' he asked softly. 'For us to be together?'

'I want Lisa back safely. That's *all* I want.'

Baxter took his arm away and stepped back from her.

'I don't want to lose her, Ken,' Julie said softly. 'I can't.'

As she stood before him, Baxter watched as a single tear trickled down her cheek.

She didn't bother to wipe it away.

6.58 p.m.

'I didn't make a mistake,' said PC Nigel Butler, forced to raise his voice to make himself heard over the din of the helicopter's rotors. 'I heard the message clearly from DS Mason.'

Butler shifted in his seat, both hands gripping the HK81 rifle.

His palms felt sweaty against the wood and steel of the weapon. Not just because the evening was fairly humid but because he was nervous.

He hated flying at the best of times. A plane was bad enough but the helicopter was even worse.

When it had taken off that afternoon, with the minimum of forward movement then straight up into the air, he'd struggled to retain control over his stomach and ever since they'd been in the air he'd felt queasy.

The Lynx was cruising at about one thousand feet and Butler was seated where the co-pilot would normally have sat. Unfortunately for him, he had an excellent view through the large windscreen of the chopper and also, when he inadvertently looked down, through the glazed nose panel.

Beside him, the pilot, Jim McBride, guided the helicopter skilfully through the air, occasionally taking it lower. So low, it seemed to Butler, that they were destined to crash into some of the capital's taller structures, but the big Scot flying the Lynx merely smiled as he saw the expression of panic periodically flash across the policeman's face.

Behind Butler, also armed with an HK81, Duncan Clark glanced into the cockpit, eyes roving over the banks of instruments which McBride dealt with almost nonchalantly. Lights flashed on and off and, throughout the flight, the muted sounds of voices floated back to him as McBride received instructions via his headset.

Above it all, the constant roar of the huge rotor blades dominated everything as they cut through the sky.

'How long before we reach Liverpool Street?' Clark shouted.

'Three or four minutes,' McBride told him.

'And you're sure you heard the order clearly?' Clark persisted, touching Butler's shoulders.

'Yes. When Doyle gets to Liverpool Street he'll be tracked by plain-clothes men,' Butler began. 'They'll tail him to wherever Neville sends him. When he makes contact with Neville we'll be notified. We move in and shoot Neville. And we shoot to kill.'

They rode the escalator from the lower platform, standing side by side.

Doyle, his long brown hair swept back from the collar of his jacket, felt his face greasy with perspiration.

Lisa, still pulling at the loose thread on her sleeve, gazed around her, taking it all in. Then she looked up at Doyle and slipped her hand into his.

He glanced down at her, feeling her tiny hand inside his strong one.

She smiled up at him and he found himself pinned in the almost luminous brilliance of her eyes.

He managed a smile in return then he winked at her.

Do you reckon she'd still be smiling at you if she knew you were going to kill her father?

Doyle brushed a hair from his face.

It isn't her father. But she thinks it is. That's all that matters.

They stepped off the moving staircase, Doyle looking

259

around the ticket hall. A flight of stone steps led up to the concourse itself.

They began to climb, Doyle deliberately slowing his pace so that Lisa could keep up with him.

She held his hand all the way up.

As they emerged on to the concourse, Doyle's eyes sought the public phones. There were four of them to the right and he headed towards them, Lisa keeping step with him.

Only when he actually reached the phones did Doyle release her hand.

All four were in use.

Doyle glanced at each user.

A youth in a blue Chelsea shirt and baggy jeans was talking animatedly into the mouthpiece of the first phone.

A young woman with a large suitcase beside her was at the second.

Then a middle-aged man who kept looking at his watch as he spoke.

At the fourth was a stunning Asian girl who was wearing a bright yellow jacket and the shortest skirt Doyle had ever seen. The garment, along with the black high heels she wore, drew even more attention to her shapely legs. He stood watching as she constantly lifted one foot from her left shoe, flexed her toes, then slid her foot back into the stiletto. She performed the movement with almost robotic precision and grace.

Aware of Doyle's prying glance, she turned so that her back was towards him.

He looked at his watch.

There was less than a minute before Neville was due to phone.

He'd get an engaged signal. As simple as that. He wouldn't detonate a bomb for that.

Would he?

Doyle licked his lips anxiously.

Time was almost up.

Pull them away from the phones. Do it now.

All of them?

The counter terrorist moved slowly from one foot to the other, the movement almost imperceptible.

Lisa watched him and giggled. To her it looked as if he was swaying gently back and forth like a tree in a breeze.

Doyle looked at his watch again.

Neville wouldn't detonate a bomb just because he got an engaged signal.

Can you be so sure? Do you want to risk it?

Doyle pulled the Beretta free

(fuck it, this was becoming a habit)

and held it in the direction of the four phone users.

'Get away from the phones, now,' he shouted.

The quartet seemed to turn simultaneously.

The youth in the Chelsea shirt dropped the receiver and ran.

The woman with the large suitcase screamed.

The man in the suit stood motionless, the receiver gripped so tightly in his hand that Doyle feared he would snap it in two.

The Asian girl's eyes bulged wildly in their sockets, her lips trying to form words but nothing would come out.

Other eyes turned towards the noise. Other eyes saw Doyle and the pointing gun.

'Get away from the phones,' he ordered.

'Please don't,' the woman with the suitcase blubbed. 'Take what you want.' She was pushing her handbag towards him.

'Just get away from the phone,' Doyle said, lowering

his voice, glancing around, noticing that other people on the concourse were running towards exits in an effort to escape this long-haired madman.

Lisa looked on in bewilderment.

She could hear the screaming. She saw the looks of terror on people's faces.

And when she turned, she was the first to see two uniformed policemen running towards them.

6.59 p.m.

The phones were within reach.

Two dangling uselessly by their cords, the others replaced on the hook. Their users were long gone.

Doyle stepped towards them, turning to look at Lisa.

He saw the policemen.

'Shit,' he hissed.

They were only yards from him now.

'It's all right,' he called, fumbling in his jacket for his ID.

'Put down the gun,' instructed the older of the two policemen, both palms extended to show he meant no harm.

Doyle pulled the ID free and tossed it at the older man, watching as he looked down at it.

'I'm with the Counter Terrorist Unit.'

'All right, son,' said the older man, taking a step towards him. 'Just take it easy.'

'Check the fucking ID, you halfwit,' Doyle rasped, the Beretta still gripped in his fist.

The phone began to ring.

The policeman kept coming.

'Put down the gun first,' said the older man. 'Then we'll talk.'

The phone rang again.

The policeman had actually stepped past the wallet now.

The phone rang for a third time.

Doyle swung the barrel until it was pointing at Lisa's head.

'Check the ID or I'll blow the kid's head off,' he hissed.

The second policeman dropped to his knees and flipped open the leather wallet, inspected the picture inside, saw the official stamp, the signatures.

Four rings.

'He's right,' the policemen kneeling nearby said, grabbing at his colleague's arm. 'Look.' He shoved the ID at the older man.

Doyle snatched up the phone.

He got the right one first time.

'Doyle,' he said, the automatic still aimed at Lisa's head.

The two policemen watched mesmerised.

Lisa's face creased slightly and they saw tears forming in her eyes as she looked at Doyle who, only now, lowered the weapon.

With the phone jammed between one shoulder and one ear, he snapped his fingers at the older policeman and pointed towards the ID wallet which the uniformed men tossed back to him.

'I want to speak to Lisa,' Neville said.

'No.'

'What the fuck are you talking about? Put her on, now.'

'Fuck you, Neville, I'm tired of this game. I'm not running around London for the rest of the night like a cunt waiting for you to do an impression of fucking Hiroshima when it gets to eight o'clock.'

'You know the rules, Doyle.'

'Fuck the rules, fuck the game and fuck *you*.'

'I'll let off another bomb in thirty seconds unless I speak to my daughter. The clock's running, hero.'

'Let it run, fuckhead.'

'You ought to know me well enough by now, Doyle. I'll do it.'

'I know you'll do it and I don't care. You can let off as many bombs as you like, you can kill however many people you want. I couldn't give a shit. You know why? Because *I've* got the only thing in this world that means anything to you. The only thing you value in your whole miserable fucking life is here with me now.'

'If you hurt her Doyle I'll—'

'You'll *what*?' Doyle hissed, scornfully. 'Bomb another part of London? Big deal. Be my guest. Now you listen to me, Neville, I'm changing the rules of this game. From now on we play my way. I don't know why it took me so long to suss this out. Are you listening to me?'

Silence at the other end.

'Neville, I hope you are listening. For your daughter's sake I hope you're listening. You and I are going to meet. But it'll be where I say and when I say. Got that?'

'And what if I don't agree?'

'I'll kill your daughter.'

'You're bluffing.'

'Do I sound like I'm bluffing? Are you willing to take that chance? Like I said, you can let off all the bombs you want but the only way you're ever going to see your daughter again is if you do what I tell you.'

'The only difference between us, Doyle, is that you've got the law to hide behind.'

'I don't need the law, Neville. Now you started this fucking game, I'm going to finish it. Any bullshit and I'll kill the girl. You let off any more bombs and I'll kill her. New rules. New game, Neville. Now listen.'

7.01 p.m.

Frank Mallory had been convinced that Doyle was going to shoot the child.

He'd seen the barrel of the Beretta aimed at her head, seen the expression on the counter terrorist's face. There had seemed only one possible outcome.

The thirty-two-year-old plain-clothes policeman had watched the entire tableau in muted shock, tempted fleetingly to draw the Smith and Wesson .38 from the holster beneath his flannel shirt, but he had watched and waited.

Watched as Doyle had spoken into the phone.

Watched as he and the little girl had headed off towards the steps which would take them back down to the station's ticket office.

Now he watched from one end of the carriage as the tube train approached Chancery Lane station, glancing up from his copy of the *Standard* every now and then, ensuring that Doyle and the girl didn't slip off the train unnoticed.

Mallory had no idea where the counter terrorist was taking his small charge.

No idea what he was going to do to her.

How could he point a gun at her?

Mallory thought of his own child and, as he glanced at

Doyle, felt a swift but overwhelming surge of hatred for the man.

The poor little sod must have been terrified.

And yet, as the plain-clothes man watched, Lisa was sitting close to Doyle.

Probably scared to move.

The carriage was relatively full so Mallory's job was made that little bit easier. When more passengers boarded at the station, most of the seats were taken.

People were moving about in the aisle, trying to find a seat or at least a hand-hold before the train lurched out of the station.

Mallory glanced across towards where Doyle had been sitting.

He couldn't see him.

The plain-clothes man tried to control the panic which struck him like a slap in the face.

What if Doyle and the girl had slipped off unnoticed?

How the hell was he going to find them now?

Mallory leaned forward slightly in his seat.

Still no sign of Doyle, but he could see the girl.

There was a young woman sitting next to her now, occasionally smiling up at Doyle, sometimes at Lisa.

Doyle stood in the aisle gripping the handrail, his other hand dug in his pocket.

Mallory breathed an almost audible sigh of relief and settled back to his newspaper, scanning the same words he'd already looked at a dozen times and still unable to remember one of them.

As the train passed through Holborn he saw that the counter terrorist and the little girl were still on board.

So too was the young woman Doyle had given up his seat for.

She had pulled a paperback from her handbag and was scanning it, pausing every now and then to point something out to Doyle who leaned close to her as she spoke.

From his position at the other end of the carriage, Mallory couldn't hear what they were saying. All he was aware of was the warmth of the young woman's smile.

Even Doyle managed a grin a couple of times.

Lisa's face never changed expression.

That look of bewilderment and concern remained etched upon her features.

Mallory glanced at Doyle once more.

What are you up to?

It was as the train approached Tottenham Court Road station that Mallory saw the counter terrorist extend a hand towards Lisa, both helping and beckoning.

She took the hand almost fearfully.

Doyle bent his head quickly and leaned close to the young woman with the dog-eared paperback.

She laughed out loud.

Doyle and Lisa moved towards the sliding doors of the carriage as the train pulled into the station.

Mallory felt his heart beating a little faster.

Take it easy.

As the train stopped, the doors slid open and Doyle stepped out, Lisa's small hand held firmly in his.

Mallory waited a second or two then followed.

7.18 p.m.

'I'm not going to hurt you,' Doyle said quietly, as they stood on the platform waiting for the train to pull in.

He looked down at Lisa who glanced up at him with watery eyes.

A man passing by heard the words and looked at Doyle warily, only continuing up the platform when he saw the steel in his warning glare.

'You told my dad you'd kill me.'

Well, would you?

Doyle looked into her eyes.

What about it, hardman? Would you shoot a kid?

He squeezed her hand a little harder but his expression didn't alter.

So? Would you? Or are you going soft? If the time came, could you put the barrel to her head and blow her fucking brains out?

'I need to see your dad,' he told Lisa. 'It was the only thing I could say to make him speak to me.'

Ah, very touching. Bottled it, have you?

Lisa didn't look too impressed.

There was a blast of warm air from the tunnel mouth signalling the arrival of the train.

Doyle took a step towards the edge of the platform, pulling Lisa gently with him.

'It's going to be OK,' he said, without looking at her.

She didn't hear him. The rumble of the tube train drowned out his words.

They stepped on as the doors slid open, Doyle ushering her towards the nearest seat.

If he noticed the thin-faced man in the flannel shirt step aboard at the far end of the carriage, a copy of the *Standard* stuck in the back pocket of his jeans, he gave no indication.

Northern line, southbound, mused Frank Mallory.

Where the fuck was Doyle going?

He stood at the far end of the carriage, not bothering with the paper this time, simply leaning against the partition, eyes scanning the other occupants of the carriage but coming to rest time and again on Doyle and Lisa.

The counter terrorist also glanced around the carriage.

Has he spotted you?

Mallory thought not. However, he had no way of being sure.

Not yet.

The train pulled into Leicester Square station, disgorged some passengers, welcomed aboard others, then pulled off once more.

Doyle and Lisa hadn't moved.

Mallory took a seat which had been vacated at Leicester Square, feeling that it was still warm when he sat on it.

This time he did pull the newspaper from his pocket but he only rested it across his lap, tapping slowly on the paper with his fingers.

He saw Doyle lean across and say something to Lisa, saw her glance at the counter terrorist briefly.

He wished he could hear what Doyle was saying. There was no way he could get closer now without alerting his quarry. The only thing to do was wait.

'So, when we see your dad, you stay close to me, right?' said Doyle, leaning close to Lisa.

'You're going to hurt us both, aren't you?' she whispered.

'Just do what I tell you and you'll be fine,' Doyle said, as reassuringly as he could.

Just don't get in the way if me or your father starts blasting.

'I need to go to the toilet,' she told him, looking almost apologetic.

'You'll have to wait,' he said, trying to soften the edge to his voice.

'But I can't.'

Doyle looked at her, pinning her in the full glare of his steel grey eyes.

'You'll have to. It won't be long now. We're nearly there.'

7.24 p.m.

Arrogant, stupid, shitheaded, fucking piece of crap.

Robert Neville gripped the handlebars of the Harley Davidson so tightly it seemed his fingers would cut through the thick leather of the gloves he wore.

Doyle.

Smartarse fucking bastard.

Who the hell did he think he was? Threatening Lisa.

Neville eased the Tour Glide around a van which had stopped close to the pavement outside a restaurant in Monmouth Street.

The traffic was heavy, as streets in the centre of the capital had been closed after the bombs. Diversions were in force. The traffic was jam-packed, bumper to bumper.

Neville guided the motorbike expertly through the traffic where he could, cursing the other vehicles, cursing the police.

Cursing Doyle.

How dare he?

Arrogant fucker.

Trying to play Neville at his own game. Trying to bargain.

The ex-para felt the bulk of the .357 beneath one armpit, the .459 beneath the other.

When he finally got his hands on the counter terrorist he'd empty both fucking guns into him.

Then he'd take Lisa.

Doyle wouldn't shoot her, he was sure of that.

Relatively sure.

Fairly sure?

Fuck it. He had no way of fathoming how the counter terrorist's mind worked. How far he was willing to push this game.

You said you were alike. How far would *he go? Would* you *kill a child if you had to?*

Some had died already in the bomb blasts earlier. They must have.

How many young lives do you want on your conscience?

How many had Doyle already got on his?

Would one more matter to him?

Neville thought it wouldn't.

As he headed into St Martin's Lane he felt, he *knew*, that the man he would shortly be meeting was every bit as ruthless as himself.

For some reason, the thought made Neville smile.

'Say that again, you're breaking up, over,' said PC Nigel Butler, the two-way held close to his ear.

He listened more carefully as Mallory repeated his message.

Through the static and beneath the steady hum of the helicopter's rotor blades, the policeman nodded, picking out the words as if he were sifting through some kind of verbal jigsaw, searching for the right pieces.

'Doyle and the kid are at Charing Cross, heading down

the Strand towards Trafalgar Square,' Butler repeated.

The pilot glanced across at him then moved the joy-stick of the Lynx a few degrees to the left, the vehicle banking.

PC Duncan Clark looked down at the maze of streets and tangle of buildings that was central London, a thousand feet below.

He gripped his rifle more tightly and swallowed hard, aware that his heart was beating that little bit faster now.

McBride spoke into his mouthpiece, replying to a question or query he'd received through his headphones. Clark saw him flick a switch to his right, saw a red light flicker on and wondered momentarily if something was wrong, but he noted with relief that the light quickly flickered off again.

'Yeah, I got it, Trafalgar Square,' Butler repeated. 'Out.'

Clark noticed that there were several beads of sweat on the other policeman's brow but he fancied they were there because of his companion's fear of flying.

Unlike the leaden feeling he felt in his own gut.

Fear?

'The plain-clothes guy following Doyle says they're heading towards Trafalgar Square,' Butler repeated.

Clark nodded.

'And Neville?' McBride enquired.

Butler could only shrug. 'Wherever Doyle is, Neville will be close.'

'I hope you're right,' Clark murmured, his face pale.

'Are you OK?' Butler asked him.

Clark nodded.

'I hope I can do it when the time comes,' he said, swallowing.

'Do what?' Butler wanted to know.

'Shoot Neville,' Clark told him. 'I've never fired at a man before. Never killed anyone.'

'I felt cold afterwards,' Butler said, looking at his own rifle, memories dancing behind his eyes. 'Like I was sitting out in a snow storm.' He shrugged. 'I couldn't stop shaking for about an hour afterwards.'

'You've killed a man?'

'About eleven months ago, over in Bermondsey,' Butler elaborated, his voice soft. 'Some nutter went apeshit with a kitchen knife, stabbed his wife and a friend of hers and took them hostage. The friend bled to death before we could reach her. He'd cut her throat. He had a gun in the house too, just some fucking old Luger, Christ knows where he got it. He managed to get off a couple of rounds then he ran for it. He ran straight at *me*. I shot him.'

Clark looked intently at his colleague.

'Caught him in the chest,' Butler continued. 'There wasn't even much blood. He didn't make a sound. Didn't go flying backwards like they do in films; that's all bullshit. He just looked surprised. Then he fell on to his face. He was dead before they got him into the ambulance.' Butler exhaled deeply. 'Like I said, I just felt so bloody cold. I got a commendation for that.' He chuckled but there was no humour in the sound.

The helicopter banked sharp right then began to descend very slowly.

Clark glanced at his companion then at his watch.

Both men checked their rifles.

7.28 p.m.

'Where are we going?'

Doyle heard Lisa speak but the words didn't seem to register.

He glanced towards Nelson's Column, which was, as usual, surrounded by tourists. The pavement was thick with pigeons, the continual flapping of their wings sounding like some unearthly round of applause. One of the birds waddled across Doyle's path until a small child came bounding out of a huddle of tourists nearby and chased it away.

Doyle glanced at the child, who promptly ran back to the welcoming arms of its mother.

He could hear the sound of the fountains in Trafalgar Square and, as he looked again, he saw two people sitting on the low stone wall around one of them, feet dipped into the water.

Close by, another couple were tossing pieces of bread to an ever-increasing multitude of pigeons.

Cameras were clicking. He could hear laughter.

He felt Lisa's hand pulling at his.

'Where are we going? I'm tired.'

'We're nearly there,' he said, pulling her along with him when she slowed down.

Nearly there.

Was it nearly over? Really over?

Would Neville be waiting or would it be as Doyle planned? Would he be a moment or two ahead of the ex-para? Would he have time to pick his ground?

He almost smiled to himself.

How many times had he done this?

How many times had he walked or driven towards a place where he knew he might lose his life?

He didn't know. Didn't care.

If death awaited him then so be it. He had no fear of death.

A man he'd once met had told him that death held no fear for someone who had nothing to live for.

Doyle had killed that man but he'd agreed with the sentiment. And for him, personally, there was *nothing* left.

Neville could be waiting for him now at the appointed place, fixed by Doyle himself.

The ex-para would try anything to get his daughter back.

Doyle had to ensure it did not end that way.

He must get Neville.

He *would*.

He didn't give a fuck about the bombs and the lost lives, or how many more would die. This was personal. He'd been ordered to kill Neville and he would.

Are your orders so important?

Doyle looked down at Lisa as they crossed the road.

Will you shoot her father down before her eyes?

The counter terrorist told himself that Neville wasn't even her father.

Who fucking cared?

She wouldn't know that.

As they crossed the road, Doyle found himself slowing his pace slightly. It was as if he wanted to delay the final confrontation as long as possible. He felt no fear. He knew that Neville would not kill him. He'd try but Doyle knew that once he had the ex-para in his sights there would be only one outcome. And even if he did die, he'd still make fucking sure he took Neville with him.

So why delay?

Perhaps Neville was right. Perhaps they *were* alike.

Mirror images of the same man with the same feelings, the same beliefs. The same needs.

Bollocks.

Doyle slipped a hand inside his jacket and felt the bulk of the Beretta there. As he walked he could feel the .45 PD Star bumping against his boot, secure in the ankle holster.

'Remember what I told you,' he said, looking down at Lisa. 'Stay close to me. Don't try and run.'

'Am I going to see my dad now?'

Doyle nodded and kept walking, eyes now alert, scanning faces, darting back and forth for the first sight of Neville.

He looked at his watch.

They crossed the road beneath Admiralty Arch and Doyle glanced up the Mall towards Buckingham Palace.

He had no idea from which direction Neville would arrive.

All he knew for sure was that he *would* come.

It was almost time.

'You've done *what*?' roared Detective Inspector Vic Calloway, taking a step around the desk, his eyes aflame.

'Neville would have set off those bombs anyway,' DS Mason said, taking a step backwards. 'Doyle won't catch him in time, and even if he does it won't matter. He'll set those fucking bombs off, Vic, I'm telling you.'

'You went behind my back,' Calloway shouted. 'You gave an instruction which could cause dozens of deaths without consulting me. If Neville is killed before we find out the location of the bombs, Christ alone knows how many more people are going to die.'

'I told you, he'll kill anyway. He'll detonate the bombs even if he gets his daughter.'

'You don't know that.'

'Well, I wasn't taking any chances. When he shows up, he's dead.'

'Call the chopper now, cancel the order.'

Calloway was standing only inches from his companion.

'It's too late,' Mason said. 'The chopper was told to break all radio links once it moved in for the final kill. It's doing that now.'

'Where?' Calloway demanded.

'Admiralty Arch,' Mason informed him. 'It's over, Vic.'

'Fucking right it's over.' Calloway snatched up the phone. 'If anyone other than Neville is hurt, I'll have your fucking badge for this.'

7.34 p.m.

The sky was mottled. A collection of bluish-purple clouds like bruises, which signalled not only the creeping onset of evening but also the inexorable approach of rain. Great swollen banks scudded across the heavens.

For Doyle the day had begun in rain-flecked darkness and it was going to end that way.

He glanced at his watch.

It wasn't even a day, was it?

Seven o'clock this morning it had all begun, hadn't it? The cramped waiting in his car.

And now, a little over twelve hours later, that waiting was almost over.

Lisa was standing close to Doyle, so close he could feel the heat from her body against his leg.

He wondered if he should comfort her.

And what will you say? That the man she thinks is her father will soon be dead? That'd be a big fucking comfort, wouldn't it?

He didn't know what to say to her.

If the truth be told he didn't really care.

Georgie would know what to do if she was here. She'd know what to say to the girl to reassure her.

But Georgie wasn't here, was she? And never fucking would be again.

Doyle ran a hand through his hair and sucked in a deep breath. He fumbled in his pocket for his cigarettes and lit one, cupping his hand around the lighter as the flame danced in a sudden breeze.

Traffic was moving swiftly up and down the Mall, the noise of the engines filling the evening air. Already most of the street lamps along the thoroughfare were flickering into life.

Doyle saw the Harley Davidson as clearly as if it had been equipped with a beacon.

He saw Neville sitting astride it.

Saw the ex-para swing the Tour Glide out of the traffic and head towards them, easing off the throttle as he drew nearer.

'Dad!' Lisa shouted and moved towards him but Doyle shot out a hand and pulled her back.

'Stand still,' he said, one firm hand gripping her shoulder.

She squirmed in his grip for a moment, wanting to run to her father who was swinging himself off the bike now, pulling his helmet free.

He stood no more than ten feet from Doyle.

'Don't hurt her, Doyle,' Neville said. 'I kept my part of the bargain, didn't I? I'm here.'

'You didn't have any choice,' Doyle reminded him.

'Why did you do it, Neville? Why the bombs here? Why the shootings and bombings over in Ireland?'

The ex-para shrugged.

'I didn't know what else to do,' he said. 'It would have worked, you know. This *peace* in Ireland is bullshit anyway. They'll never stop fighting.'

'And you wanted to make *sure* they didn't?' Doyle said, pulling the Beretta from its holster, levelling the weapon at his opponent.

'Do *you* think they will then? Do you want them to? You didn't want an end to the fighting any more than I did because you know that, just like me, you're finished without it. What else have you got, Doyle? How long before you go off your head? This peace is no good to you either.'

The counter terrorist held his gaze.

'They might give you a desk job if you're lucky,' Neville continued. 'Is that what you want?'

'You're right, it's finished for both of us,' Doyle said quietly. 'Now drop the guns. Take them out slowly with your left hand.'

'And if I don't?' Neville said.

Doyle pulled back the hammer on the automatic and pressed the barrel lightly against Lisa's right temple.

'Then I'll kill her.'

Neville reached inside his jacket and first pulled out the .459 then the .357. He dropped both on the pavement at his feet.

'Are you going to shoot an unarmed man?'

'It wouldn't be the first time,' Doyle informed him.

'Dad,' Lisa said tearfully and Neville smiled at her, took a step forward.

Doyle held on to the little girl.

'Don't move, Neville,' he said through clenched teeth. 'Now tell me, where's the bomb?'

'It doesn't matter now. It's too late. Even if you kill me it'll still detonate. The others were activated by remote control. This one is on a timer. It goes up at eight o'clock no matter what.' He smiled. 'The big one.'

'How big?' Doyle wanted to know.

'One hundred and thirty pounds,' Neville said. 'Or think of it as fifty car bombs all going off at once. I know you're familiar with car bombs, Doyle.' Again a crooked smile.

'Where is it, Neville?'

'You'd never disarm it even if you found it in time. I've still beaten you.'

'Well, you won't be around to enjoy it, will you?' said Doyle, raising the Beretta so that it was level with Neville's head.

'No!' shrieked Lisa.

'Not in front of my daughter, Doyle.'

'*Your* daughter,' Doyle taunted, and it was his turn to smile. 'Wrong. She's not *your* kid, Neville. You should have asked your missus or that good, close, trusted friend of yours, Kenneth Baxter. She's *his* kid, Neville, not yours.'

'You fucking liar,' Neville snarled, taking a step back towards the bike.

Doyle shook his head. 'She's Baxter's kid. Trust me.'

The gunshot was deafening.

It was followed by another and another.

Bullets struck the pavement and screamed away, ricocheting off the concrete.

Doyle lurched backwards.

Neville leaped towards the bike, both men looking up, towards the direction of the shots.

Towards the roar of rotor blades.

The police helicopter descended slowly, hovering barely fifty feet above the ground.

The air was suddenly filled with the crackle of firearms.

7.37 p.m.

Doyle had dropped to his knees when the first shot struck the ground, pulling Lisa with him, but she shook loose and scrambled to her feet, running towards Neville who was already at the Harley Davidson.

He dragged open the top box and pulled the Steyr MPi 69 free, his finger jerking on the trigger.

The staccato rattle of automatic fire filled the air as he sprayed the ground close to Doyle, bullets singing up from the pavement.

As Doyle ducked down, amazed that he hadn't been hit by the fusillade, he heard the roar of the Harley's engine, even over the droning rotors of the Lynx.

There was a scream of spinning rubber and, for a long moment, the bike seemed to hover on its churning wheels, motionless.

Doyle raised the Beretta and squeezed the trigger, three shots blasting off in quick succession, the automatic slamming back against the heel of his hand.

Then, the Tour Glide's wheels gained purchase and it shot off as if fired from a cannon.

Doyle scrambled to his feet and fired off two more shots at the speeding bike, ducking involuntarily as the helicopter suddenly roared over his head, also in pursuit of Neville.

Lisa was lying on the pavement sobbing.

Doyle pulled her to her feet, saw that there was blood on her cheek.

A tiny sliver of concrete, blasted free by a bullet, had cut her skin.

Otherwise there seemed to be no damage. She just stood there sobbing uncontrollably.

Frank Mallory saw her as he ran towards the two figures, shouting something which Doyle couldn't make out.

He saw the man in the flannel shirt gesturing towards him but he didn't hear what he shouted. He had other things on his mind.

Neville was already halfway up the Mall by now, the helicopter still in pursuit, hurtling along so low it seemed to brush the tops of the trees which lined the thoroughfare.

Traffic travelling in both directions slowed down, mesmerised or terrified by the spectacle.

Doyle ran into the road, the Beretta still gripped in his fist.

The driver of a Cortina slammed on his brakes in an effort to avoid this madman, the car skidding, missing Doyle by inches.

Two more cars behind him also slowed up, one of them bumping the back of the Cortina.

It was the vehicle behind that which Doyle wanted.

The driver of the red Nissan 200 SX was in his late thirties, smartly dressed and, when he saw Doyle running towards his car, he immediately slapped on the central locking.

His companion, a young woman in her late twenties with long hair and an impossibly tight black dress, screamed as she saw the leather-jacketed, long-haired man approaching the driver's side. She realised instantly he was carrying a gun. She'd seen enough Sylvester Stallone pictures to recognise one when it was waved at her.

'Get out the fucking car,' shouted Doyle, levelling the Beretta at the driver.

Neither occupant moved.

Doyle fired once, the bullet shattering the side window. The glass fractured, splintered and sprayed inwards.

The counter terrorist punched through what was left of it and yanked up the locking depressor, tugging at the handle, then grabbing the driver, hurling him into the street.

'Get out!' Doyle shouted at the woman who was still screaming.

She tumbled out of the passenger door, one of her high heels skittering across the pavement behind her.

Doyle floored the accelerator, twisting the wheel, allowing the car to complete a one-hundred-and-eighty-degree turn.

A van travelling in the other direction struck the rear of the Nissan, shattering a back light, but Doyle pressed down harder on the right-hand pedal and the SX roared off up the Mall.

He could see Neville up ahead of him, weaving in and out of traffic, the helicopter skimming low as it followed him.

Doyle jammed the Beretta into his belt, using both hands to grip the steering wheel.

He slammed into the side of a blue car in the opposite lane, ripping off a wing mirror, the squeal of metal on metal almost deafening. Paint was stripped from the nearside of the Nissan as surely as if someone had attacked it with a blow torch.

Ahead of him, Neville swung right into Marlborough Road, cutting across the path of a taxi, which was forced to mount the pavement to avoid him.

The helicopter banked right too and Doyle heard another shot.

What were those dozy fuckers playing at?

As he himself sent the Nissan screaming around the bend, the needle of the speedo touched fifty.

The car barely held the road.

Doyle fought and regained control of the wheel.

Air from the shattered window gushed in, sending his hair flying behind him like incensed reptilian tails, but he cared about nothing except that motorbike rider ahead of him.

Doyle pressed down even harder on the accelerator and eased the automatic free.

He was ready.

7.42 p.m.

'This wasn't supposed to happen,' PC Duncan Clark panted, gripping the back of his seat as the helicopter swung low between two buildings before rising sharply again, always following the fleeing motorbike.

'We were told to get Neville,' Butler reminded him. 'We've got to.'

The pilot looked down at the small infra-red image showing on the console beside him, checking that Neville was still within their reach.

The Lynx was flying at around a hundred feet, rising and dipping where necessary, McBride constantly aware of the proximity of so many buildings.

Neville was roaring up St James's Street now, hunched low over his handlebars, the Harley Davidson swerving in and out of traffic as if it were on some kind of maniacal slalom.

Butler pulled the HK81 up to his shoulder once more and squinted into the telescopic sight, trying to draw a bead on Neville.

'Take her down a little.'

'I can't take her any further, we'll hit something,' McBride told the marksman.

Butler tried to hold the rifle steady. His finger pressed more firmly on the trigger as he waited until he had Neville squarely in the cross-threads of the sight.

The bike veered left slightly and Butler lifted his finger from the trigger.

'Jesus,' he snarled. 'I can't get a clear shot.'

Clark was breathing hard, his heart pounding madly against his ribs.

He raised his own rifle and drew a bead on Neville.

He tried to swallow but it felt as if someone had filled his throat with chalk.

There were so many other vehicles in the road. So many other targets he might hit by accident.

Dare he shoot?

He kept the rifle pressed to his shoulder.

The chopper dipped low once more.

As Doyle roared along in pursuit of Neville, he could see the Lynx above him, drifting up and down like some toy dangled on a string. Many of the pedestrians he sped past had stopped to look at the spectacle hurtling past them, marvelling at the wildly moving helicopter and the speeding motorcycle it pursued.

Fucking police, Doyle thought angrily.

They were told to keep out of it.

Without their interference he'd have got Neville.

Fuck it. He *had* him. Helpless before him until the bloody chopper arrived and fucked everything up.

If Neville got away the police would be to blame.

Let that bomb that was due to go off in just over fifteen minutes be on their conscience.

But where?

One hundred and thirty pounds of Semtex. Where the fuck had Neville hidden such a prodigious supply of the explosive?

Doyle shook his head as if to clear away the thought, concentrating his mind on the fleeing motorcyclist, using all his skill to weave a path through increasingly heavy traffic.

The counter terrorist knew that Neville had an advantage.

His manoeuvrability.

The Nissan Doyle was driving was fast but cumbersome compared to the swiftly moving Harley Davidson. If the ex-para should swing the bike off a main road then Doyle knew he was fucked.

Ahead of him two cars were blocking the road.

Doyle twisted the wheel and sent the Nissan hurtling up on to the pavement.

He heard someone scream, saw a dark shape dive away from the onrushing car.

Doyle stayed on the pavement, realising it would give him easier access along the thoroughfare.

There was a loud clang as he struck a waste bin, ripping it from its position on the pavement.

It flew into the air, spinning, sending its rotting contents scattering in all directions.

He hit the next one too and heard one of the Nissan's headlights shatter.

Still he drove along the pavement, finally guiding the vehicle back into the road as Neville reached the junction of St James's Street and Piccadilly.

The lights were red.

7.46 p.m.

Neville glanced up at the red light then sent the bike hurtling left into Piccadilly, oblivious to the frantic blasting of horns which greeted his arrival.

The Harley swept across the path of two cars, both of which braked hard to avoid collision with the bike.

They managed that but not with the vehicles following.

A bus slammed into one, shunting it several yards further down the road.

The other, a Fiesta, shuddered as another car struck it hard in the rear, the metal crumpling like paper, back lights shattering under the impact.

Doyle sent the Nissan after the bike, slamming sideways into a Cortina in the process, the impact jarring both cars momentarily, but Doyle gripped the wheel, pressed down on the accelerator and roared off once more, noticing that the helicopter was now able to swoop even lower in such a wide thoroughfare as Piccadilly.

It was no more than fifty feet above Neville, the skids moving downwards until it looked as though they could merely bump the fleeing ex-para off the Harley.

Neville heard the deafening roar of the rotor blades and glanced up. The Lynx hovered over him like some massive metallic bird of prey.

287

He worked the throttle of the Harley and coaxed yet more speed from the bike, whose speedo was already pushing seventy.

There was an ear-splitting bang and a bullet sang off the road no more than ten feet from the Tour Glide.

Then another.

The second struck the front grille of a stationary Mercedes and punched a hole through the metal.

In the chopper Clark cursed and took aim again.

Ahead on the left Neville saw the brightly lit frontage of the Ritz Hotel.

He swung left sharply, across the path of a taxi, whose driver blasted its horn angrily.

The Harley hit the kerb, rose into the air for precious seconds then slammed down again, skidding momentarily on the pavement.

Neville hunched over the handlebars and rode fast through the horde of pedestrians on the pavement outside the hotel, scattering them as a dog does sheep.

Some even ran screaming into the road.

He looked up and saw that the Lynx was almost level with him now, dropping ever lower until it seemed the thing must strike the ground.

Behind, Doyle floored the accelerator and also sped up until he was virtually alongside Neville.

A parked Jag whose driver seemed oblivious to the pandemonium around him flung open his door, preparing to step out.

Doyle tried to swerve but it was too late.

The Nissan struck the Jag's open door and tore it free, sending it skidding across the road.

The other headlight shattered, more paint was stripped from the body of the SX, leaving a great furrow in the red paintwork of the vehicle.

Doyle reached for the Beretta, watching as Neville swung back into the road only yards ahead of the Lynx.

The traffic on both sides of the road was slowing down, those facing the speeding procession aware of the danger they faced.

The bus driver who found himself heading towards the helicopter screamed and covered his face, convinced that the chopper was going to plough into him but, at the last moment, McBride sent the helicopter into a steep climb, just clearing the double decker.

One of the skids actually scraped along the roof of the bus, tearing paint free, causing the chopper to lurch violently to one side.

McBride fought to control the Lynx, its rotor blades spinning only feet from the front of the buildings to his right.

The bus went out of control, ploughing across the road.

Doyle saw it coming and floored the pedal again, aiming for a gap between the front of the oncoming bus and a Cavalier which was blocking his path.

He slammed into the front of the car, knocking it aside, screeching through seconds before the bus crashed into the car behind him, the massive red bulk of the vehicle now blocking traffic in both directions.

Those queuing outside the Hard Rock Café turned to watch the suicidal chase.

A couple even applauded.

Neville was approaching Hyde Park Corner.

The underpass, Doyle thought. The bastard was heading for the underpass. He could lose the helicopter that way.

Wind poured through the broken side window of the

Nissan and Doyle stuck a hand out, wondering if he could get off a few shots before Neville sent the bike hurtling below ground.

No. The traffic was too heavy. The danger of hitting others too great. Besides, even a shot as accomplished as Doyle would have little chance of hitting a target moving so quickly.

The Lynx swooped low again.

Doyle heard another loud crack as one of the armed policemen fired.

They obviously didn't care about hitting innocent bystanders, Doyle mused.

The entrance to the underpass was approaching.

To Doyle's surprise, Neville suddenly veered right, across the traffic, straight into Old Park Lane, a small side road leading off the main thoroughfare.

Fuck it.

Doyle hit the brake, turning the wheel, clipping the front of an oncoming Astra in the process.

The collision caused the Astra to spin and Doyle himself grunted as the impact slammed him back in the driver's seat but he gripped the wheel and drove on, aware that Neville was doing what he'd feared.

The road and streets leading off from this part of Piccadilly were narrow, mostly one-way . . .

. . . (the *wrong* fucking way for Doyle) . . .

. . . and some were barely wide enough to accommodate a car.

Neville was having no trouble on the motorbike apart from having to slow down.

The helicopter had risen high into the darkening sky now, unable to get close due to the proximity of the buildings, but McBride tracked Neville on the monitor, the fleeing ex-para appearing as a small red shape on the infra-red.

Doyle could see the motorbike, no more than ten yards ahead of him, twisting and turning effortlessly through the narrow streets while he fought with the Nissan, trying to coax it, at speed, through the same thoroughfares, striking the kerbs frequently, forcing pedestrians into doorways for safety.

But the counter terrorist wouldn't give up. Perspiration was beading on his forehead, some of it running down the side of his face as he used all his concentration to keep on Neville's tail, all his driving skill just to stop himself ploughing into a building.

There was an empty stretch of road ahead, narrow, cobbled but free of people.

Doyle stuck the Beretta out and gripped firmly, firing off three rounds.

The pistol slammed against the heel of his hand with each recoil, empty shell cases spinning into the air.

One shot screamed off the concrete, another parted air and the third punched in the window of a shop, glass shattering noisily.

Neville turned a corner into Derby Street and again Doyle wondered what the hell he was playing at.

If he'd shot right into Shepherd Market it would have been impossible for a car to follow him but he didn't, he chose to ride on into Curzon Street.

Back into traffic.

What the fuck was he playing at?

Twice now he'd refused the opportunity to shake off or at least delay his pursuers, first at Hyde Park Corner and now here.

Doyle could hear sirens through the roar of engines.

He knew there must be police cars on the way by now, joining the chase.

Neville sped across the road, looking back quickly, almost as if to ensure that Doyle was still following.

The counter terrorist saw him reach back with one hand, flip open the top box and reach in.

He pulled the Steyr free and fired one short burst in Doyle's direction.

Bullets peppered the front of the Nissan, drilling holes in the bodywork, punching in a portion of the radiator grille, another shattering the windscreen.

Another spiderwebbed it and, for precious seconds, Doyle could see nothing except cracked glass.

He was about to punch a hole in the opaque mess when another bullet sent the whole lot spraying inwards.

Doyle hissed as a thin sliver sliced open the flesh on his jaw and he shielded his eyes from the pulverised crystal flying at him like transparent needles.

Cold air rushed through the gaping hole but at least he could see again.

See Neville speeding up South Audley Street.

See the Lynx dip low once more to join in the chase.

And now, what had begun to scratch away in the back of Doyle's mind became not a scratch but a great churning.

There was something wrong here.

Very wrong.

Twice Neville had been in a position to avoid pursuit. Twice he'd chosen to continue the chase.

Doyle glanced down at the dashboard clock.

Jesus Christ. Less than twelve minutes to detonation.

There was a method in this apparent madness from Neville, Doyle was sure of it.

But why?

Had he one last trick left?

As Doyle drove on he was gripped by an almost unbearable conviction that Neville was leading them right to the bomb.

When *it* went up, they'd all go with it.

And no matter how hard he tried, he couldn't shake that belief.

7.51 p.m.

The Lynx had stayed roughly level with the tops of the buildings as it had skirted South Audley Street but now, as Neville emerged into Grosvenor Square, the helicopter swooped towards him, free to dive and turn in the open area.

Doyle saw it dip towards Neville.

Saw Neville slow up slightly.

Saw him fumbling with the Steyr.

A loud bang sounded as one of the police marksmen fired at Neville.

The bullet struck the ground close to him.

Another loud retort.

Another miss.

Doyle swung the Beretta up and fired off more shots until the slide flew back signalling that the pistol was empty.

He pulled a spare magazine from his pocket and jammed it into the butt of the pistol, forced to slow down as he worked the slide, chambering a round.

As the Nissan slowed, Doyle saw what was happening.

'No!' he roared. 'Get away from him.'

His shout was directed at the helicopter which was dropping still lower, the noise of its rotors now deafening.

'I've got him,' said Clark, eye pressed tight to the telescopic sight.

Neville swung the Steyr upwards and tightened his finger on the trigger.

The fusillade raked the chopper, blasting in the windscreen, punching holes in the co-pilot's door. Bullets drilled the length of the helicopter.

One struck Clark, stove in part of his ribcage then erupted from his back.

He slumped forward in his seat as more bullets dotted the chopper, piercing the cabin door, drilling through the tail boom. One struck the tail skin and blasted it clean off.

McBride struggled with the controls, tried to lift the Lynx free but Neville jammed in a fresh magazine and opened up again, once more raking the helicopter from end to end.

Bullets screamed off the hull, punctured the cabin and tore through the vertical fin.

The tail rotor gearbox was hit. Pulverised by a concentrated burst of fire.

The chopper lurched violently in the air and McBride felt his stomach tighten as the instrument panel suddenly flashed with a dozen red warning lights.

The chopper began to spin hopelessly out of control, the end swinging round madly.

It was as if someone had nailed the main rotor to the sky and the chopper was turning around that central point.

It dipped crazily, the pilot yanking so hard on the joystick that it seemed he would wrench it free.

Then, with alarming speed, like a puppet with its strings cut, the chopper plummeted earthward.

It struck the ground in the centre of Grosvenor Square.

The explosion was massive. A conflagration so powerful it blew Neville over, spilling him from the bike.

The concussion blast even moved Doyle's car and the counter terrorist covered his face with one arm as a wave of intense heat rolled across the square.

An enormous cloud of black smoke and flame rose into the air as the chopper exploded with such ferocity that every window in the buildings around the square was blasted inwards.

Huge, twisted pieces of metal were hurled in every direction by the cataclysmic blast, spewing through the air like lumps of flaming shrapnel.

A piece of the main rotor, as if fired from a cannon, shot across the square and smashed through a parked car, impaling the vehicle which also exploded, adding its own chorus to the already ear-splitting hurricane of fire belching upwards into the darkening sky.

Blazing petrol ejaculated into the air and spilled across the ground, igniting everything it touched.

More cars began to burn. A whole series of secondary explosions were triggered, as if someone had let off a great chain of venomous and extremely powerful firecrackers.

The sky turned orange, then red, then black.

Noxious smoke rose and hung over the square like a reeking shroud.

Doyle saw Neville roll over on the ground, struggle to his feet, hurrying to pull the Harley Davidson upright.

The counter terrorist floored the accelerator and the Nissan hurtled towards Neville and the bike.

Neville spun around, had time to fire one single burst from the Steyr.

Doyle shouted in pain as a bullet tore through his left shoulder, cracked the collar bone and punched its way out of his back, ripping through the seat in the process, but he held on to the wheel, seeing Neville's face illuminated by the fire.

He saw the look of horror on the ex-para's face.

Then the car hit him.

Neville was catapulted ten feet into the air, such was the impact. He crashed earthward, landed on the roof of the car and rolled off, the Steyr falling from his grip.

Doyle slammed on the brakes and tumbled out of the car into the road, aware even more of the unbearable heat, which rolled across the square like a wave.

Blood was running freely from his shoulder and he could feel it beginning to stiffen, his left hand already going numb. He clutched the Beretta in his right hand and advanced towards Neville, who was lying on his back a few yards away.

Doyle stood over him and looked down at the ex-para.

His eyes were open, blood was running from his mouth and nose and, when he tried to speak, all that escaped was a liquid gurgle.

Doyle figured the impact of the car must have pulped his ribs, driven them into his lungs. His face was splashed with blood.

The counter terrorist knelt beside Neville and lifted his head with one hand, groaning with his own pain.

The visor of Neville's helmet had been broken. What remained of it was flipped open.

Doyle pushed the Beretta against the ex-para's cheek.

'Where's the bomb?' he grunted through clenched teeth.

Neville's eyes rolled and Doyle thought he was going to pass out but, instead, he realised that the dying man was trying to direct his attention to something.

'You're looking at it,' Neville managed to say before blood filled his mouth and he coughed, his face twisting into an agonised grimace. As he coughed, blood and sputum showered Doyle.

'Where?' Doyle demanded. 'Don't fucking die yet, you bastard.'

Neville coughed again, tried to turn his head then vomited a foul mixture of bile and blood, most of which spilled down his chest.

'The bike,' he whispered, and Doyle was sure he saw a smile flicker across those bloodied lips. 'It's packed with Semtex. It's *all* there.' He was gripped by a great fit of racking coughs and Doyle stood back as more blood and vomit spilled from his mouth. Great crimson clots splattered on to the road beside him.

Doyle could hear the wail of sirens more clearly now, even over the roar of flames from the wreck of the blazing helicopter.

'I won,' Neville grunted.

'Fuck you,' hissed Doyle.

He shot Neville three times in the face, each impact causing his body to jerk wildly, every bullet staving in another portion of his features.

'Cunt,' Doyle rasped at the corpse.

He turned towards the bike, running across to it.

Could Neville be bluffing?

He doubted it.

He pulled open the top box.

The entire cavity was filled with long white packages. Doyle drew a finger over the nearest and sniffed. He recognised that marzipan smell of plastic explosive only too well.

He tugged one of the panniers open.

More Semtex inside.

Doyle dragged the bike upright, shouting in pain as he was forced to put pressure on his left shoulder but he finally managed it, opening the other pannier.

That too was filled with Semtex.

He could only guess at where the rest of the explosive was.

Packed inside the fuel tanks? Hidden in the frame itself?

That didn't seem to matter.

What did was that the whole fucking lot was going up in five minutes.

Come on think. What do you do?

His head was spinning, he was having difficulty breathing, as if the raging fire was sucking all the oxygen from the air.

Think.

There was only one chance and *that* was slim. But it was all he had.

As the first police car pulled into Grosvenor Square, Doyle swung his leg over the Harley Davidson and started the engine.

7.56 p.m.

Doyle saw a policeman gesturing wildly at him as he swept past on the Harley.

Maybe the man thought he was Neville, he mused,

twisting the throttle harder, trying to coax more speed from the bike.

His shoulder hurt like hell.

More pain.

But he seemed able to grip the handlebars tightly enough and the sight of blood running on to his left hand didn't bother him.

He had other things on his mind.

Or, more to the point, under his arse.

One hundred and thirty explosive fucking things to be exact.

If he didn't make it he'd be vaporised. The equation was simple.

They wouldn't need a coffin to bury him in next to Georgie, a fucking matchbox would probably do the trick.

He sent the Harley Davidson screaming along Brook Street, the fire from the blazing remains of the helicopter still sending shrieking plumes of fire into the sky. He passed several fire engines travelling towards the carnage. Ambulances too. They'd find Neville. It might take a little while to identify him with most of his face blasted off, thought Doyle, but by the time they did identify him, it might not matter anyway.

If *he* couldn't reach his desired destination in time then fuck all would matter any more.

Across New Bond Street, through Hanover Square towards Regent Street he sent the bike.

This had to be the quickest route.

The needle on the speedo was nudging seventy and, when he couldn't get a clear run on the street, Doyle guided the bike up on to the pavements.

Where he could he gestured wildly for those blocking

his path to get away. If they didn't he'd ride the stupid fuckers down.

Time?

He couldn't even look at his watch. He could only guess at how close to oblivion he was.

Could only surmise how long he had before the one hundred and thirty pounds of explosives beneath him went up.

He roared into Regent Street, saw the crush of traffic and, again, mounted the pavement.

All along the route people screamed as they tried to get out of his way.

Doyle looked down at the speedo as he sped through Piccadilly Circus, running a red light, almost going under a bus which was moving ponderously towards Shaftesbury Avenue. The driver hit his horn but Doyle barely heard it as he went roaring down the Haymarket.

More blocked traffic.

Again he took the bike up on to the pavement, each jolt causing fresh waves of pain to throb in his shoulder and arm.

He noticed with concern that his left hand was now quite numb. It felt as if someone had dipped the entire appendage in iced water and the feeling was spreading inexorably up his forearm to his elbow. He realised that the bullet must have severed a nerve or tendon somewhere and there wasn't a fucking thing he could do about it except hang on. Grip tightly to this vast moving bomb which he straddled like some suicidal cowboy.

His long hair flowed out behind him, the wind chilled his face and made his eyes water and, all the time, the numbness crept further up his arm.

He shot across Cockspur Street, past Trafalgar Square, Admiralty Arch on his right.

It should have finished there less than an hour ago. It should never have come to this. *But it had, hadn't it?*

But very shortly it wouldn't matter.

He chanced a look at his watch and wished he hadn't.

He was about to swing into Whitehall when he realised that Northumberland Avenue would be quicker. It would take him straight to the Victoria Embankment.

Straight to the Thames.

Straight to his only chance of saving himself and Christ knows how many more around him.

He worked the throttle, looking down to see the needle on the speedo touch ninety.

It was as he did that he saw the needle on the other dial.

The one on the fuel gauge.

It was hovering over empty.

7.59 p.m.

Not now, you bastard.

Doyle looked down at the fuel gauge again.

'Not now,' he roared, still twisting the throttle as hard as he could.

How far to the river?

Half a mile?

Less?

The bike was running on fumes. The needle had dropped into the red by now.

The speed was dropping.

Eighty-five.

Doyle was standing, the Embankment coming into

view. He gripped the handlebars and lifted himself up on the footrests, as if removing his weight from the bike slightly would cause it to gain speed again.

Still the speedometer showed a slowing of speed.

Eighty.

But he was close now.

Don't look at your watch.

Time was running out.

It may even have run out.

Any second now there would be one vast, apocalyptic blast and that would be it.

Seven hundred yards to the Embankment.

Doyle saw people in front of him.

He bellowed at them to get out of his way.

Six hundred yards.

The bike juddered. The speed fell to seventy-five.

Five hundred yards.

He could see a train moving across Hungerford Bridge, could hear it rumbling away, even above the roar of the Harley's engine.

Four hundred yards.

Ahead of him he could see the *Hispaniola*. The old ship anchored there in the Thames for ever now. A tourist attraction.

There was a ramp leading up to it, a sloping gangplank which allowed visitors access.

Three hundred yards.

'Come on,' Doyle roared to no one in particular.

If he'd believed in God he might have said a prayer.

The Harley was screaming along at seventy now.

It was still fast enough. That fucking fuel gauge needle was still dropping but, Doyle thought, not fast enough to stop him.

Was it?

One hundred yards.

He heard more screams. Somewhere in the distance he heard more sirens.

He missed a man by inches as he wrenched the throttle one last time, rising again from the saddle of the bike like a cavalry officer leading his men into battle.

Into hell?

He hit the ramp doing sixty-five.

The bike hurtled up the slope and went flying out over the Thames.

Doyle let go, felt himself falling.

The bike was still hurtling through the air, spinning over and over on its upward arc.

Doyle was hurtling towards something.

Water? Earth?

Who cared?

The bike was at the highest point of its arc when it exploded.

Doyle struck something solid and lay still.

The explosion was deafening. An eardrum-shredding eruption of noise which was joined, simultaneously, by a blinding flash of white light. It was as if a supernova had exploded over the Thames and the entire sky seemed to turn first white, then yellow, with the intensity of the blast.

Those nearby dropped to the ground as the motorbike simply evaporated, a few tiny pieces of metal spinning off into the air, others dropping, hissing, into the water of the Thames.

The concussion blast spread out and rattled windows in their frames.

The train on the Hungerford Bridge rocked for a second.

Even the waters of the Thames were forced into small waves for about a hundred yards around the epicentre of the fearsome explosion.

Black and red smoke spread across the sky like blood across blotting paper and the air seemed to be filled with millions of tiny black cinders, which floated on the breeze and settled on the clothes of those nearby.

Doyle included.

He had no feeling at all in his left arm or shoulder now but he *could* feel the burning sensation in his right leg where he'd fallen heavily on it. It wasn't a break, that much he was sure of. There was a cut across his forehead just below his hairline which was weeping blood down his face.

He could hear screams, shouts.

And sirens.

There were always bloody sirens.

Sean Doyle passed out.

Redemption

It was going to rain. He was certain of it.

Doyle glanced up at the threatening banks of cloud and turned the key in the door of the Datsun.

He winced slightly as he did.

He'd left hospital two days ago with his shoulder heavily strapped.

More pain.

They'd wanted him to stay longer, make sure that the fracture of his collar bone was only hair-line, but he'd discharged himself after less than thirty-six hours. He wanted to be out of the hospital; he hated the fucking places even though it seemed, sometimes, as if he'd spent half his life in one or another. They all looked the same, they all smelled the same and he hated them.

Better off at home.

Better the solitude. He didn't want to be around other people any more than he had to be.

He opened the rear door of the car and carefully laid the bunch of red carnations on the back seat, gazing down at them for a moment.

Why did it always rain when he visited Georgie's grave?

He grimaced to himself and walked around to the driver's side.

'Doyle.'

The sound of his name made him turn and he noticed that a car had pulled up across the street.

Detective Inspector Vic Calloway was walking towards him, collar turned up against the wind that had sprung up, bringing an unexpected chill with it.

'How's the arm?' asked the DI, nodding towards Doyle's injured shoulder.

'Stiff,' Doyle told him. 'But it could have been worse.'

'You were lucky,' Calloway told him.

'So people say,' said Doyle wryly.

The two men looked at each other, the ensuing silence awkward. It was broken by the DI.

'Look, Doyle,' he began, the words faltering. 'I'm glad I caught you, I wanted to say thanks.'

'No need. I was doing my job.'

'If it hadn't been for you, Christ knows how many people would have been killed. That last bomb you—'

'Forget it.'

Doyle pulled open the driver's door, slid behind the wheel and lowered the side window.

Calloway watched as he dug in his pocket for his cigarettes and lit up.

'Was there anything else?' Doyle asked, starting the engine.

Calloway shook his head and stepped away from the Datsun, catching sight of the carnations on the back seat.

'Who are the flowers for?' he asked.

Doyle answered without looking at him.

'A friend,' he said softly. Then he guided the car smoothly away from the kerb.

Calloway watched until the car reached the end of the

road, the indicator winking, then headed back towards his own vehicle.

When he looked again, Doyle was gone.

The first spots of rain had begun to fall.

'Don't ever try to change what you don't understand.
Live your life on the sharp edge . . .'

– Sword